OLD MONEY

BOBBY COLE

OLD MONEY

A JAKE CROSBY THRILLER

THOMAS & MERCER

Published by Thomas & Mercer, Seattle
www.apub.com

Amazon, the Amazon logo, and Thomas & Mercer are trademarks of Amazon.com, Inc., or its affiliates.

ISBN-13: 9781503954779
ISBN-10: 1503954773

Cover design by Jason Blackburn

Printed in the United States of America

This story is dedicated to the brave men and women of law enforcement, who work tirelessly and without much thanks to catch the bad guys.

For the love of money is the root of all evil: which while some coveted after, they have erred from the faith, and pierced themselves through many sorrows.

—1 Timothy 6:10 (King James Version)

CHAPTER 1

The cold, misting rain forced the tired hunter to hurry back to his truck in the darkness. His wife had recently texted that she was leaving her Pilates class and supper would be ready when he arrived home. Mud slurped with each step as he picked up the pace even further, knowing his dry vehicle and favorite sports radio show were waiting.

The doctor had enjoyed the damp afternoon in his dry deer blind, though the hunt had produced only a sighting of two small bucks and not the big eleven-point he was chasing. Deer hunting was a reliable source of relaxation for him, a necessary relief from the extreme pressure of his daily surgeries.

Free of worries, the doctor displayed no caution as he walked the old logging road to the property's edge. He wasn't afraid of the dark, and the place was so remote he'd never encountered anyone else around. Since purchasing it a few years prior, the doctor had frequented the property as often as he could slip away. He was so comfortable there he didn't need to use his flashlight. The doctor knew where he was going and hurried to get there.

Waiting near the truck, hidden behind an ancient water oak, was a very calculating armed robber who had been observing the doctor's habits and planning this crime for some time. This would be the fourth robbery of a deer hunter in two years, and it fascinated the robber that none had gone to the police. The chosen targets—doctors, lawyers, or rich businessmen hunting by themselves—offered fewer unseen complications and always had valuable gear that was easy to turn into cash. It wasn't out of the question to get thousands of dollars' worth of gear, and the risks were quite low, as each crime was carried out in the dark of early morning or evening and from behind both a mask and a high-tech voice-distortion device.

Cold November rain slowly dripped off the brim of the lurker's hat as the silhouetted image of the target approached in the darkness. All the others had used flashlights. The absence of light could only help matters.

A slight pull of the sleeve revealed a watch. "Right on time," the robber muttered, then snuffed out a damp cigarette against the bark and smiled as the mask was pulled down into place.

The doctor wasn't trying to walk quietly. He was in a hurry. A backpack slid off one shoulder, and his scoped rifle was slung barrel up over the other, inviting the rain to flow down it.

"Novice," the robber whispered. *Probably buys a new gun every year anyway.*

Reaching his truck, the doctor opened the gas flap to retrieve his hidden keys. Clicking the remote, the doctor unlocked the doors, and the inside of the truck illuminated. The robber used these noises to cover any sounds of the final approach, thumb cocking a .357 Magnum pistol in the doctor's ear. The chilling metallic sound had its intended effect, and the doctor froze in his tracks.

"Don't move a muscle, and don't turn around," the robber said through the voice-distortion device.

The doctor had never heard a voice so evil sounding. The robber calmly took the rifle from the shocked man and leaned it against the truck.

"What do you want?" the doctor asked.

"I'll only say it once," said an awful, otherworldly voice. "Drop to your knees!"

"Okay, don't hurt me." The doctor dropped obediently to his knees. "I don't want any trouble."

"Do you have a pistol on you?"

"No. No, I don't."

Silence only deepened the doctor's anxiety.

"I swear."

Assured of the man's total submission after carefully searching the doctor's sides and waist for a second weapon, the robber clicked on a bright cap light that would temporarily blind the victim if he looked into it, and reached for the man's wallet. Peeling out the obvious cash, the robber searched for the hidden stash, knowing all men hid money in their wallets. Sure enough, several hundred-dollar bills were quickly discovered folded in a pocket. The wallet was dropped to the mud. The doctor's backpack was certain to hold a treasure trove of items that could be turned into cash. Given the doctor's penchant for nice toys, there would likely be expensive German binoculars, a range finder, and at least one knife. After tossing the backpack beside the scoped rifle, the robber then bent down closer to the victim.

"Your watch." A blinding light beamed into the side of the doctor's face. "Give me your watch!"

"You can have it, just don't hurt me," he said, raising his left arm. The doctor could only think of self-preservation. He was a hero in the operating room, but not out here. He wisely understood he could replace everything that might be stolen from him.

The Rolex Submariner was plucked from the doctor's wrist. The robber smiled at the weight of it, knowing it was real.

Next: "Keys and phone!" The doctor hesitated long enough to earn another distorted hiss: "Keys and phone. Now!"

"My phone's in my jacket pocket. Here are the keys."

After a search of the man's pocket, a smartphone was retrieved, leaving the man with no form of quick transportation or communication. His assailant's getaway plan depended on having at least fifteen to twenty minutes to escape, as well as what needed to be done next. Quickly pocketing the victim's phone and keys, the robber hurriedly raised the butt of the pistol and struck the doctor on the side of his head, knocking him out.

Satisfied the doctor was out cold, the robber took a moment to admire the Browning rifle and Zeiss scope, then grabbed the doctor's gear bag and started for another vehicle, hidden down the road, never once wondering if the man had been hit too hard and was actually injured.

At the truck the keys and phone would be tossed in the ditch, where they would eventually be found. The funds from the doctor's weapon and gear would of course be welcome, but it and the stolen cash was all really just folding money, extra funds for recreational drugs and gambling. The righteous glow delivered by stealing from the rich and entitled was the primary reward.

Nearing the hidden getaway vehicle, the confident, happy robber was one step closer to vaporizing into the damp, dark night.

* * *

Jake Crosby had yet to become accustomed to the pistol on his hip, but its presence was reassuring to him. Each time he moved, the leather holster creaked just loud enough to remind him it was there. Carrying it gave Jake confidence; he felt equipped, like a Boy Scout prepared for whatever may occur. Covering the firearm from public view was a dark-green waxed cotton jacket that was fashionably faded from years of wear. The coat was old and symbolized the affluence he had once tried to attain. The Glock pistol was new and represented the danger Jake could potentially face.

Much had happened to Jake in the two years since his almost-lifeless body was pulled from a cold drainpipe in a Mississippi swamp. Two surgeries and multiple stainless steel pins had healed his broken leg. A slight limp that was more pronounced in cold weather reminded him of the evil that is always out there waiting for an opportunity. Several counselors had tried to unburden his tormented mind, which was far more damaged than his fractured femur. Unfortunately, Jake didn't like to open up and talk about anything. He preferred to suppress his feelings, deal with his nightmares, and assure everyone he was fine. He did this in his marriage, much to his wife's dismay, and especially with the violent incidents of his past.

Sipping coffee in a gas station dining area just north of Columbus, Mississippi, Jake patiently waited for the man who had requested that they meet. The topic hadn't been discussed, but Jake could sense the urgency in his voice. His recent training had taught him to listen carefully and key in on certain voice inflections. He had been taught that it could mean the difference in life and death. Unless he missed his guess, this was a problem that would be better explained in person than over a phone line.

Gas station customers hurried in and out. Cigarettes, soft drinks, sausage biscuits, and gasoline proved to be the most popular items of the day, but Jake was also amazed at how much fried chicken the convenience store sold so early in the morning. He gently blew on his hot coffee while he tried to analyze customers. All seemed engrossed in their day, and most seemed in a hurry to get somewhere. *Life shouldn't be this rushed,* he thought, watching them.

Judge Ransom Rothbone rolled into the parking lot and waved at Jake through the windshield of his Land Rover. The gray-haired gentleman glanced nervously around the gas pumps before locking the vehicle doors and heading inside to the wooden booth and Jake.

"Good morning, Jake," the judge said with a smile and a handshake.

"Morning to you, sir," Jake responded.

Judge Rothbone groaned as he slid into the hard booth and then smiled warmly across the table at Jake.

"Looks like life's treating you well, Judge," Jake said with a nervous smile.

Ransom smirked and exhaled deeply. "I'm healthier at this age than my father was, God rest his soul. I'm trying to eat better and exercise, but my wife has limited my fried foods, and it's about to kill me."

"They say if the lightning don't get you, the thunder will," Jake responded with a twinkle in his eye.

"My wife reads a health magazine, and next thing I know I'm eating steamed broccoli and a fruit medley for supper. I used to never lie to her. Now I lie about what I ate for lunch," the judge explained with a chuckle.

Jake had always liked Judge Rothbone. It had been about twenty years since he had been around him regularly. That was back when he had dated his daughter. Through the years they had been on a few dove shoots together, seen each other in passing at football games and restaurants, but their circles didn't provide opportunity to socialize. The judge was sort of a local legend. He'd been a federal judge in Aberdeen, Mississippi, a small river town about twenty-five miles north of Columbus and West Point, for as long as most people could remember. He was a no-nonsense, presidentially appointed judge who didn't like the direction the country was headed and spoke his mind—regularly and fervently. He didn't like Republicans and didn't like Democrats; he liked people and supported those with good ideas, the best intentions, and a hardy willingness to work. No one was ever convicted in his court without a good scolding when it was all said and done. Even those who were vindicated were often the recipients of the same tongue-lashing. Many a defendant had broken down under the weight of a verdict and the judge's verbal thrashing about how they had personally let down their families and society. To Judge Rothbone, all people played an important role in a community. Their complete participation included working, paying taxes, voting, school attendance, and church leadership—all were needed to keep the community, state, and country strong. "Frustrated" would be a major understatement in describing his daily attitude. Jake remembered his extremely high expectations of everyone and his talent for cussing like a sailor. He made Jake nervous when Jake was a teenager, but now, twenty years later, he didn't seem so bad. *Probably because I'm not making out with his daughter right now,* Jake thought, and fought back a smile.

"How's the new job?" the judge asked.

"I'm enjoying it. It's way different than watching Wall Street and consoling a client when their stock portfolio takes a nosedive."

"It's a dignified profession that's more important than lots of people realize," the judge said, then shot a glance over his shoulder as a big man walked by their booth. Jake couldn't help but notice his nervousness.

Then a stooped-backed older lady who ran the cash register brought the judge a large coffee and set it down with a respectful smile. They obviously knew each other. Jake watched as the judge thanked her, and she walked off. He admired the respect that the judge received. *The local folks really love him,* Jake thought.

The judge leaned over the table and said to him in just above a whisper, "Her husband lost a limb in a farming accident. He got a fair settlement, I suppose. I always struggled with putting prices on arms and legs."

Jake didn't know what to say. He remembered the anxiety he'd felt when he was sixteen and met the judge for the first time. Jake was picking up the judge's daughter for a movie date. A younger, stern-faced judge wasted little time asking about Jake's recent run-in with the police. The story involved a very mad bobcat, a suitcase, and a carload of brightly dressed mourners from Detroit, Michigan, as they left a funeral. Jake remembered the judge tried not to smile as he explained what happened, but the concerned father still acted as if he were suspicious of Jake.

The judge still made him nervous. "I'm hoping to make a difference," Jake said. "I mean, as a game warden." He realized his words sounded very cliché. He wished he had thought of something more substantial to say. *You probably will later,* he thought.

"You better not waste any time," the judge said, "'cause the world's going to hell in a hurry. I try to do what I can, but it's damn tough in this day and age. The world ain't what it was when I was getting started. So much has deteriorated. Hell, these days most of these young people ain't even got simple basic manners."

Jake nodded and wondered where the conversation was heading. He watched the judge and sipped his coffee. He was in no rush. Jake wasn't officially on the clock yet.

The judge patiently looked Jake over for a moment, and then a knowing smile emerged and disappeared behind his Styrofoam cup.

Jake sensed something was amiss and shook his head. "What's so funny?"

The judge pointed at Jake's collar. "You got a blonde girlfriend these days?"

Flustered, Jake looked down and tugged his corduroy jacket collar out so he could see what the judge was talking about. Jake's hair was much darker than the blonde hair stuck there. "More like a blonde nightmare," he said, brushing it away.

"Do tell," the judge said with a smile.

"I'm having so much fun. I never thought I would again after my last one passed. That was tough on me."

"Does she mind good?"

"It's a he, and to be honest, he doesn't. He takes suggestions instead of commands."

"I know the type well. Sort of thinks he is self-employed?"

"That's him. He's a year-old yellow Lab, but he's still just a big puppy," he said with a laugh. "He's gonna be a great hunting dog, but he is unbelievably mischievous, troublesome, and hardheaded."

Judge Rothbone smiled again. "All the good ones are, son."

"Not like this one. He has intense separation anxieties. Just last week he chewed the leather steering wheel cover off my wife's car when she left him to run in the grocery store."

The judge chuckled.

"Two days before that he pulled up nearly every bush in our yard because he saw me leaving the house wearing camo. My wife's about ready to get rid of him, or maybe me."

"He just wants to go with you," the judge said with certainty. "That's normal." He clearly enjoyed talking dogs, but Jake saw him decide it was time to get down to immediate matters.

Leaning forward, the judge made eye contact. "Jake, you're probably wondering why I asked you to meet me here and not in my office. I'll cut to the chase. I've always liked you. I've kept up with you, and it's no surprise that you've turned out to be a fine young man. A good reputation is a helluva handy thing to have."

"Yes, sir. Thank you."

"I'm in a bind because I think someone has betrayed me."

Jake leaned forward. His holster creaked. "Go on."

"As you know, I've been a federal judge for a long time, put away a lot of criminals, and made a lot of enemies. I have always known the convicted and their families who left my courtroom were pissed off at me. Like I made 'em do the crime? Anyway, some time back I sent away a guy from below Columbus that had embezzled millions in fake insurance premiums. He ruined a bunch of good, hardworking people when they needed and expected financial help. It's a long story involving some sorry kids and just plain old-fashioned greed."

"I think I remember it," Jake said. "Was his name Bolivar?"

"That's right. Bronson Bolivar was his name, and he was a real piece of shit. His family had a furniture factory for almost eighty years before it closed its doors. His daddy employed a bunch of folks for years before he retired. Bronson ran it in the ground in less than four years. So he started a septic tank business, which made money, but just not the kind of money he wanted. That's when he started selling insurance, and evidently he was really good at it, or his premiums were just lower than everybody else's. Anyway, all Bronson ever did was cheat good folks outta their money, whether it was his family's furniture business, his questionable septic tank business, or his insurance scam. The sombitch was consistent."

"Didn't the old man—Bronson's father, I mean—eventually commit suicide?" Jake had just started his career as a stockbroker when the story of the man's son's embezzled millions ran wildly through his office.

"That's right. He was very upset with Bronson. After the trial he sold everything he had and put it in a fund for the victims. Then he prepaid for a funeral, walked out back, and climbed into the dumpster with a pistol so he wouldn't make a mess. He was just plain ashamed of what his son had done."

"I remember. I didn't know all that, though."

"That was a sad situation, and somebody kept the details pretty quiet. The Bolivar family was very well connected, since they were from old money, with 'was' being a key word. After his conviction, Bronson pledged that he would get even with me, but I saw to it that he wasn't gonna get out of prison in time to enjoy any of his stolen fortune, most of which they never recovered." The judge grimaced at his coffee.

Jake stared into the bottom of his own cup. "How much?"

"They don't know exactly, but they figured it was about three million dollars, and that was almost twenty years ago."

Jake whistled. His mind couldn't help but calculate the commissions on managing that kind of cash. It was an old stockbroker's habit. "That's a lot of money. So what happened to it?"

"I don't know. Bronson had a high-society lifestyle with lots of leeches he was supporting that did all his dirty work. During the trial the prosecutor could only account for about a third of the money, and there was always a rumor that he had a pile hidden away somewhere. Still to this day folks talk about it." The judge smiled. "It was even thought to be stashed in a septic tank. The kids—they're twins, by the way, a brother and a sister—have dug up nearly every shitter their old man installed looking for it. I can't even imagine searching through used septic tanks."

Jake envisioned millions of dollars waiting to be found and the elation someone would feel upon seeing it. That much money could really change the course of a life for the good or bad. Could it really be hidden in a septic tank?

Waving his hands like a traveling preacher, the judge exclaimed, "The good news is, Bronson is no longer a drain on Mississippi's taxpayers, since he conveniently died in prison. The bad news, his deadbeat young'uns seem even more obsessed with finding the money than ever before. Evidently their daddy knew they would screw up their lives worse if they had access to that kinda cash and hid it from them. So now both of these septic tank divers are forevermore pissed off at anything resembling authority."

"They sound pretty dysfunctional."

"Yeah, they hated their daddy for not giving 'em the money and detest me for putting him away."

"Is there a Mrs. Bolivar?"

"No, she passed away giving birth to the shitheads. I'm sure that probably contributed to their many problems. Bronson married and divorced several women through the years, and they took their fair share of his wealth. But at the height of this scam he was living with a Gypsy woman. She was pure coast trash, and nobody knows where she is now."

Jake watched the judge stir his coffee to cool it down.

"Since I presided over the trial and there had been rumors of threats against me, the Columbus police have kept me informed of any events that might be of interest. Now they think the twins are up to something," the judge explained, and looked down at his coffee.

"So what's happening?"

"Jake, they invited their dad's longtime cellmate to come see them this weekend. He just got out a few weeks ago. They said they wanted to take him hunting. It was kinda out of the blue, and it sounds suspicious to me."

"What do you need me to do?"

"I want someone to watch 'em. The local police can keep an eye on 'em around town, but I need someone who can watch 'em while they're in the swamp. They're capable of anything."

The judge watched Jake soak in this information for a long moment, waiting until Jake looked up to go on.

"The guy's name is Perry Burns. He's a slick one too. He did fifteen years in Parchman for embezzling state funds. He had a phony construction company and was getting paid for maintaining roads that he never maintained. Evidently he was making good money until he got caught. It seems he started billing for roads that didn't even exist."

"Good grief," Jake said. "He sounds brazen."

"Greed got him. He paid bribes to elected supervisors in about a dozen counties. When the grease got hot, one came up missing and was never found. The rest suddenly got quiet. Bronson and Perry had a lot in common, and I figure they probably became fast friends. I'm sure the twins think he knows where the money is hidden, and they may very well be right."

"How old are these Bolivar twins now?"

"I suppose they're at least forty now and well educated in all things illegal. They've never had real jobs. They're scam artists and trouble with a capital *T*. They share the same DNA, and it ain't from the deep end of the gene pool."

Jake shook his head. The Golden Triangle of the West Point, Columbus, and Starkville area was small enough that he had heard many of the rumors about the Bolivar family and the missing money, but large enough that he had never met or even, to his knowledge, laid eyes on the twins.

"If he's a convicted felon, he can't have a firearm or even be around 'em," Jake said as a matter of fact, showing his knowledge of the law.

"The intercepted message indicated they invited him to bow-hunt, but I seriously doubt that's the main focus of the meeting."

The laws were fresh in Jake's mind. "He can have a bow—even a crossbow—but not a firearm."

"Jake, I'm not worried about the sombitch hunting illegally. They're up to something else. It's gotta be about the missing money."

There was a long pause while the judge sipped his coffee and made a frowning face.

"Jake, I don't trust many people. There are a lotta folks looking for that money. I need you to be discreet. The Bolivar twins have been bragging about knowing where I live. That's supposed to be protected information. So I fear someone near me leaked it. I may just be paranoid. Hell, I mean they could simply follow me home after court and find out. After all, I do live a normal life here. But they just seem to know too much, and it makes me nervous."

"Believe me, I know what you mean," Jake said. He understood all too well the danger of the wrong person having his home address.

"What you don't know is that Rosemary and my grandson are coming home to live with Mary Margaret and me. They'll be here tomorrow. I can take care of me and my wife . . . but I don't want my baby girl to live in fear. You understand, son?"

"Yes, sir," Jake responded while his mind wandered.

Jake nodded, while his mind raced with questions he wanted to ask. He clearly remembered Rosemary Rothbone, a free spirit who stole the hearts of many young men in the area. They dated his senior year of high school and part of his freshman year of college. She was Miss Everything at Mississippi State, and Jake wanted to marry her, only she couldn't be tied down. Rosemary needed to see all life's options. She broke up with him and left for a summer mission trip to South America. Jake wasn't mature enough yet to understand her reasons; he was just smitten and confused. It had been an unanswered question in his life for many years before he came to understand it was just part of growing up. For years he had tried to purge her from his mind, but he never quite deleted all the memories. There were too many, buried too deep. He wondered why she was moving home but felt uncomfortable asking. The Rothbones had always been intensely secretive and rarely volunteered much information.

The judge folded his hands and lowered his voice. "Jake, your new job is gonna have you around a lot of law enforcement personnel from different agencies. I'm asking you to keep your eyes and ears open. Somebody close to me, somebody that should know better, has told them things about me."

Jake leaned in, and his holster creaked. "Yes, sir. I understand. You can count on me."

"Thank you, son. I'll call and let you know when Perry gets here and where they are hunting." The judge slid a card with his phone numbers across the table.

"They'll never know I'm around," Jake said confidently while dropping the card in his chest pocket.

"Be careful who you trust, son."

"Yes, sir."

The judge smiled appreciatively at Jake. He seemed relieved. It was a strangely familiar smile to Jake, although he hadn't seen it in many years.

"By the way, Rosemary's doing good now, Jake. I'll let her tell you about it. She's been pulled through the knothole lately."

Jake smiled politely, but his mind hung on the judge's words "Rosemary's doing good now." Jake wondered what "now" meant.

The judge slowly stood up and glanced around the surroundings. Jake finished his coffee and started to slide out of the booth.

"Hey Jake, you haven't put any more bobcats in a suitcase, have you?"

Jake was embarrassed but smiled slightly. "No, sir."

"I suppose most anyone would stop and pick up a suitcase that was in the middle of the road."

Jake smiled sheepishly. "Yes, sir. Apparently."

"I gotta ask. I've always wondered—how far did they get down the road before they opened the suitcase?"

"Not very far. After about a quarter mile all hell broke loose, the car slid in a ditch, and everybody bailed out, hollering."

"Just so you know, down at the police station they still talk about that story," the judge said with a smile. "Take care, son."

Jake watched the judge walk away and remembered the trouble he got into for the bobcat prank. He was trying to play a joke on a friend. He had no idea the funeral was going on and the brightly dressed out-of-town mourners would be the first to stop. Jake smiled and finished his coffee.

CHAPTER 2

Morgan Crosby pushed the stack of bills away and sighed. Frustrated, she chugged the remainder of the chardonnay she had been sipping. Staring at the ceiling, she contemplated giving up her twice-a-week yoga classes to save the couple some money.

Since Jake had resigned from his job as a stockbroker nine months ago, money had gotten even tighter. He had been miserable in the job and running in the daily rat race. Morgan had known that for a while. Sometimes miserable is hard to cure when you have a mortgage, car payments, private school, and the expenses of a teenage daughter and now a newborn. Without a safety net, you just have to dig in and make the best of the situation. That's what Jake had done for the last five years, and she loved him for it. But still, she wished he could have stuck it out a few more years.

Jake had thoroughly researched his career change, and they had talked it through for months. With help from a friend close to the governor and fresh funds from the BP oil spill earmarked for wildlife protection, Jake Crosby became a Mississippi game warden after months of extensive training. It was his dream job and allowed him to be a part of protecting something he dearly loved. If he had waited one more year, he would have been over the age limit. It had been a now-or-never decision. While Morgan fretted over their family finances, showing Jake it could never work on paper, he begged relentlessly. Jake was a hopeless optimist and believed things would always work out. Morgan wasn't nearly as optimistic.

Morgan thought he would basically be a park ranger that spoke to grade school kids and rescued orphaned fawns, while occasionally writing a ticket to someone who had killed too many ducks. She really didn't understand modern poachers and law enforcement. She now feared that he was going to be used as an undercover agent, and that scared her. It seemed the higher-ups in Jackson thought Jake's career in money management had made him comfortable with a special vernacular that would be authentic and extremely useful in certain situations. Jake looked and sounded like a businessman, not a law officer, and that was appealing to the agency. Ironically, that was Jake's appeal for Morgan when she first saw him. She pictured him as a stockbroker, rubbing elbows with doctors and making a secure six figures. She had finally agreed to his career choice as long as he promised to stay out of life-threatening situations. He responded with a promise and a smile, and Morgan naively believed him.

Jake and Morgan had a growing small family. Katy was now thirteen, in the seventh grade, and Covey was almost ten months. She would be walking any day now if Morgan and Katy would ever put her down. Katy was beginning to notice boys and cared about her appearance now more than she ever had. This change in attitude allowed Morgan and Katy to bond through shopping. They both had expensive tastes in brand-name clothes, and shopping was one thing that made Morgan happy. It was a sport to her.

Wearily, she poured another glass of wine and began to pay what bills she could.

* * *

The judge and his wife, Mary Margaret, sat patiently at the Golden Triangle Regional Airport and awaited the arrival of Delta Flight 1552 from Atlanta. The small jet was an hour overdue, which caused him excessive frustration. The airline conveniently blamed bad weather. The judge was convinced it was another sign of the times; lost was the willingness to be punctual.

Rosemary Rothbone had married a fast-talking pharmaceutical salesman who would do anything to make the sale. They met at the Columbus Air Force Base during a Fourth of July air show. He noticed her arrive by herself and park next to him. Smitten, he spent the afternoon observing her with friends from a distance. After the Thunderbirds performed and it appeared she was about to leave, he hurried ahead of her to her car and stabbed one of her tires with a knife, then waited patiently to play the role of hero and change her tire. That's how a doomed relationship, born in fraud, was formed.

The Rothbones had barely approved of the young man, who the judge thought was more interested in himself than was healthy for a marriage to his daughter, or to any woman for that matter. Noting his future ex-son-in-law's capitalistic ambition, the judge also worried that he was more interested in appearances than true happiness. When Rosemary announced they were moving, the judge was not pleased. No part of him wanted his daughter to move away. That was difficult for him and Mary Margaret Rothbone. The first move was to Atlanta, and then on to Washington, DC. Farther away from the Rothbones.

While Rosemary was living in DC, the judge helped her land a job with Senator Thad Cochran, and she loved being involved in political activities at the highest level. When their grandson was born, however, it was obvious that Rosemary's husband wasn't going to be much help. During their daughter's frequent trips home over the last five years, they noticed Rosemary appeared increasingly tired and stressed. They both worried but remained proud of the woman she had become, especially in her role as a mother to young Luke.

For decades the judge sat stoically on the bench listening to awful, depressing stories and irrational decisions. After hearing the pain in his daughter's voice and knowing what her jerk husband had done, he finally understood the desire for revenge. He could see how it would be satisfying.

About a month back she had called and tearfully explained that her husband had left her for a young nurse he had met at one of his clients' offices. Stunned, the Rothbones did what they could to help her get her life back on track, including an unsuccessful attempt by the judge to talk some sense into the husband. They were both excited when Rosemary later called and said she wanted to move home. She missed Mississippi and the slower way of life. She wanted "Daddy" to instill his values in young Luke. She also wanted him to teach Luke about the outdoors, which was something he completely missed out on in Washington, DC. She wanted the same community that had been a part of raising her to help raise her son.

The judge had endured a rough six months and finally had something to smile about. Ever since his wife's diagnosis, their life had been a bundle of doctor's appointments, as they desperately sought an opinion that had a better outcome. He was destined to be alone soon, and Rosemary and his grandson's return made his hurting heart leap. With so much going on at this stage of his life, he applied for senior status so his workload could be lightened. He now had a project: the judge had a young, impressionable mind to shape instead of punishing deviant ones every day.

As the jet loudly rolled to the gate, a lump formed in the judge's throat. He sensed this was a life-changing moment. He placed his arm around his sick wife as they waited for the airplane door to open. The judge felt a sense of guilt that his daughter's sadness could provide him an opportunity to be happy.

* * *

Jake read the report on the doctor who had been attacked. This was not the sort of event that happened to deer hunters. He couldn't get the story out of his mind as he checked e-mails, read reports on illegal activities in the Northeast Mississippi area, and filled out endless forms explaining his daily activities. He hated the redundancy of the paperwork already. His immediate superior was a ladder-climbing career state-government employee who did everything exactly by the book with painstaking detail. Jake knew he was eventually going to disappoint his boss, because Jake hated details and flew by the seat of his pants. He was a spontaneous reactor and bounced through life dealing with whatever came his way.

The Mississippi Department of Wildlife, Fisheries & Parks had hired Jake in a very untraditional way. He had a friend who was very connected to the governor, and a favor was asked. Elizabeth Beasley's father was extremely appreciative of Jake's efforts to protect his daughter several years ago at the place that now was simply called the Dummy Line. When he learned what Jake was trying to do, he intervened without Jake's knowledge. Never had a candidate been fast-tracked through the approval process like Jake Crosby. Many of the higher-ups resented being forced to hire him. Jake, being totally new to bureaucracy, hadn't anticipated the problems but now sensed there were issues as he navigated his daily duties, sometimes without the support he felt he needed. Jake wanted to protect wildlife and help preserve the rich tradition of hunting and fishing that meant so much to him. Being a game warden allowed him to feel that he was doing something good, and he thought it was his aptitude and qualifications that had led to his fast track into the department.

Jake and his warden colleagues fought the usual game violations that plagued most states. Deer were poached and sold for meat; fish were illegally netted from the local rivers and sold to deceitful restaurants. Modern wildlife criminals used all the latest high-tech equipment to help them be successful and elude capture. Game wardens now also faced encounters with portable meth labs that popped up on remote farms, hidden in old barns and abandoned houses. Danger was abundant in the swampy woods of rural Mississippi.

Today was different, though, since they had received word that the popular local doctor had been robbed at his hunting club and beaten unconscious. The doctor remained in serious condition at Baptist Hospital while the staff worked nonstop to reduce the swelling on his brain. Information had been somewhat foggy since the event. When the doctor wouldn't answer his phone and didn't arrive home, his wife had freaked out. His partner, who knew the property, had discovered him, and instead of waiting for an ambulance, managed to load him into a truck and get him to the hospital. The crime scene had been seriously violated, but boot prints and three cigarette butts told part of the story. Jake and his partner were trying to absorb details that had been shared by the sheriff's department, which was handling the crime.

Jake had been paired with Virgil Fain, a man who found his niche in the bureaucratic state-government forty-hour workweek. Lately, he had been nursing a bad back that he claimed was from chasing alligator poachers in the mud but was more likely caused by his extended belly. He'd become the butt of many jokes in the department because the lawbreakers quickly realized they could run from him. He could not catch anyone on foot, and since the department was already short-staffed he oftentimes didn't have any assistance. He'd invest hours observing duck hunters shooting over the limit and sneak right up to the hunters. When he emerged, the guilty parties would take one look at him and immediately take off running. His prosecution rate had kept sinking, until he started concentrating on catching the guys at their vehicles.

That seemed to level the playing field. Nobody ever said Virgil wasn't smart. He'd been with the department fifteen years and knew more about wildlife and the laws than anyone Jake had ever met. He also entertained Jake with constant useless trivia. Virgil arrived on time and left exactly nine hours later after he took his mandatory one-hour lunch break. He was a pure government employee and a product of the system.

Virgil sprawled in a chair in their small office and gulped his morning breakfast, which consisted of a sixteen-ounce Red Bull, a honey bun, and a banana.

"That's not exactly a healthy breakfast, you know," Jake said, as he had almost every time he'd seen the meal.

"I gotta have sugar for energy. It kick-starts my brain, and I get a headache if I don't."

"How many bananas are you up to now?"

"Thirty-three," Virgil explained with a sigh, as if he were tired of explaining. About a month before he had announced that he was on a mission to eat three hundred and sixty-five bananas in a year.

Jake looked at his gut. "I bet your doctor would be interested in you eating a little better."

"My banana diet is going to get me into shape."

Jake looked at him stuffing his face and laughed. "You're already a shape," he said. "Round."

Virgil just shook his head and brushed the fallen sugar crumbs from his chest. "Not only were you a terrible stockbroker, but you're also not a comedian."

Jake went back to reading the report and reflecting on his own near-death experience that had started as a robbery. When he'd finished reading, he looked up at Virgil. "You ever heard of a hunter getting robbed like this?"

"No, but it doesn't surprise me, though. Hunters have a lot of resalable guns and gear that could be turned to cash pretty quick."

Jake knew all too well just how possible it was, especially in today's world, where drug users would seemingly do anything to buy another hit of their preferred drug. "I wanna see that crime scene."

"Yeah, me too," Virgil said.

"Swelling of the brain sounds serious."

"It is. We'll need a big break to solve this one, since there are conveniently no witnesses." Virgil took a bite of honey bun and washed it down with Red Bull. "So, what was your day looking like before we got this news? You got your monthly paperwork done?"

Jake slumped a bit. He hated mundane paperwork.

"No, no, I haven't. I need to learn about the Bolivars from Columbus. You know anything?"

"Chance and Chase Bolivar? Now that's a pair. They're always in some kind of trouble, but nothing ever sticks on them. And they've been in some sticky situations. They are slicker than greasy BBs."

"So you know of 'em?"

"Oh yeah. Last I heard, they were making moonshine and tried to get a permit to do it legally. The state alcohol control board turned 'em down because of their shady past. That just pissed 'em off."

"You have any idea where they hunt? I got a tip that I need to check up on them."

"You haven't ever heard the story?"

"I don't think so. Tell me."

"Their daddy owned a bunch of land south of Columbus on the Tombigbee River. He basically swindled it from a family that had owned it for generations. That's a whole 'nother story. Anyway, Bronson, their daddy, died in prison a few years back and left 'em the land, but when the will was probated, he shocked everyone by giving lifetime exclusive hunting rights to his lawyer! Chase and Chance had a screaming fit. The will also specified that they couldn't sell the land, and he put limits on how much timber they could cut."

"No way! I've never heard that story," Jake said with a shocked look.

"Of course they contested the will, saying that the lawyer added that language when their daddy was out of his mind, but nonetheless it held up in probate court."

"So they can't even go hunting on their own place?"

"Nope. Not legally. It's a mess."

"That just doesn't seem right," Jake said, shaking his head.

"It was in the will."

"I can't even imagine owning a place and not even being able to hunt on it."

"Or sell timber when you wanted to," Virgil said. "They started selling dirt and gravel, though, and they figured ways to get under the lawyer's skin. I heard the lawyer has worked out a deal with them that lets 'em hunt some of it. Heck, he doesn't even hunt; he's too busy chasing ambulances."

"That's a crazy story," Jake said, laughing.

"And it's a sweet property on the river. Great zip code for lots of wildlife."

Jake nodded. "Can you show me?"

"Can you tell me why?" Virgil asked as he peeled a banana.

Watching Virgil begin work on his banana, Jake remembered the judge asking him to be discreet. *Surely I can trust him,* he thought. Virgil was one of the most trustworthy guys he had ever known and had never given Jake any reason to doubt him. Jake had known him only a few months, but he didn't appear to be motivated by money. His interests appeared limited to heirloom garden vegetables and cooking.

"They are meeting a known felon," Jake said. "I have a tip that they may be up to more than just a friendly hunt."

"It must have to do with the missing money."

Jake nodded. "You know about the money?"

"Everybody knows about the money."

"Well, I didn't."

"You're a sheltered enigma."

"Whatever."

"That's why I think the lawyer got the hunting rights," Virgil said. "It was clearly to give himself a reason to be able to snoop around."

"You think he tricked Bronson into signing the new will?"

"Yeah, I do. Everybody does."

Jake shook his head again. "So can you show me on a map where it is?"

"Yeah, I can show you after we look around the doctor's crime scene. There's a great place to eat lunch down there too. Meat and three cooked the old-fashioned way, and they make a mean banana pudding that will put me over my daily requirement."

"I'd like to learn more about their dad, the missing money, and this lawyer."

"Buy me lunch and I'll tell you everything I know."

Jake looked at the lazy warden, who tried to find a free meal every day, and shook his head. "You got a deal," he replied. Dealing with Virgil was more exciting than investing little old ladies' retirement funds. So far Jake wasn't missing the rat race of the stock brokerage business. He grabbed his truck keys and jacket.

"Let's go help that doctor. I heard he's a good guy," Jake said.

* * *

As children, Chance and Chase Bolivar never really looked alike. Chance always had a muscular structure that most people found menacing. Chase worked hard to keep herself in some resemblance of shape and could turn heads if she wanted to. However, in the last few years their differences in lifestyle had begun to accentuate certain features. Chance was sixty pounds heavier and rarely was seen without a ball cap and some form of tobacco in his mouth. He drove a GMC four-wheel-drive truck with just enough lift to allow him some larger rims and tires. His truck was a big part of his personality. For him, bigger was better. Chance was either dead broke or had a pocket full of cash. When he had cash, he was on a fast track to being dead broke.

Chase wore only the latest fashionable brand-name clothes, because looks were important to her. A solid half hour of her day was spent on a treadmill, burning calories. The thinner twin drove an older Mercedes and had always been the smarter of the two. Chase hated the woods and anything that didn't involve trying to make money.

Between the siblings they had been married and divorced three times. Missed alimony payments were the norm for Chance, who had a teenage son and preteen daughter by different wives. Chance was beginning to like his young son now that he was getting older, but he had very limited access to his kids because of previous behavior issues. Chance was a dad in the biological sense, but that was about as far as it went. Therapy had been a disaster, and while Chance completely blamed his ex-wives for his problems, the wives and the Lowndes County courts pointed their collective finger at him.

Chase and Chance originally pooled their resources, living together in their late father's outdated house on the Tombigbee River to cut expenses. The siblings got along most days, but under the surface, waiting to expose itself, was a deep resentment.

Chase was bitter at the world and the hand of cards that she had been dealt. She was angry at their dad for not leaving them the mysterious fortune, which she considered their birthright. Chance just floated through life doing whatever he was told. Everyone could tell he wasn't wound as tight as his sister. But what he lacked in motivation he made up for in pure meanness. The Bolivar twins were each scary for different reasons.

To no one's surprise, they both equally hated the attorney, who in their minds had manipulated their dad into signing a will that clearly benefited him. They had spent too much money contesting the will and had finally worked to make peace with the lawyer, even though they both still loathed him. Chance loved to hunt, and it frustrated him that they couldn't hunt on their own property without permission. Chase wanted the land as an asset that could be sold. The big kicker was the burden of inheritance taxes, and they really needed to sell timber to help pay the taxes down. Their dad had basically given them debt, and they were convinced he wouldn't have done that on purpose. There had to be some kind of mistake.

Bronson Bolivar also left them the only legitimate business that he owned, the septic tank repair and installation outfit. It was a license to steal. Customers never asked many questions; they just wanted their sewage problems solved as fast as possible. The Bolivar twins knew how to work the racket, yet because of their poor management skills the company made only enough money to help them stay just barely ahead of their bills.

While the twins had their differences of opinions, for different reasons they chose to look out for each other. They had been a part of schemes ranging from staging false accidents to selling moonshine whiskey. Recently, they had been studying a scam that involved selling the idea of a chain of pet cemeteries to the sharks on *Shark Tank*. Chase wanted to meet Mark Cuban. On a napkin in a bar, she had done the math that would allow them to sell over eight hundred burial plots per acre. At a minimum of five hundred dollars a plot, they quickly realized ten acres of pasture could yield them more than four million dollars. If they could be selective about buying rural land outside of metropolitan areas, they thought they had a formula to make some serious money. Though neither had the skillset to execute the plan, Chance thought it was brilliant, and Chase wanted to be on national television. Chase was desperate for a big financial windfall to hit them in a hurry, lottery-style. Chance, however, appeared to be just along for the ride.

As hard as she'd worked at trying to make money, Chase had worked even more tirelessly for almost twenty years trying to find the rumored fortune in cash their dad was supposed to have hidden. The thought of the money tortured her day and night. She had no real proof that it existed, and their dad had never spoken of it, but it would have been just like him to hide it. For his part, Chance knew the money existed and enjoyed searching for it. But more than anything, he relished seeing his sister tortured by the thought of the money. She would get physically sick worrying about it and the idea that someone else might find it first. Though they had looked everywhere they could think of, searching remained a weekly ritual, and each day she cussed their dead daddy, his cheating lawyer, and Judge Ransom Rothbone.

CHAPTER 3

Rosemary walked into her room and was comforted by the familiarity of it. She knew each picture and stuffed animal, remembered each plastic trophy and poster that still hung on the walls. Each had a specific memory. The room seemed smaller now, but it felt good to be home. She sat on the edge of her bed and smiled at her dad as he placed her bags down. She could hear Luke and her mother in the room down the hall.

"We fixed up the guest bedroom for Luke. He should have plenty of room in there," the judge explained.

"Dad, I really appreciate y'all letting me come home."

"This will always be your home. You're always welcome here."

"We won't be in your way long. I promise. I plan on getting a job, and I'll find us our own place. I just need to start over."

"Take your time. I'm looking forward to getting to know Luke better."

"Thanks, Dad. I know he's going to enjoy that too."

"I'm sure you've both had a rough go of it lately. It's good to have you home."

"I'm just craving some normalcy. I just want my world to slow down and for Luke to experience being a boy in Mississippi."

The judge smiled and nodded. He sat down on the bed beside her and squeezed her knee. He wanted to tell his daughter about her mother, but he had promised Mary Margaret he wouldn't. She had her reasons, and the judge respected his wife's wishes.

"Oh," he said, "and I've got a friend that's got some Labrador retriever puppies. They are the perfect dog for a youngster and will show him a lot more affection than my bird dogs. Anyway, he's promised me one. Tomorrow I'll take Luke and let him pick one out. Every boy needs a dog."

"Oh, he'll love that, Dad!"

"Your mother may not be as excited about a puppy as you are, so let's go easy on her at first. Okay?"

Rosemary grinned at her dad and remembered how they had always teamed up against her mom to get their way. "Okay, Dad." Rosemary already knew her mother would welcome anything that would make Luke happy.

Luke ran into the room excitedly and laughed when he saw a picture of Rosemary in her high school cheerleading outfit. Rosemary was just happy to see him smiling. The last few months had offered little opportunity for happiness. It was difficult for Luke to understand his dad leaving them. Rosemary worried that he would blame himself for his parents' divorce. She repeatedly explained to him that it was not his fault, and she hoped he believed her.

Rosemary's mother walked in and smiled. "It's just like you left it."

"Yes, Mom. It sure is," she replied, glancing around, experiencing a trickle that would eventually turn into a flood of memories.

"Luke, I have some chocolate cheesecake downstairs. It's your mama's favorite, Mississippi Mud."

"That sounds delicious," Rosemary exclaimed with wide-open eyes.

Luke and her father hurriedly left the bedroom ahead of her, and as she started to leave she noticed a framed photograph. It was a high school photo of Rosemary and a boy her age on an old trestle bridge that was a teenage hangout. She smiled at the memory as it fogged her mind. *Those were fun days,* she thought.

* * *

Chance and Chase planned out a meeting with their late father's cellmate. They wanted to win his trust and use him for information. Neither one had the patience or the skills to have a healthy relationship. Everything they did was based on their wanting something, and they weren't very good at hiding that fact. Because of this, neither twin had a dependable friend, and they often wondered why.

"Do you really think he knows where the money is?" Chance asked as he guzzled a cold beer and burped.

"Who knows? I don't know what else to do. You've looked everywhere. But if he does know, he'll look for it while he is up here. We have to keep our eyes on him so he doesn't slip off on his own."

"Hellfire, he could already have the money! Dad could have told him, and he has already found it. I wouldn't put anything past our old man."

"In my opinion, if he comes up here, he ain't got the money," Chase responded, staring out the window.

"How do you figure?"

"If you had a couple million in cash and you were his age, would you do anything you didn't want to do?"

"Yeah, you may be right, I dunno," Chance answered while he played a game on his phone. "Maybe he's playing us to try and learn where the money is."

"I doubt that, since *we* called *him*," Chase explained, more than a little disgusted at both the situation and her brother.

Chase looked thoughtfully out the big glass windows at the river. "All those years they were in a cell together, they had to talk about the money at some point. He may not know exactly where it's hidden, but I'm betting he can verify it exists."

"Last night he said he'd be here tomorrow about noon."

"That's good. So let's be real friendly with him and show him a good time, get to know him. Let's fry some catfish, y'all drink some moonshine and get him loosened up. If we find the money, he may be a victim of an unfortunate hunting accident."

Chance considered the idea. Hunting accidents were tough to prove as anything but accidents. "Chase," he said, "I have an idea. Why don't we offer to split it with him if he'll just tell us what he knows? That might speed this whole process up."

"That's not a bad idea. It's just that we've been looking for this for so long I'd hate to give any of it up."

"We have been looking for so long, I'd hate to not find anything!" Chance was enjoying the search, and he didn't want to share any of the found money with his sister, much less an ex-con that he didn't even know. Chance knew that if Perry led them to any money, he would never leave with it.

She sighed. "You make a good point."

"And anyway, I just said *offer*; I didn't mean we would actually give him his share." Chance knew where a deep, remote well was located that would be perfect for disposing a body. The thought of the dark well made him smile.

"Let me think on it."

"You're the brains," Chance replied as he opened another beer. "It might work if he knows something."

* * *

34

Judge Ransom Rothbone had grown up in Amory, Mississippi, just down the river from where he now worked in Aberdeen. He didn't come from a family with social status. His dad had been a high school football coach and science teacher. His mother had been a stay-at-home mom. Ransom had worked his tail off to graduate from Mississippi State with no student loans, and then had attended law school on scholarship at Ole Miss.

He loved criminal law. He was fascinated by people who labored so hard to be criminals. He couldn't understand why they didn't apply their talents to honest work. His defense skills were flawless, and he went on to serve in a local circuit court and constantly made headlines. He insisted that the Ten Commandments be on display in his courtroom and challenged anyone to take them down. Ronald Reagan took notice of him in his last year in office and appointed Ransom to the Northeast District Federal Court. It was a lifetime appointment that provided a platform for Judge Rothbone to have a heavy hand in the Northeast Mississippi area's justice system, and the judge took his role very seriously.

Yesterday he'd learned his senior status was likely to be approved, allowing him to lighten his workload. Suddenly being a judge wasn't nearly as important as it once had been to him. He had a wife who was sick, and there weren't many options for her. His stomach was in knots as he constantly worried for her. Now he had his grandson, and he intended to spend as much time as possible with him, teaching Luke how to be a boy and forget the bad situation he'd recently endured.

Standing in the kitchen, the judge watched Luke devouring a piece of cheesecake and smiled. Raising two girls had been a challenge, and he had always wanted a boy. The girls were great and he wouldn't trade them for any reason, but he wanted a boy to talk guns with and take on hunting trips, where they could fish all night for crappie and not be worried about bugs, mud, and fingernail polish. Girls and boys were different, or at least the ones he was around were. He smiled, and his hands shook with excitement.

"Luke, tomorrow we'll get up early and go to the rifle range. I have a few guns I want to teach you to shoot, and then we're going to pick out a puppy for you. I'll help you train him, and he'll be our duck dog."

Luke's eyes widened, and he looked at his mother with enthusiasm. Rosemary beamed, excited to see his smile.

"What color are they?" Luke asked.

"Either solid black or solid yellow. You have a preference?"

"Yeah," Luke said with a nod.

"Yes, sir," his mom corrected immediately.

Luke looked up, embarrassed at having forgotten his manners. "Yes, sir. I think black would be my favorite."

"That's a fine choice. I like a black dog myself, son. These pups come from hunting parents and should be good dogs."

"Yes, sir!" Luke replied. "Can I name him too?"

"Why, hell yes—I mean, absolutely." The judge knew the women in the room wouldn't approve of his language around the boy. He made a motion to let them know he understood and would try harder to control his language.

Judge Ransom saw his wife and daughter smiling as they looked at Luke. The judge was feeling important, like he was needed for more than just his wallet.

"Is there anything else to look for in picking out a dog, Grandpa?"

"There sure is, like how he carries his tail. You don't want one that carries its tail too high—he's an alpha male, and he'll be really hard-headed. But you don't want one that carries his tail too low. That means he's too submissive. It's gotta be right there in the middle," the judge said with certainty as he used his hands to demonstrate how the dog's tail should be.

Luke seemed to be absorbing every word his grandfather said. He had no idea what "carries his tail" meant, but he knew he would find out tomorrow. He'd also shoot a rifle for the first time tomorrow. He looked past the kitchen into the den with curiosity. The mounted deer heads and ducks had his young mind racing with visions of his own frosty morning hunts. He already liked Mississippi. Tonight he had a big mental project for such a young boy. He had to think of the perfect name for his new puppy.

* * *

Bronson Bolivar's attorney, Billy Joe Green, was a fast-talking, opportunistic lawyer who was always looking for a way to make money. He would negotiate a settlement the way a major league baseball pitcher faced a batter. Most of his pitches were strikes, thrown right down the middle, but he also tossed strategically placed balls that were setting up a later strike. Occasionally, a wild pitch hit a client.

He became Bronson Bolivar's attorney of record when the FBI developed a sudden interest in Bronson's unique business strategy, which was to simply charge premiums that were cheaper than all the other insurance companies and then—and this was the part the feds were interested in—never, ever pay a claim. Unsurprisingly, his discounted prices generated a sizable book of business in a short time.

Defending guilty clients was Billy Joe's forte, which made him a perfect match for Bronson Bolivar. The two of them fought hard and frustrated everyone they encountered.

His last defense of Bronson was exhausting, and he always thought that Judge Rothbone had railroaded his client. In his mind, the judge went out of his way to allow the prosecution to present evidence that would have been tossed out of most courtrooms. Through it all Bronson and the lawyer bonded. Bronson needed legal help, and the lawyer smelled cash. It was easy to act as if he were Bronson's friend, and the lawyer was convincing to the end.

The Bolivar twins started off being fans of their dad's lawyer. After all, he tried to help him. But once the will was probated, they felt betrayed. They never believed it, and a battle ensued that lasted for years. The lawyer carried a pistol everywhere he went in anticipation that one day they might try to kill him.

During Bronson's trial, Billy Joe realized there was still money missing. Bronson would only smile when asked about it. After a few years, when it became clear the twins hadn't found it, the lawyer became even more interested and prepared a will that gave him lifetime access to the property. Bronson Bolivar didn't realize what he was signing, and Billy Joe Green didn't give two shits about hunting. He just wanted to find the missing money. The rumors of millions in cash being hidden somewhere continued to swirl, and he needed an excuse to be on the property. He figured there was a good chance it was hidden on the swampy river property the locals called Boogie Bottom, after an urban legend that a mysterious boogeyman was seen crossing a road in the area numerous times. Bronson laughed when he told his lawyer that he had created the story of the legend himself to keep the local folks off his place.

* * *

Jake was growing exasperated as he drove to the crime scene. He tried to tune out Virgil's ramblings about people not planting gardens anymore. Virgil explained that the secrets for canning vegetables and whipping okra stalks for maximum production were slowly being lost.

"Did you know okra originated in Africa?"

Jake was bored and stared straight ahead at the road, then reached down and made sure the warden radio was working. He wished for a radio call. Finally he responded in monotone, "Really?"

"That's right. There's a lotta what we eat now came from over there. Did you know that Delta State University's mascot is the Fighting Okra?"

"You're full of it."

"I swear it's their mascot, but it's unofficial. The Fighting Okra— now that's funny."

"Well, if it's not official, what . . . ?" Jake let it go. He wanted to circle back to the Bronson Bolivar story, but Virgil frequently went off on tangents. Jake suspected he had ADD or ADHD or something like that. It was hard to keep Virgil on topic. Jake was beginning to wonder why the department had partnered him with Virgil. Someone some-where was extremely relieved to have passed him off. Jake sighed and turned the volume up on the radio when he heard one of his favorite artists, Gordon Lightfoot, singing "Sundown."

"Even I don't listen to that old music," Virgil said when the music began.

"Yeah, well, I'm cultured."

"You're boring."

"I like Adele too."

"That's a little better."

"And Shakira."

"You like to look at Shakira."

"What do you listen to?"

"I'm in an NPR phase."

Jake sighed and adjusted his sunglasses. He liked National Public Radio also, but he wouldn't let Virgil know, not today anyway. "Tell me about Bronson Bolivar."

"You know I *almost* arrested him once."

"Really?"

"Now, this was a long time ago. I was a new warden, and we had a report of some folks shining deer near Barton Ferry Road. It was about midnight, and me and my partner were parked behind some hay bales so our truck was hidden. We were watching the horizon for lights when this truck comes by pulling an old cattle trailer. It seemed odd that someone would be hauling cattle that late, and there had been reports of cattle being stolen in the county. Whoever was doing it was just taking six or eight cows at a time, and the farmers weren't immediately noticing they were gone, you see. Anyway, when we saw the truck we pulled in behind it to see where it was going, because that's what good law officers do—they follow their instincts. We let it get way ahead of us so it wouldn't be suspicious when we followed behind."

Jake was paying close attention. "Go on."

"I'll never forget it, 'cause we found a muscadine vine where we were hiding, and they were all over the ground. They were the best I ever had. You like muscadines?"

"Yes, I do, Virgil. But stay on the story."

"Okay, well, we purposely can't see the truck. That's another trick; you have to stay far enough behind they don't know you're following 'em. You'll learn. Anyway, after we crossed that old bumpy bridge spanning a creek we started seeing brake lights, and they eventually turned in a pasture that had some beautiful Angus cows. You know, they are black as night themselves. We cut our lights and pulled in there, and old Bronson was just opening up the cattle trailer. Turns out he had two horses back there, and when he opened the door a bull he didn't know was in the pasture charged him. Anyway, he was trying to shut the gate to protect his horse, and the bull pinned him against the cattle trailer."

"What did y'all do?"

"We finally got to him after I Tasered the bull and he ran off, but Bronson was messed up. In the headlights he looked dead. The horses were freaking out, and it was pretty dicey there until we got everything calmed down. He ended up having internal bleeding, crushed ribs, and a broken leg. We evacuated him to the hospital and probably saved his life."

"Son of a—" Jake said, in shock.

Clearly on a roll telling his story, Virgil interrupted and continued. "Yeah, I mean it was real bad. We were certain Bronson was gonna steal the cows, but since we didn't catch him in the act he was able to talk his way out of it. The cattle stealing stopped after that night, though. He knew that we knew what he was doing."

Jake was stunned and found himself at a loss for words.

"It was one of the scariest things I ever saw, Jake. I still can't look at a bull without thinking about Tasering that one. I couldn't get him off Bronson, but that Taser sure did."

Jake adjusted his Costa sunglasses again and exhaled. He had a Taser on his belt and had seen it demonstrated and knew how well it worked.

"Electricity is an attention getter," he said.

"Yes, it is."

Jake thought about Bronson and wanted to know more. "Tell me about this missing money."

CHAPTER 4

Rosemary enjoyed the comfort of her old room. She sat on her bed and looked around at her memories. She looked at the George Strait and Nirvana posters hanging on the closet door and smiled at the eclectic musical tastes of her youth. She flicked a switch on her old clock radio, and suddenly the Band Perry was singing "If I Die Young," and Rosemary left it on.

A Rubik's Cube that she had conquered one summer night sat right where she'd left it. It was as if her room were frozen in time. Sitting on her bed, she felt like the last fifteen years of her life hadn't occurred and she should be studying for a high school test. Rosemary felt at home, and most importantly, she felt safe.

The judge tapped gently on the door, and she knew it was him. "Come in, Dad. I guess I'm just reminiscing."

"I saw you slip out of the kitchen. You okay?"

Rosemary studied her dad's face. He looked older than he had just a year ago, and she imagined the stress of the bench was showing. She remembered him from when she was a young girl, and it pained her to see him age.

"I am. It just feels so good to be home."

The judge wanted details, but he knew he couldn't push. She'd tell him what she wanted him to know. Rosemary was a very private person, and she got that trait from him. When she was in high school and dating, he'd wanted to know every detail that she hadn't wanted to share. Of course Rosemary provided only enough information to make him have more questions.

"Do you have a plan? I guess what I'm asking is, what can I help with?"

"He's already filed for divorce, and I'm okay with it. I can't lie: the fact that he left me for a younger woman hurt at first. But I'm getting over it."

The judge clenched his jaw muscles when he thought of his daughter hurting and her ex-husband's actions.

"Do you know why?"

Rosemary sighed and then almost laughed as she wiped a tear from her eye. "He said she made him feel alive again, and he hated that I vacuumed at night." She did laugh then.

The judge stared at his daughter. He had so much he wanted to say.

"She is twenty-five and I'm thirty-nine. It's obvious."

"Some men just can't deal with responsibilities and commitments."

"One night my phone died and I asked to borrow his. He freaked out but eventually let me use it, and that's when the text came in that made me suspicious. He had been texting at all hours of the night, saying that doctors keep crazy hours, to pacify me, I guess. I finally confronted him. He was having a hard time once the drug companies started cutting commissions. His self-worth was totally wrapped up in how much he made. I think this young nurse was a distraction from his responsibilities—or his problems, as he viewed them."

"I don't know what to say, Rose."

"It's okay, Dad. I probably wasn't the best wife, and he certainly wasn't the best husband. He was much more interested in his career than in Luke and me. He didn't understand being a father. It was just a burden to him. He actually told me it took away his edge, whatever that means."

The judge clenched his teeth and exhaled deeply. "Do you have an attorney? I know some good ones. That's something I can help with."

"Yeah, I do, but I'd really need to get a local one to help also."

"I know just the one. She's a bulldog in divorces. She's only been practicing a few years; nevertheless, she's plenty seasoned, and I guarantee you'll like her."

"Thank you, Dad."

"You're welcome. I'll call her tomorrow."

"And thank you for taking care of Luke. I can tell he's so excited."

"He can't be more excited than I am."

"His dad never did anything with him. They rarely ever played ball. I've had to be a mom and a dad."

"It's hard to figure why, but maybe all this is for the best. I'm sure it's painful, but let's make the most of it."

Rosemary hugged her dad and wiped another tear. She noticed a picture of Jake Crosby and her from their senior year in high school. The green water of the Tombigbee River flowed lazily in the background of their sun-tanned, smiling faces. They both looked so young. The picture brought back so many memories, she could almost smell the river.

"Do you ever see Jake Crosby, Dad?"

"I saw him yesterday, matter of fact. He's had a rough time too, but for different reasons. He turned out all right."

"What happened?"

The judge welcomed a change of topic to something that didn't make him want to punch the wall. "A group of sorry-ass white trash tried to rob him a few years back. Jake was at his hunting club with his daughter and it got ugly. He killed 'em, or most of 'em, and one came back a year or two later for revenge and tried to kill him again."

"Oh my goodness!" Rosemary exclaimed.

"It was a helluva story. He's okay now, or at least he says he is. The events of that night would have messed up a lot of people." He shook his head. "Yeah, you could Google it and probably learn more. That's what I do these days."

"I may do that." Rosemary had more than once considered friending Jake on Facebook but had so far decided against it. As much as she would enjoy catching up with him, after their tumultuous past she didn't think it would be proper. She knew she had hurt him, and popping back into his life wouldn't be fair to his wife. Rosemary genuinely hoped Jake was happy, and smiled at the picture of Jake and his wife at the beach.

"Or ask your mom about the Jake business," her father said. "Mary Margaret knows everything that goes on in this part of Mississippi."

* * *

Perry Burns had excitedly accepted the invitation from Chase Bolivar to come and visit. He had planned to travel to the area and search discreetly, but now he had an open invitation. Before his death, Bronson Bolivar had spoken of a hidden fortune and where it lay waiting to be found. Though Bronson was known to spin a yarn, Perry was intrigued. Maybe it did exist, and the kids hadn't found it.

He didn't have much going on to keep him in Hattiesburg, Mississippi. His wife had divorced him and taken almost everything the state hadn't seized. He still had a credit card and enough cash to last a few months, he figured. His kids weren't thrilled with the idea of having to take care of him. They had disowned him after his disgraceful conviction. Most nights found him sitting here at the bar of the Purple Parrot Cafe, eating and drinking his way through an extensive menu and trying to make a plan for the rest of his life. He needed quick cash. Many times he'd wondered about his cellmate's supposed hidden fortune.

Earlier in the day Perry had called in a favor and borrowed a small .357 revolver from an old friend. The gun's serial number had been filed off. He packed it carefully, taking care to hide it well while knowing he might need to reach it quickly. The pistol could protect him but would also send him straight back to prison.

Perry had heard stories about the Bolivar twins. They had grown up with access to money and spent every dollar they could get in their hands. The only reason they ever showed any affection for their dad was to get more money. Perry knew this to be a fact because Bronson had told him. He had given much thought to the events that forced Bronson to the realization. Parents almost always were forgiving of their own children and wanted to believe the best of them. Oftentimes a parent couldn't or wouldn't admit their children's faults, just made excuses. Not Bronson Bolivar. He readily admitted his kids were sorry and always had their hands out. He told Perry stories of their greed that amazed him. The Bolivar twins had a motive to ask him to visit. Perry had nothing but time and thought through every conceivable angle his mind could imagine. He concluded they didn't know where the money was hidden and their hope was that Perry knew. They hoped to learn something from him. The ex-con smiled between spoonfuls of gumbo. *This is exactly the opportunity I have been looking for,* he thought.

Perry began to think back to the conversations that Bronson and he had had while alone in their cell for all those years. His mind wandered back and processed the conversations slowly. Bronson had made and lost small fortunes, and Perry had heard all those stories. He heard about the family furniture business and how that lasted only a short while, with Bronson sucking the life out of it, firing long-time employees to save a few bucks that didn't need to be saved. He also heard about the insurance business that printed money for Bronson and allowed him to purchase land, boats, expensive vehicles, and grown-up toys that were pure wastes of money. "What's the use of having it if you can't show off and make people jealous?" he would say.

Perry ordered a cold beer and thought more about past conversations with Bronson. He knew he had to go to visit the property. He had always planned on it but was waiting for a good time. When the time was right, in the dark of the night he would look for his friend's hidden money. He had yet to meet them, but by reputation the Bolivar kids weren't known for their smarts. Perry was slick—city slick—and his time in prison had heightened his greed for cash. They would be no match for his wits. He just knew he needed to wait for the right time.

* * *

As they approached their destination, Jake finally got Virgil to focus on the topic he was curious to learn more about: the missing money. Extracting information from his coworker could be painfully frustrating.

"I don't have a clue if the money exists," Virgil muttered as he leaned back in the truck seat, "but I'll tell you lots of people do believe it's out there, and I personally think it makes the world a lot more interesting to believe it does. Kinda like Bigfoot."

"So through the years nobody has claimed to find it, or started spending money like a drunken sailor?" Jake asked as he passed a tractor hauling hay. "You know, making crazy purchases beyond their means?"

"Not that I am aware of. Nope. That case is old and cold. I wouldn't imagine anyone is watching that close anymore." Virgil looked at him. "Why are you suddenly so interested?"

"I'm just curious."

"Uh-huh, don't do me like that. Just tell me."

Jake really didn't want to tell Virgil; however, he was his partner. If he couldn't trust him, who could he trust? He glanced at Virgil, who had his eyes closed. The only threat he posed was to take a nap on government time. Jake decided to tell him just enough to keep the information flowing but protect Judge Rothbone's identity.

"Okay," he said at last. "The truth is I got some info that the cell-mate of Bronson Bolivar just got out of prison and is coming up here in a few days to do some hunting."

"This story just won't die," Virgil said with a smile.

"It's supposedly a lot of money."

"Enough to burn a wet cow," Virgil replied with his eyes still closed. "That's Southern for 'a lot.'"

Jake chuckled at Virgil's country expression.

"Those kids have had almost twenty years to look for it," Jake said, "with access to all his property, and they haven't found it."

"Maybe they already have. They'd never tell."

Jake pulled his truck over to the side of the road. His eyes watched a trail of migrating starlings that stretched as far as he could see. "Do you know something you're not telling me?" he asked.

The sound of the truck tires on gravel had caused Virgil to rise up. "That's the first murmuration I've seen this year. Bunch of birds."

"What?"

"Murmuration is what you call a flock of starlings. Although those may be blackbirds. I can't tell from this distance."

"You're avoiding the question."

"Seriously," Virgil said. "Google it and click on 'Images.' They're fantastic."

Jake sighed loudly with obvious exasperation and pulled the truck back onto the road.

"Look, Jake, if you ask me, the money exists. Folks like Bronson didn't trust banks, and most buried cash in Mason jars in their back-yards for a rainy day. With Bronson it was probably Igloo coolers of cash."

"I know folks like that, but that doesn't prove anything."

"That's just it, you can't prove anything. That's why it's a local mystery that's borderlining on being a local legend. But a lot of smart people think it's out there somewhere waiting to be found."

"Like who?"

"My old boss wasted a lot of his time looking for it," Virgil said. "Almost cost him his career."

Jake stared out the windshield as he drove, deep in thought. This sounded like a wild-goose chase, but he knew he would trail the ex-con like the judge had asked. He had to admit he was very curious himself.

"So do you think it exists?"

Virgil watched the flight of the dark birds that were motivated by some internal age-old instinct to gather in huge groups and migrate together in order to be safer. Safety came in numbers and trusting others to be watchful.

"Bronson was the opposite of those birds," Virgil said. "He didn't have a lot of people he trusted or that even liked him. That tends to make me think the money is out there somewhere waiting to be found, if it hasn't been already. Heck, it may never be found."

Jake's heart skipped a beat, and he began to consider that the story just might be real. As his mind began to wander, his eyes spotted a sheriff's patrol unit and a uniformed deputy standing guard at the entrance to the injured doctor's hunting property.

CHAPTER 5

Since the kids had been born, Morgan Crosby had been perennially late to most of the events of her daily adult life. She woke up early enough every morning, but the unanticipated needs of two kids kept her constantly behind the clock. Jake's forgetfulness added to her daily stress. Each day there was something. Today he had forgotten to take the trash to the street. It was a small thing, but they all added up. She was ready to leave the house when she heard the approaching garbage truck and then noticed their oversized rolling plastic refuse container was sitting near Jake's parking spot. He had brought it from the rear of their home last night so he would remember to roll it to the street this morning.

She grunted and cussed under her breath as she placed the baby carrier and diaper bag down. Kramer, the yellow Lab pup, instantly stuck his nose in the diaper bag to enjoy the fresh smells and find something to chew.

"No, Kramer," she scolded.

The young dog looked up, wagged his tail, and then stuck his nose back in the bag.

"Kramer, I said no!"

The dog now had a new diaper in his mouth and ran away with it. Glancing at the foyer clock, she knew she would be late for Covey's doctor's appointment. "Damn that dog," she growled while following him into the den, where he had planned to destroy his find. Snatching the diaper from him, she said no a little louder than usual. The dog dropped his head, and his tail gently thumped on the floor. His eyes said, *I'm sorry.*

Morgan continued to glare at him, and his tail thumped faster. He was a charmer and almost impossible to stay mad at for longer than a few minutes.

"Not the baby's stuff. You need to be outside anyway. Go chew on Jake's boots," she said as she opened the front door and the dog raced out. Maybe the underground fence would fail today and he would be gone when she returned.

Gathering up her armful of baby and her daily necessities, Morgan rushed to get on with her day, knowing all too well that the dog would be there when she returned. Tonight she would talk to Jake about Kramer. He needed some training or discipline; the dog was driving her crazy. She would talk to Jake right after she dropped the bomb that Katy wanted to go on her first date Friday night. Jake would have an interesting reaction, she knew. She smiled as she locked the front door. *Tonight will be fun.*

* * *

Jake parked the truck and was surprised by the amount of law enforcement personnel on the site. The sheriff saw them pull up and immediately walked over to bring them up to speed. He was a typical Southern law enforcement officer who was overworked and underpaid. An older man with almost thirty years of civil service, he rarely wore a uniform. Today he was in jeans and a heavy brown insulated coat. His tan cap had a gold star shield embroidered on the front.

"Virgil, Jake, glad to see you boys."

"How's the doc doing?"

He took his cap off and ran a hand hard through his hair, clearly agitated. "He's in bad shape. He's in a coma right now. They're keeping him in one to allow the brain swelling to go down."

"You seen anything like this before?" Virgil asked as he zipped his jacket.

"Nope, and these wet woods are a tough crime scene."

"Anything new?" Virgil asked.

"We think we figured out where the perp parked his vehicle, and we know he hid behind that tree waiting on the doc. We found four cigarette butts. They were chewed on. Very unique looking but also very soggy, which hurts our chances for DNA."

"Menthol?"

"No, just plain Marlboro Lights. Most popular cigarette made," the sheriff answered as he waved at an evidence technician.

"Where did he park?"

"Right through those woods about a hundred yards, on the edge of the county road. We're taking pics of the tires' tracks, and we also found the doc's cell phone in the ditch there."

"Somebody may have seen the vehicle."

"Maybe, but these county roads aren't heavily traveled. We might get lucky, though."

"Could the guy not sell the phone?" Jake asked, knowing they were expensive.

"Not really. Today's phones aren't nearly as easy to do anything with. You can track down exactly where it is, and most are electronically locked. It's just not worth it."

"I hope this was a random act," Jake said as he studied the doc's pickup truck. It was new and didn't have any scratches. He wondered why the perp hadn't stolen the truck.

"You got any hunches, Sheriff?" Jake asked.

The sheriff exhaled. "No, son, but you can bet it was drug related, and I'd bet the perp knew the doc somehow."

Virgil shook his head. "This is gonna make a lot of hunters and wives nervous."

"Me too," the sheriff said. "But that's where you guys can help. Y'all know who hunts around here who might have gone down this road to their hunting club. If you guys can ask around if anyone saw anything, I'll get my boys to ask the local folks that live in the area. I'd like to get some answers fast."

"You got it, Sheriff," Virgil said as he reached out a hand to shake. "Thank you."

Jake nodded his willingness to help and then shook the sheriff's hand also. When he and Virgil looked around at the scene one more time before leaving, Jake had to push aside a sense of foreboding.

* * *

Virgil's double-wide trailer appeared well kept on the outside but was full of clutter on the inside. The longtime bachelor had turned borderline hoarder after his wife had left him ten years ago and took everything including the dog. The stuff he accumulated somehow comforted him. After walking in from an eight-hour shift with Jake, he tossed his keys into a pickle jar of loose change and quickly undressed. He smelled his loden-green uniform shirt and decided he could get one more wear out of it and its matching pants. He lifted a couch cushion and neatly inserted his folded pants beneath it, then hung his shirt on a treadmill that hadn't been used in years.

Standing in his boxers, he poured himself two fingers of whiskey and plopped down on the couch to press his pants while watching the Weather Channel. The weather highly influenced Virgil's mood each day. Weather changes impacted wildlife movements, poacher activities, and his gardening projects. Virgil had become a game warden right out of college. He also had a biology degree that he'd hoped would move him up into the federal ranks one day. That had been his dream. Now he was eyeing his retirement and just doing what he had to do to get by. The state and an ex-wife had broken him. At one point in his life, protecting wildlife was motivation for Virgil; today he was much more interested in growing hot peppers and heirloom butter beans and drawing a paycheck.

After Virgil watched the local and five-day forecast, his mind turned toward supper. Tonight's would include canned corned beef with runny fried eggs, eaten straight from the pan to save washing dishes. Virgil was capable of cooking meals that would make most Southern chefs envious, but most nights he just cooked what was easy.

Usually after supper Virgil checked his online dating account, surfed Facebook, and called his mama. But tonight he pulled old case files he kept in his home office on Bronson Bolivar and the missing money. Jake Crosby had renewed Virgil's curiosity in the area's biggest mystery. The memories of the old case flowed through his mind effortlessly. The more brown water he drank, the more he recalled. By the time he finished reading files and searching Internet news stories, he was half-drunk and fully informed.

His back pain went unnoticed as he thought about what he could do with the money. He pondered the big question: What would he do if he found it—turn it in or keep it for himself?

* * *

Jake's mind had been replaying the day's events while he ate supper with his family. In between he listened to Morgan explain her day and complain about Kramer, who sat watching Jake eat, clearly expecting him to slip him a piece of food. Drool pooled beneath him, and Katy rolled her eyes at the sight.

"Dad, that is so gross!" she exclaimed.

Jake looked at Kramer and sighed. He loved that dog, but he wished he didn't drool at the sight of food. "Katy, he's just a puppy. He'll grow out of it."

"He's a year old, Jake," Morgan said, "and today I caught him chewing on the car tires." She shook her head darkly. "Yesterday he tried to jump on top of the birdbath and knocked the whole thing over," she added while she fed the baby mashed carrots.

"What do you want me to do?"

"He needs discipline, and he needs to live outside in a pen."

Jake had known this was coming, but he loved the idea of having a dog in the house. It was a great deterrent and first-alert alarm system. Once his old dog, Scout, passed away, he'd moved fast to get another dog. He just didn't expect this dog to be such a handful. "I'm working with him. He's just—he's a challenge. It's taking some time, and we agreed it would be a good thing to have him inside. Anyone breaks in the house, he's gonna let us know," Jake said proudly.

"Unless they have food, and then Kramer would probably be glad to see them," Katy said with a laugh that Morgan joined in on.

"Very funny," Jake said. "Don't you have some homework or something you need to do?"

"As a matter of fact I do," Katy responded smartly as she stood to leave the table. As she passed Kramer, she dropped him a part of a roll, and he caught it in midair. "He knows *that* trick," she said, laughing again as the dog swallowed the roll without chewing.

Katy had really grown in the last year. She was almost as tall as Morgan. In a few months she would be fourteen. She'd suddenly started to develop female curves and was beginning to lose the kid look. *About time to build a moat,* Jake thought with dread.

"You worry about school, and I'll worry about the dog," he called after her. "I heard you have an English paper that's due soon," Jake said in his best dad voice. "You have to have good grades to get into college."

"Yes, sir." Katy placed her dishes in the sink and began to rinse them.

"I'll clean those, Katy, if you have homework you can get started," Morgan offered. "Just call me if you need any help."

"Thanks, Mom!" she said as she started up the stairs to her room.

"Yeah," Jake called over his shoulder, "and I'll come help!"

"I'd rather have Mom," Katy called back. Jake hadn't been known for his good grades in school.

Morgan fed Covey a spoonful of mashed peas and wiped the baby's chin. Kramer could be heard lapping water loudly from the commode in the downstairs half bath.

"Jake, we need to talk," Morgan said bluntly.

Jake didn't like the way this conversation was starting. He'd been the recipient of many we-need-to-talk discussions and couldn't recall any that ended well. Most pointed out something he was doing wrong.

"It's my fault," he said as a preemptive strike. "I'll start closing the lid."

"That's not what I'm talking about. I'll save that one for later."

"What then?"

"You might want to sit down for this," Morgan said with a smirk.

Jake's mind raced from the dog to the kids and to their marriage as he wiped his hands and sat next to Morgan at the table. He sighed.

"Katy has a date Friday night."

"A *date*?"

"Yes. A boy from her class asked her to go to a movie Friday night."

Jake leaned back in the chair and swallowed. "She's only fourteen!"

"I know."

"How old were you when you went on your first date?"

"Fourteen," Morgan said confidently as she folded her arms. "We went to see *Jurassic Park*."

"You remember?"

"It was my first date. Yes, I remember."

"Well, she can't go."

"Jake, he's a nice boy."

"She still can't go. I have to work Friday night. I can't supervise them that night, and I need to meet the kid first."

"Jake, you know him. It's the Housels' son, Will. They've grown up together."

"That doesn't matter. I still need to chaperone them," Jake said as he stood up and raked his hand through his hair.

"Will's mother is going to pick her up, take them to the movie, and bring them back."

"Is she going to sit with them?"

"No, she's not, and neither are you. Jake, you sound deranged," Morgan said with a grin, obviously enjoying Jake's frustration. It was clear to Jake that Morgan felt the time had come. She trusted Katy. There was no reasonable reason to tell her she couldn't go.

"Doesn't she need to study or something?"

"Good Lord, Jake, it's Friday night. The child gets to take a break sometime!"

Jake slung the refrigerator door open, looking for something to take his mind off the situation. He didn't want to think about Katy on a date and all the worries that would follow. He was so disoriented he almost grabbed a container of Greek yogurt. Wiping his face, he grabbed a bottle of Coors Light and twisted the top off.

"She's old enough, we know the boy and the parents, and it's just a movie," Morgan explained with empathy. "Maybe dinner too. I don't know for sure. I think she can handle it."

"She can handle it, but what about us?" Jake said after a swig of beer.

"You mean you. I can handle it," Morgan said calmly.

Jake looked at Morgan, the mother of his two children, and shook his head. She wouldn't let Katy go anywhere or do anything that would put her in danger. That thought was very reassuring to Jake, and he smiled at her.

"Are you sure?"

"I'm positive."

Jake sighed. He couldn't think of anything to say, and his mind was swirling with new concerns. "What movie?"

"I don't know," Morgan said as she stood up.

"It can't be a romantic love movie."

"I'll let you know. They are kids; it'll probably be a Disney flick." She rubbed his back. "Relax, Dad, I got this."

The stunned father stood staring out the kitchen window into the darkness. His world was rapidly changing. He had known it was coming, but still he wasn't ready. The silence was suddenly broken by the sound of Kramer upchucking in the next room.

"Jake!" Morgan said in an exhausted tone.

"I know, I know," he said as he ran toward the dog.

Morgan stayed behind, wanting no part of cleaning up whatever had just occurred in the other room.

"Are you missing a yellow highlighter?" Jake hollered.

"As a matter of fact I am," Morgan muttered.

Jake shook his head at the big puppy. Kramer thumped his tail on the floor and looked pitiful, as all dogs do after they throw up.

"I found it."

CHAPTER 6

Chase and Chance Bolivar felt like they had nothing to lose in inviting Perry Burns to visit them. The man had spent more than five years as their father's cellmate, and it made sense that at some point they had talked.

Chance suggested they beat the information out of the ex-con. Chase smiled at the idea but insisted they try a more sophisticated approach. If that didn't work, they could always fall back on violence.

When Perry's beat-up truck pulled in their driveway, both twins were energized with anticipation. A wild-eyed dog with one ice-blue eye barked incessantly as the older man sat in the truck determining the dog's intentions. The twins studied the old man. It didn't appear he had money, judging from the vehicle he was driving.

"That junker could be a trick to make us think he's broke. That'd be actually smart," Chance said, being somewhat analytical. Something he didn't do often.

"Chance, help him, and don't let that crazy dog bite him just yet," Chase said after lighting a cigarette.

Chase watched them walk toward her and the river house, the dog trailing them nervously and barking occasionally. Another dog was peeing on the truck tires. Chase noticed nothing special about Perry Burns as he approached the house. Simple clothes that probably came from Kmart, topped with a Saints baseball cap that appeared to be as old as the truck. Chance was carrying an old overnight bag. The kind you could purchase at any thrift store for five bucks. Perry Burns was also wearing a bulky jacket, which left Chance wondering if he was carrying a pistol.

"Hello, Mr. Burns. Welcome to our father's river house," Chase said with as much sincerity as could be mustered.

The old man smiled and looked around at the eclectic furnishings. At one time it had probably been very nice. Now it looked more like a college dorm room with old, mismatched family heirlooms.

"Thanks. It was a pretty long drive up here."

"How about a cold beer?"

"I thought you would never ask."

Chase headed to the refrigerator, while Chance continued to glare at the guest.

"Bronson talked about this house all the time," Perry Burns said. "He loved the peacefulness of the river. We sure didn't have a view like this from our prison cell."

"It's been in the family a long time," Chase said. "I like the idea of keeping things in the family. My father didn't really seem to share that sentiment about everything," she added.

Perry took a long swallow of his beer. He knew he was being studied. He knew they wanted something from him. The Bolivar twins were not the type to be social without an agenda. He knew that much from his time with their father.

"Maybe he didn't have time to prepare. You know?"

"Maybe," Chase answered.

"Some people don't think about the future."

"Obviously. This house was one of the few things we got free and clear."

"It's more than a lot of kids get."

"We had to fight to keep it," she said, "and there should have been more."

"A lot more," Chance added emphatically.

Chase and Chance were both standing and studying their guest. They didn't realize he was studying them also.

Perry sat down in an old leather chair and looked around the room before saying, "Inheritance is a funny thing. Between my ex-wife cleaning me out and the state seizing my assets, my kids won't get much of anything from me. They know it and won't hardly speak to me. Like Baptists at a liquor store."

Chance and Chase didn't answer, and the quip was wasted on them. They were incapable of feeling sorry for someone. They just drank their beer and tried to learn.

Chase offered a can of peanuts, and Perry immediately put his hand up to stop any peanut offerings. "No, thanks. I am highly allergic. I even carry an EpiPen with me just in case."

Chase placed the peanuts at the far side of the bar and processed the EpiPen information while Perry continued talking.

"Yeah, well," he went on, "they pretty much disowned me before I was ever convicted. They liked the money and lifestyle well enough before I was indicted, but then they suddenly didn't like my business practices."

"You were guilty?"

"Oh yeah. Unlike most convicts, I'll tell you the truth. I was guilty of being greedy. It cost me everything, including my family. Crazy thing is they were the reason I did it. I was just trying to keep them happy."

"Our dad was bitter that he got caught."

"Hell yeah he was, and I can tell you he didn't expect to die in prison. He was looking forward to getting out. He talked about it all the time."

"You guys got pretty close in prison?"

"We spent a lot of time together, over five years in the same cell. Yeah, I would say we got close."

The excited glance Chance and Chase exchanged at that comment didn't go unnoticed by Perry. It confirmed to him that they had not found the money. The thought made him excited. He felt like he was back in the con game—the only way he knew to make a living. Sipping his beer, he decided to wait and see what they had in mind. He would also wait for an opportunity to search on his own. Suddenly, he felt alive, and he knew he just had to be patient. *I wonder how much is out there waiting to be found,* he thought.

* * *

Judge Ransom Rothbone barely slept that night. His mind raced with thoughts of his new houseguests and his wife's diagnosis, and he also considered Bronson Bolivar's missing fortune. Though during the trial it became obvious he had hidden away a chunk of cash, neither search warrants nor plea bargaining had uncovered a clue. The guilty man tried to hide his smirk when questioned, but the judge could see it and the jury could sense it. Back in the day he'd hated the idea that Bronson would one day walk out of prison with access to the hidden cash. Many times since the trial he'd wondered about the money and if the twins had found it, or if anyone had found it for that matter. No one knew for certain, but the judge figured it to be close to two million dollars. Even if it was a half a million in cash, that was still a remarkable sum of money.

To all who looked, the Rothbone family gave the appearance of comfort and status yet maintained an air of modesty. The judge valued a conservative lifestyle, but his job allowed him to afford a beautiful four-thousand-square-foot plantation-style home on one hundred acres of pristine pasture and woods. His wife, Mary Margaret, had insisted on a swimming pool to make the Mississippi summers more bearable for the children, and he'd happily complied. Since learning she was pregnant with their first baby, she had always been a stay-at-home mother. Now that the kids were gone, she'd focused her attention on furnishing the house with exquisite English antiques. It was a hobby that had almost become a full-time job. The judge didn't enjoy antiquing in the least, but he did enjoy collecting vintage double-barrel shotguns. He had quite a collection. His wife didn't realize how many he had stashed in two safes, and he often hoped that if he passed away first, she wouldn't sell his guns for what he told her he paid for them.

Retirement had been discussed, and the judge hoped to execute his plan in the next few years. He wanted to train bird dogs, specifically English pointers. He always had good dogs, and folks constantly asked him to help with theirs, but he never had enough time. A well-trained started puppy could bring a nice price. The folks that still quail-hunted didn't really care what a dog cost. They just wanted the best dog. That was his kind of customer.

The judge had no idea how many pieces of Blue Willow china his wife had accumulated. Both collections were significant. Most nights he stayed in his study, reading and polishing guns, while she enjoyed the latest HBO series and her Moscato wine. They had secrets, but they weren't toxic to their marriage.

Having Rosemary and their grandson around was going to make their life change. The judge welcomed the modifications to their sedentary marriage, and he sensed his wife did too. Now if only he could find a way to keep his wife healthy. He wanted her to be able to enjoy Luke and Rosemary. Somehow, someway the judge had to find a treatment that would work.

* * *

As daylight broke, Jake pulled his truck onto a muddy two-track road that led into the land next to the Bolivars' family property. He had gained access to an old lock through Virgil's giant key chain. With the access point he could drive in and hide from prying, gossiping eyes, park and walk into the property. After concealing his truck in some wild river cane, he checked his weapon and locked the truck doors. His iPhone glowed as he studied his GPS position to familiarize himself with the direction of the Bolivars' river house. He had three bars of service and realized that cell phone coverage had improved greatly since his deadly night on the Dummy Line years ago. Confirming the direction, he zipped his jacket and set a course. The air was fresh and cool with a smell of damp leaves. *Much better than watching the stock exchange ticker,* he thought.

Normally the late-November woods were dry, and it would be difficult to walk undetected with new-fallen leaves crunching beneath every step. With the rainfall over the last three days, though, Jake could move almost silently. He turned the radio volume down as he walked and admired the beauty of the mature hardwood forest. The property line was obvious. The Bolivars had been cutting trees since as soon as they legally could, and the trees were large enough to generate cash. The neighbors had not. As a result the Bolivar property's timber was nothing like the woods he first entered. Jake looked back at the neighbors' trees before attempting to penetrate the Bolivars' thicket of sweet gum and ash saplings, so thick he could barely see forty yards.

Jake knew he was approaching the river when he heard the steady drone of a diesel engine barge pushing up the waterway toward Columbus, only fifteen miles north. The barge appeared to be moving slowly when it drew into view, but it was gone in only a few minutes, leaving an eerie silence in the woods.

A dog barked and caught Jake's attention. Too far away to be an immediate threat, the dog was most likely at the river house, and Jake cautiously continued his push to the site. He hadn't considered they would have a dog, but he should have. *I still have a lot to learn,* he thought.

When the river house came into view through the trees, Jake rubbed mud on his face to darken his skin, then crawled to a stump that allowed him a good vantage point. Through binoculars he could tell the house had once been a fine structure but had clearly seen better days. A misty fog boiled just past the roofline, indicating the banks of the river. A light illuminated one window, and Jake noticed shadows moving occasionally. Outside were several vehicles, and he realized he hadn't thought to familiarize himself with what the twins might be driving, or Perry Burns for that matter. He noted the license numbers so he could sort it out later. Halfway up the outside stairs sat a mixed-breed-looking dog that must have been what he'd heard bark. The dog lazily looked at the house as if he were waiting on something. In makeshift kennels next to the house, Jake could see several dogs that appeared to be pit bulls. Most were lounging, but two of the dogs were pacing like caged lions. He was glad they were in behind a fence.

Jake was trying to get comfortable against the hard stump, thinking he might be here awhile, when the side door slid open. A white female approximately thirty-five years of age in workout clothes bounced down the stairs. She placed her ponytail through the back of the cap and took off at a slow jog with the dog leading the way. She appeared to be about the age of the twins. Had to be Chase Bolivar, he concluded.

When it became clear the woman's path would bring her toward him, Jake assessed his surroundings. He was well hidden; if he stayed in his current position, she should jog right by him. Unless the dog smelled him. It was a cool morning. When Jake lightly exhaled, he watched the plume of warm vapor drift away like smoke at a right angle. It would be close, but if the wind held, the dog probably wouldn't smell him.

Jake hunkered down and watched her approach. As she got closer, he silenced his radio in an effort to take no chances. The gravel crunched with each step, and the dog was already panting when they moved past him less than a dozen feet away. Jake did not recognize the woman.

Turning his attention back to the river house, Jake could see two figures moving inside. He couldn't get any closer without being spotted and didn't have any good options for closing the distance. He really didn't know what he could accomplish from here, though. His binoculars helped, but it was still difficult to identify anyone through brief glimpses. At best they would walk outside, and hopefully Jake could overhear what their plans were for the day, but that was a long shot and asking for too much pure luck. At the worst he would report back to the judge that they stayed in the house, but Jake didn't want to have to sit here all day. He had duties and responsibilities and knew he had already missed calls on his cell phone. Seven missed calls to be exact; he'd checked the list before he hunkered down behind the stump. One of them was from a rich landowner who would call Jake's boss if he didn't hurry up and return the call. Jake sighed as he tore open a peanut butter Clif Bar for a snack.

After about twenty minutes he began to hear gravel crunching and knew the runner was returning. Pluming his breath again, Jake was unnerved to see it drift in clear view toward the gravel road. He quickly gathered his binoculars and tried to think of what he should do next. Move? Hunker down and hope the dog didn't see or smell him? As the jogger approached to within fifty yards, Jake tossed the remainder of his snack ten feet in front of him, where the dog would find it if he investigated Jake's scent, then slowly backed away, doing what he could to keep trees and thick brush between them.

The jogger slowed to a walk, and Jake's heart raced. The dog slowed also and looked around curiously. The runner took a phone from her pocket and said, "Hello?"

Jake pushed closer to an oak stump and listened. He could see her trying to catch her breath while she listened to the caller.

"You have to find a way," she said. "Let's sue his ass or something. He has our assets tied up, and we need to cut some timber and pay some bills. It's our timber!"

As Jake listened, he kept a wary eye on the dog, which had his nose to the air. The jogger kept walking slowly while on the phone, but the dog stayed behind. Sniffing loudly, the canine approached Jake's position, and he noticed he had two different-colored eyes, and both looked cold. Jake didn't like the situation he had gotten himself into.

The jogger, holding the phone to her ear, looked back for the dog, and when she didn't see it, lowered the phone and called, "Here, boy."

Jake watched the dog continue to sniff and close the distance. His hand slid to his pistol. He didn't want to shoot a dog, but he had to be prepared for anything.

"Here, boy! Come here!" the jogger yelled.

And still the dog continued to slowly approach Jake's position, then sped up when he smelled the protein bar.

The jogger was walking toward Jake now. "Come *here*!" she yelled.

At last the dog turned and looked toward her. His urge for food was stronger than his urge to please, though, and he quickly lunged for the unexpected treat before loping back toward her.

"There you are. What in the world are you eating?" Jake heard her say as he breathed a sigh of relief.

From less than twenty yards away, Jake watched the unknown jogger and hoped he had successfully muted his cell phone. He held his breath until slowly she turned and began to walk away.

"Call me when you know more," she said into the phone. Jake couldn't hear her last sentence clearly. He watched her walk away and return her phone into her sweat-jacket pocket. Then she abruptly started jogging again, with the happy dog leading the way.

Looking at his own phone, he saw he now had nine missed calls and a text from Morgan stating that Kramer had knocked the next-door neighbor's elderly father down, and they were taking the man to the emergency room.

Knocked the neighbor down? Jake sighed and cautiously looked around before he stood slowly. Morgan would be furious, especially if the man were hurt. *Dammit!*

Jake's right leg, injured from the drainpipe incident two years ago, was sore from the awkward stance he'd had to hold over the last few minutes. Rubbing his knee, he thought about the one-sided conversation and decided to leave. The judge would want to know what he'd heard. Just as he was about to turn away, the sun hit the front yard of the house, and Jake noticed unusual colors. Through the binoculars he could see various blue-colored bottles stuck on the ends of a cedar tree's dead branches. Maybe thirty bottles in all. Jake knew this to be a bottle tree meant for decoration, but some seriously believed such a tree kept evil spirits away from an area. The Bolivars must be superstitious. Above the house, two crows sitting in trees caught his attention. Their jet-black plumage shined in the sunlight, contrasting with the glowing light-blue bottles. The whole setting, with fog rising in the background, looked ominous to Jake.

"I gotta go," he said softly.

CHAPTER 7

Virgil had tried to call Jake several times that morning. He wanted to talk about the missing money. He'd spent much of the night thinking back over the case and reading fifteen-year-old newspaper clippings from the *Commercial Dispatch*, the Columbus newspaper.

Jake wasn't answering his phone, and he hadn't told Virgil where he was going this morning. That wasn't good. He could be at his daughter's school watching her in a play, on a routine patrol, or he could be doing something stupid. Virgil had seen his share of fresh new wardens fail to take precautions. Wardens were most often alone when they encountered people, and almost 100 percent of the people they approached daily were armed. It was serious work that required much diplomacy and the ability to very quickly evaluate people and their motives. Most people you approached were law-abiding citizens, but with meth labs popping up in the remote areas of the county, you never knew when you would walk straight into a dangerous situation. When an officer is alone, a group of reprobates always think they can attain the upper hand.

The old-school warden looked at his watch and wished Jake would call, the same way a parent of a teenage daughter worries when she is out past her curfew.

To distract himself, Virgil sipped a Red Bull and read about Bronson Bolivar's love interest, who disappeared prior to the trial. She was known to be of Gypsy descent—in fact, said to be a direct descendant of the queen of all Gypsies, who was buried in Meridian, Mississippi, in 1915. Her grave had become a landmark around the small Southern town now known as the Queen City. People traveled from all over the world to leave trinkets in exchange for advice for their problems from beyond the grave. It was rumored she was buried with a small fortune of silver.

Virgil wondered if she was still alive, and if so, where she lived. That would be a good lead to chase down and see how she was living. He typed her name—Eva Marie Mitchell—into the browser window of Google and hit "Enter."

It appeared he had the wrong name, or Eva Marie Mitchell didn't want to be found.

* * *

Rosemary had decided to legally take her maiden name back. She wanted as little to remind her of her sorry-ass ex-husband as possible. It might cause some headaches for her young son, but she would help him deal with the problems as they arose.

She sipped her morning coffee and looked out the windows of her parents' home. There were so many good memories here. Even though it had been torn down, she could visualize the playhouse where as a child she'd played with her dolls for hours on end. There was the pine tree she remembered backing into on her sixteenth birthday. Her used new car was less than a day old, and she crunched a fender and taillight. Her father never said a word and had it repaired the next day. It took her having her own child to really understand unconditional love, but still she was surprised she didn't get a lecture that time. Her father was famous for his berating sermons.

Out another window she saw the old swing, whose frame was covered in a wisteria vine that she remembered bloomed purple each spring. She had many memories of lazy Sunday afternoons with Jake Crosby in the wooden swing. She would try to kiss him, and he was constantly worried about her dad seeing them. That memory made her smile. She had enjoyed making him uncomfortable but always appreciated his respect for her parents. He was raised right.

Rosemary had often wondered what her life would have been like if she had stayed with Jake. It would have been easy. It was a safe, comfortable relationship, and maybe that's why she wanted out. She always thought there had to be more to life than the status quo. Now, though, she wondered. She had friends who'd married their college sweethearts and quickly obtained the 2.5 kids and a mortgage. Many were happy, and a few were like her, starting over after love turned to something that was far from love and civility occurred only because of the kids. *How do you really know a person?* she wondered. *How do you know that they aren't going to change and cheat or otherwise prove themselves untrustworthy?* It seemed like churches or maybe even high school should have classes on what life is really like and how to determine what you need in a mate. *Maybe they do and I just missed it,* she thought as she sipped her coffee.

* * *

Judge Ransom Rothbone had a very enjoyable morning with his grandson. They started the morning at the gun range, where he taught Luke to shoot a .22 rifle. They went over the basic firearm safety issues first, and he was pleased to see the young boy embrace them with determination. The judge would later recall the scene with the pride of a grandfather.

"Guns are not toys. You never touch one when I am not with you. You understand?"

Luke nodded his head, absorbing the judge's words.

"Never, ever point a gun at anything you don't want to shoot," the judge said with total seriousness. "That's a very important lesson you have to always remember."

"Yes, sir, I promise," the wide-eyed boy answered.

"As you get older, you'll hear people saying bad things about guns. Guns are our right and are protected by the Constitution. You'll learn about that soon in school, but always remember guns aren't the problem. People with no moral compass are the problem."

"What's a moral compass?"

The judge realized he was talking over the kid's head. "It's when somebody doesn't know right from wrong. There are some idiots who don't know how to behave. Do you understand?"

"Yes, sir."

After they left the rifle range, the two drove to the nearby city of West Point to look at puppies. The judge had a friend who raised and trained high-dollar British Labradors to be fine hunting retrievers. Young Luke sat in the grass with a giant smile, trying to remember everything his grandfather had told him about picking out a puppy as five six-week-old pups swarmed him in a frenzy of puppy excitement. He finally selected a small black male. Or the puppy picked Luke out. The judge wasn't certain. It was a fun process, though. There wasn't one inch of Luke's exposed skin that hadn't been licked. Both men enjoyed teaching the young boy about dogs and watching his enthusiasm.

The man who owned the puppies wouldn't take any money from the judge. He was glad to do a favor for his longtime friend.

On the drive home, the judge began explaining to the youngster some of the finer points of manhood.

"Luke, there are three things a man doesn't loan out," the judge explained. "His shotgun, his hunting dog, and his wife. Not necessarily in that order. Remember that."

The judge was about to continue when his cell phone rang. He first turned the radio down and then reached for his phone. Jake Crosby's name displayed on his caller ID, and he quickly pressed the green button. "Hello."

"Judge, I have some information for you."

Judge Rothbone smiled. "Let's hear it, son."

"This morning I walked in through the woods and observed the Bolivars' river house. There were three vehicles, and I could see at least three subjects moving around inside the house. I couldn't get very close because they had dogs, and I didn't want a confrontation."

The judge was picturing the scene in his mind. He had viewed the property on Google Earth and was familiar with the remote location. "Go on."

"After I had been watching for a while, a female about midthirties left the house to go jogging." Jake explained all that had occurred and the conversation he'd overheard.

"That had to be Chase Bolivar."

Jake agreed with the judge and added, "I plan to drop back in on them, but it's going to be hard to get close with the dogs around."

"You need to find a way to get close, Jake."

"It's hard to know what exactly is going on until I actually see them doing something." Jake then explained how he had overheard Chase Bolivar talking to someone about some legal action. The details were sketchy at best, since he'd heard only one side, but the potential of the conversation intrigued the judge.

"Keep an eye on 'em. I'm counting on you, Jake."

"Yes, sir."

"I know. They're pretty smart. They know the value of dogs. Just do the best you can, son."

"Judge, what do you expect or hope I'm going to see them doing?"

The judge thought for a second and finally said, "I don't know exactly, but you'll know it when you see it."

* * *

"Your old man loved his money," Perry said. "I remember him saying many times how he missed carrying around folding money while he was in prison."

"Yeah," Chance said as he exhaled smoke from a cigarette, "he always had a pocketful of hundred-dollar bills."

"He liked other people's money too," Perry added, and snorted an odd chuckle before he took a sip of apple pie–flavored moonshine.

"Did he ever mention the missing money?" Chase asked bluntly.

Perry paused for a few seconds as if in thought. "Not directly, but he always said he had enough stashed away that he wouldn't have to worry about anything after he got out."

The twins made eye contact. But neither made any gestures.

Perry leaned forward and swirled the shine in a ceramic cup. He could see curiosity and a strange hunger in their eyes. "So it's true then?" He wanted to know as well.

"What's that?" Chase replied coldly.

"His stash of cash. Y'all haven't found it? He didn't leave any instructions in a will?"

"Our dad wasn't much for planning or instructions or thinking about anybody other than himself," Chase explained as a matter of fact.

"Yeah, I could see that in him. I suppose you've looked in the obvious places. Safes, safety-deposit boxes, old mattresses."

"Of course. We've turned his world upside down and don't have anything to show for it."

"How much do you think we're talking about?"

Chance was not the talker of the two. He didn't understand the strategies that Chase was always trying to deploy. So he joined Perry in watching Chase as she measured her answer.

"Millions, we think. There's no way to know for sure."

Perry took a slow sip and grimaced as it burned his throat. "That's a lot of cash."

"That's why we invited you here," Chase said. "You got any information that might help us?"

Now Perry Burns was trying to deploy his own strategy. He needed them to be convinced he could help, to buy some time and trust until he could look where he wanted. He would do whatever it took to get the money, all of it. Remembering the pistol in his luggage, he knew he was prepared for anything. For millions in cash, he was capable of anything. Prison had taught him that.

"He was always talking about money," said the old convict while the twins watched his eyes with growing anticipation. "He was probably giving me clues and I just didn't realize it. I had no idea that you guys were, you know, looking for it."

"We need you to think back," Chase said. "Remember some of those conversations."

"I've been so busy just trying to adjust to life outside prison without a job, I haven't thought about it," Perry lied convincingly.

"We'd like to make you an offer. You help us find Daddy's money, and if something you know helps us locate it, we'll cut you in."

"What's a cut look like up here?"

"We're offering ten percent."

"Ten points, huh?"

"All you gotta do is remember. Chance will do all the work."

"But what I remember is probably going to be pretty critical. I mean, you haven't found it yet, and I figure you've been looking for years."

"What do you want?"

"Thirty percent" came out of his mouth, even though *All of it* was on his mind.

Chase looked at Chance and exchanged a look that only they understood. Chase then looked back at the convict with solemn eyes.

"Seriously, you got some ideas?" Chance asked, knowing he intended to drop Perry down an old abandoned well after they got what they needed from him. He would be in control of the situation and the number of people who lived after the money was found.

"Hell yeah I do."

Chase exhaled and looked at her brother with a nod. "Okay, if you contribute and we find the money, then twenty percent, but not a penny more."

"And y'all take care of me while I'm up here. Place to sleep and three squares. I don't have any money, you know."

"You can stay in the guest bedroom and eat all your meals with Chance."

For a convict who was just released from prison with no means to support himself, this was a pretty sweet deal. It wouldn't take long for him to gain their trust. Perry smiled and leaned forward. "You have a deal."

CHAPTER 8

Jake started returning calls while he drove his official duty truck about twenty miles south of Columbus toward the small community of Brooksville, Mississippi. Virgil anxiously answered his first call on the second ring.

"You want anything from the Mennonite bakery?" Jake asked.

"Yeah, get me an apple fritter."

Jake shook his head. "That on your health diet?"

"It's made from fruit, Jake; it ain't all that bad for you."

"Right."

"Where have you been? My phone's been ringing with people looking for you, and I had no idea what to tell 'em."

"I took a walk through the Bolivar property on the river."

"You shoulda told me where you were going."

"You sound like my wife."

"You forget I'm your partner. If you get in a bad situation, it would be helpful for me to have a heads-up as to where you are."

"Yeah, you're right. Sorry, I'll let you know next time. What's up?"

"Some poachers worked the north end of the county last night shooting deer. Couple of landowners reported it. Our boss called and asked me about how you were doing. I take it you guys still aren't getting along."

Jake groaned. He did not like his immediate supervisor, and the feeling was mutual. "What did you tell him?"

"I told him you were the best thing since Sherlock Holmes."

Jake smiled. "Yeah, I bet he bought that."

"You need to call in today and get your reports up to date."

"Yeah, I will," Jake said with a sigh.

"You workin' something?"

"Not really—maybe."

"You know that Chance Bolivar is a thoroughly dangerous man. If I had known you were going to his place, I woulda put a stop to it."

"You really think so?"

"He has been involved in several suspicious incidents, but he always has some miracle that keeps him from being prosecuted."

"Really?"

"They had an employee that Chase caught red-handed stealing from them. She fired him. Chance was outta town gambling and boozing it up with his buddies. When he got back, the guy, who was now out on bail, suddenly went missing. They found his johnboat on the river, so there was this possibility that he had an accident and drowned, but everyone with common sense was looking at Chance."

Jake processed what he was being told.

"A week or two later a ten-foot gator shows up near the bridge in town and has a weird taste for wanting to eat people. Unfortunately, it had to be killed, and an autopsy finds the missing man's wedding ring and watch in the gator's gut, but they never could prove Chance had anything to do with it."

Jake stared out the windshield a few seconds, considering how the missing man came to be inside an alligator's stomach.

"They are pure trouble," Virgil said. "What are you up to? It's that missing money, ain't it?"

Jake was pulling into the parking lot of the Mennonite bakery, but his mind wasn't on doughnuts now. "Yeah, it is."

"People have been looking for that a long time."

"I went to observe Bronson's cellmate at their river house. It's suspected that he knows something."

"Do the police know this?"

"Yeah, I think so."

Virgil's suspicions were right. This missing money would never go away. It fascinated him as much as anyone.

"You at the bakery yet?"

"Yeah, I just pulled up."

"Hurry up and meet me at the boat ramp south of the Highway 82 bridge. I'll talk to you then. There are some things you need to know. And bring me a lemon square also."

* * *

Perry Burns sat in an Adirondack deck chair, sipping coffee that tasted like it had been filtered through a dirty sock. He was, however, enjoying watching the river meander its way south. He pondered the thought that the water passing in front of him would find its way into the Alabama River and eventually flow into the Gulf of Mexico. The flowing river sure beat the memory of his view from the prison cell. After being incarcerated for over ten years, he never took a sunrise, sunset, or good view for granted.

Prison had afforded him lots of time to reflect. The parole board heard him say he was reformed and rehabilitated. Even more, Perry said he was repentant. It was all a lie that he had rehearsed thoughtfully and delivered skillfully. He was sorry that he had gotten caught, and he constantly replayed events in his mind that he wished he could change.

He knew that greed had gotten him. There was always someone with a bigger house, more money, or newer cars. He eventually realized he couldn't keep up, even though he tried gloriously with crimes of deceit. Each one hardened him to do whatever needed to be done to preserve his lifestyle.

Perry knew he was capable of murder, and he would kill the Bolivar twins when the money was found if he needed to. He wouldn't suffer through poverty during his golden years. This time he would be satisfied with the money and live within his means. With no wife to siphon off the money, he figured he could make a few million last the rest of his days. Maybe the kids would actually come back around. He felt rational and clearheaded and considered that perhaps he had actually learned something in prison after all.

Watching Chance approach the deck, Perry Burns knew what was on the man's mind. Yesterday after arriving, Perry did his best to get a read on Chance. He had the appearance of someone who didn't care about anything—what he did, how he dressed, what he said, what he ate, or what anybody thought. Chance Bolivar did not give a shit and had the air of someone who was fearless. He wasn't full of bravado, but rather a quiet confidence in anything physical. It was obvious he wasn't the smartest of the twins, and he looked at his sister for instruction and affirmation. This surprised Perry, but he was already scheming how to take advantage of the weakness.

Chance looked like he hadn't bathed in a few days, and Perry thought he saw a tick when he raised his shirt to scratch an itch. Slurping coffee that was undoubtedly spiked with some form of alcohol, Chance mumbled something about beating a dog that barked all night.

"They're pit bulls. I use 'em for catch dogs."

"Whattaya catch?"

"Mostly wild hogs."

"They make good guard dogs too, I'll bet."

"You don't want to run from them; they'll tear your damn arm off," Chance said, and cleared his throat and spat on a nearby tree.

"I'll keep that in mind."

"I have to keep 'em penned up or they'd hurt somebody."

They both turned when they heard the door creak, and watched Chase emerge. She was sweaty from her run and was drinking cheap bottled water.

"So do we still have a deal?" she asked Perry.

"We do. I've been thinking about where it might be hidden and conversations I had with your dad."

Chase looked out over the river and then turned so she could see both men clearly. "And what's your thinking got you so far?"

"I would think it's obvious that he would want to hide the money someplace he knew he would have access to when he got out. Something that would not be sold or developed that could have someone accidentally find it."

Chase sipped water and listened. So far nothing he'd said was of any value.

"He also wouldn't hide it where it could be found by a dumbass with a metal detector. That's too easy."

"We have almost a thousand acres here," Chance said, "and Dad had a bunch of rental properties, an antebellum house he wanted to restore, the old furniture factory, and the septic tank business. He had lots of places to hide something."

"You still have all those?"

Chase sighed as if she were exhausted. "We sold the rental houses and the old house downtown after we searched it. We haven't been able to sell the old factory."

"It's a shithole," Chance added.

"He probably expected you to sell the factory and rental properties, but do you think he expected you to sell that old house?"

"Dad always loved anything old," Chase said, "and especially anything that went back to Civil War times. He bought that old house with the intentions of restoring it and making it part of the spring pilgrimage of antebellum homes."

"He wanted to live there," Chance blurted.

"He did, but restoring it was more expensive than he thought, and that's about when he started having legal issues."

"He did talk about the Old South all the time," Perry said, remembering. "That old house could have been a hiding place."

Chase scowled. "A doctor and his wife bought it and have totally restored the place. If they found the money, they kept it quiet."

"I searched all over the place before we sold it," Chance said as he stared at the floor. "Inside and out. Only thing I found was some Confederate money in a wall. Nothing valuable."

Perry was in deep thought. Bronson Bolivar had talked about the Old South all the time. He'd even talked about moving to South America. He had explained that after the Civil War about ten thousand Southerners had packed up and moved to Brazil to start a new life, and according to Bronson, remnant communities still existed and cherished the old Southern ways. Bronson called them Confederados. Perry struggled to recall relevant parts of past conversations.

"He did love anything old," Perry said. "That house seems to be the best potential location, if you ask me."

Chase looked at Chance, and he looked away and shrugged. Chase knew they had already searched the old antebellum house thoroughly.

* * *

Rosemary listened to Luke tell about his morning while the puppy excitedly jumped all over everybody in the room. She couldn't remember the last time she saw her son so excited. Her dad looked like he was enjoying the moment also. Luke babbled nonstop about shooting a

.22 rifle and told her in great detail about how he picked out the black puppy.

"His breath smells funny," Luke said with a giggle as the dog licked his face.

"He has puppy breath," his mom explained with a smile that had been rare of late. She was enjoying watching the puppy's tail wagging like a windshield wiper on high speed.

"They say money can't buy happiness," the judge said with a chuckle. "Whoever said that never bought a boy a puppy."

Mary Margaret Rothbone enjoyed watching Luke's excitement but worried the puppy was going to pee on her antique pine floors. She and her husband had raised many bird dog puppies, but none in her house. She had drawn the line with her husband but moved it quickly for Luke.

"His name is Shadow," Luke announced.

"I love it," his grandmother said. "It's perfect."

"The man at the kennels said it would be really good for me to have a dog. He said that a dog brings out the best or the worst in a man. Just like a woman," Luke said with remarkable clarity.

Rosemary and her mother instantly glared at the judge. The judge nervously shrugged his shoulders and dropped down on a knee to pet the puppy.

"Well, Luke," his grandmother said, "you're still a young boy, and you shouldn't be worried about women."

"I know. I'm just saying."

"What else did the wise man tell you?" his mother asked.

"We have to keep the puppy warm, so he needs to sleep in the house."

Rosemary looked at her mother and then at her father, who was nodding his head. She knew her mother wasn't excited about having a puppy in the house, but—the consummate grandmother—she wasn't going to say no either.

"Is he housebroken?" Mary Margaret asked.

The judge shook his head from side to side.

"And he is gonna be lonely, because this is the first night without his mama," Luke explained without looking up from the puppy.

"We'll fix a spot in your room, Luke," his grandmother said lovingly.

The judge tried to tamp down his smile. He'd known she would be agreeable once she saw how happy and excited the puppy made Luke. His wife was the most compassionate person he knew, and Luke was her only grandchild. Luke could ask to keep a baby skunk in the house and she would have agreed.

The judge watched her smile and could tell she was tired. Luke and Rosemary arriving had given her a new purpose, but the failing kidneys were taking their toll. Soon they wouldn't be able to hide this from Rosemary. The judge worried what his life would be like if they didn't get a donor kidney soon. He had recently made calls and was seriously considering taking her to a specialty clinic in France where he could purchase anything she needed medically. The price tag was staggering, but he loved his wife, and he would find a way to pay. He had to.

* * *

Virgil sat at a cold metal picnic table overlooking the Tombigbee River as he waited on Jake to arrive. With his smartphone, he checked his Farmers Only dating service account, only to find he didn't have any messages. It was the last service he hadn't tried, and he hoped he would find a country girl.

Jake was approaching the bridge and boat ramp in his state-issued patrol truck. He'd just gotten off the phone with his very unhappy wife. Morgan was still at the ER, dealing with the fallout of the Kramer incident. Evidently, the dog had gone after the tennis balls on their elderly neighbor's walker as he walked by their house. Kramer loved tennis balls, and seeing two attached to the bottom legs of the walker must have driven him crazy. He kept tugging on a ball, while the older man pulled back until he finally fell. His head was bruised, but not seriously, and the neighbors weren't too upset. They seemed to understand what had happened. Jake promised to come home as soon as he could.

Seeing Virgil sitting on the picnic table made Jake forget the dog problems. He wanted to learn more about the Bolivars. He pulled the truck in next to the table and radioed the county dispatch his location. His leather belt and holster creaked as he got out of the truck.

"So how did you learn the cellmate was in town?" Virgil asked immediately.

Jake handed him the bag of pastries and looked into his eyes. Could he trust Virgil? He had been on the force in the same capacity for over twenty years. He could be frustrated that his career had never allowed him the opportunity to advance. It had taken only a few months to learn that Virgil was very good at what he did, but he did only enough to get by. He never worked fifteen more minutes a week than his forty-hour minimum. Nevertheless, Virgil did know many relevant people in Northeast Mississippi, and he could probably help Jake.

"I got a lead that they were meeting."

Virgil was wearing jeans and a fleece jacket, since his shift didn't start until later in the day. He pulled an apple fritter out, and crusted sugar dropped onto his jacket as he took a bite. "You got a lead?"

"That's right," Jake answered, knowing he was going to have to tell Virgil more information if he expected to get some help.

"This lead, was it anonymous?"

"No." Jake leaned against his truck and looked at the ground.

"Can you tell me who?"

"I'd rather not. They asked that I keep it quiet."

"And you don't trust me, your partner?"

"I didn't say that. I'm just trying to do what was asked of me." Jake didn't like being secretive. It wasn't his style.

Virgil took another bite of his apple fritter. The silence was awkward.

"Jake," Virgil said at last, "the Bolivars are not good people. Their grandfather was a wealthy businessman. Somehow their dad pissed away the family fortune and embezzled another fortune, and they missed out on it too. They are sorry white trash from old money, and they're bitter. Bad bitter. You can't snoop around on them and not be prepared for a confrontation that could get very ugly. They are dangerous."

"What about the female, Chase?" Jake asked. "Is she dangerous too?"

"Yep. She's cold-blooded and calculating."

"What's she done?"

"For starters, about ten years ago she caught her second husband cheating on her. He had a fondness for hookers and made regular business trips to Atlanta. She hired a private investigator, got pictures and video, all the proof she would ever need in court, but she had no intentions of going to court."

"So what happened?"

"A few weeks later he was found dead on the bench press in his weight room. It appears about two hundred pounds dropped on his neck and broke it. His friends say he never talked about working out."

"Did the police investigate?"

"As far as they could. They uncovered the private detective, but he was so scared of Chase he wouldn't talk. So it eventually got ruled an accident."

"So you think she dropped the weights on his neck?"

"I'm very suspicious. It was all too convenient."

Jake stared at him in shock. This was the same woman he had watched jog this morning.

"He probably got a little drunk, and she lured him into the weight room, and when he wasn't paying attention a loaded barbell crushed his neck."

"So she could pick up two hundred pounds?" Jake hadn't spent much time in a weight room but knew two hundred pounds would be heavy for a female.

"All she had to do was get it up out of the cradle, and then gravity did the rest. Or maybe her brother helped her. Both scenarios are very possible."

Jake shook his head, looking at the slow-moving, peaceful river and back at Virgil as he stuffed his breakfast in his mouth. He took inventory of the situation: somewhere out there was a couple million dollars just waiting to be found. Jake figured the judge wanted justice for the people who'd lost their money. The twins wanted the money and were willing to do whatever to get it. Who knew what Perry Burns wanted? But he probably wanted the money. Virgil wanted to make his eight hours and go home. Jake wanted to resolve a high-profile cold case to prove to his bosses, Morgan, and everyone else that he could be a good law enforcement officer. He also had a deep desire to please the judge, just like he did when he was sixteen. Finding the money would be nice too.

"You know I'll help you," Virgil said, "but what specifically are you trying to accomplish?"

Jake watched Virgil take another bite of fritter and figured he might as well trust him. He didn't want to get caught in a bad situation around the Bolivars without backup.

"They've brought Perry Burns here to see if he knows where the money is hidden. We just need to monitor them. See what they find out."

Virgil thought for a few seconds. "This could be big. I have some listening devices we could install in the house."

"Is that legal?"

"No. But I won't tell anyone if you won't."

Jake loved the simple idea but wondered how they could possibly install listening devices without being seen or shredded by a crazed dog. How would they get inside the house? This was all new to him.

"I got a buddy that can help us," Virgil said as he brushed off the sugar chunks on his chest. "We also need to help find the doc's assailant. I made a few calls this morning, and so far I'm not coming up with anything."

"Have you heard how he is doing?"

"Still in a coma," Virgil said as he reached in his truck for a Red Bull.

"Dammit."

CHAPTER 9

The robber had watched the local television reports and scanned the local newspaper for any mention of the recent robbery. There had been none. It had been the best haul yet—about eight thousand dollars—and such easy money, easier even than the others. It left an itch begging to be scratched.

Then like a gift, later that same day, the robber was eating sushi and overheard a children's dentist describing his bad day. He had been bitten by a four-year-old several times during a dental exam. They'd had to retrieve the child's mom from the waiting room to convince the child to release his last bite. Displaying the bite marks on his finger, the dentist loudly self-prescribed an afternoon deer hunt for himself in front of his friends and the eavesdropping robber at the next table.

The dentist's Rolex Yacht-Master watch looked brand-new. A quick smartphone search of Amazon determined it would be worth almost ten thousand dollars. The dentist looked like he had just stepped out of an Orvis catalog. There was absolutely no doubt that the man would be decked out head to toe in the most expensive of hunting gear.

The short fuse was a challenge, especially given everything else going on in the robber's life at the moment. The previous jobs had been meticulously planned and preceded by days of surveillance. But the robber was feeling invincible and liked the idea of being spontaneous. It was a simple business, really. *Why overthink it?*

* * *

Chase Bolivar spent half a day at the office just trying to keep their business, Septic Tank Services, from unraveling. Payroll, inventory, and employees with little work ethic constantly challenged her ability to keep the doors open. Fortunately, if customers needed their services, they really needed their services. The surrounding counties they serviced had plenty of rural customers with septic tanks. Tree roots grew into waterlines, tanks got old and needed to be replaced, and every few years tanks needed to be pumped out. It was not a pretty business, but it was steady.

When she returned to the river house, she marched up the stairs and found Perry Burns watching *True Detective* on HBO. Ever since his prison exit, he loved watching the premium movie channels when he could. Prison television was mostly soap operas and game shows.

"Where's Chance?" she asked.

"He said he had to help the tank installers fix a winch that was broken."

Chase hadn't heard anything about that, but it didn't surprise her. Their front-end loader and work trucks were always breaking down. She blamed the crews, who clearly didn't care. A broken winch meant more money going out. *Dammit!*

She quickly turned her mind back to matters at hand and matters that could prove to be much more profitable. She grabbed the remote and turned off the television.

"Okay, here's the deal, Perry Burns. You stay here in the guest bedroom; you can't go to any of the properties without either me or Chance. I can leave work pretty much anytime, and Chance doesn't work more than half a day anyway, so one of us will always be available."

"That sounds fine," he replied as he reached for his beer.

"I hope you won't be wasting our time."

"I don't intend to." He gave the can a shake to confirm that it was empty. "I'm recalling old conversations right now."

"Can you do that while you're watching television?" Chase asked sarcastically.

"Actually, I can. I'm always thinking. I will figure this out," Perry answered, and then popped open a new beer.

Chase looked at her watch. She had a busy afternoon and was frustrated at the old man's attitude, and Chance was supposed to have already been back. "Don't go searching without us. Chance will be back soon, and y'all can search together."

* * *

The judge spent the afternoon surfing the web for options. There weren't many. His wife needed a kidney, and her history of cancer and chemotherapy ruled her out as a transplant candidate. He had promised her that he would take care of her for better or worse, and this was as bad as he could imagine. He didn't intend to let it get worse. He had found a facility in France that sounded promising. He just needed to come up with almost five hundred thousand in cash, since they didn't take insurance. An extra one hundred and fifty thousand would move the operation up three weeks. It all seemed shady to the judge, but he didn't know any other options. None that were legal.

He made notes and dreaded how he would explain all this to his wife. She wanted to live, but she would never agree to the money, knowing they didn't have all of it. The judge considered asking friends to help, but he really didn't know anyone with that kind of cash lying around. He would gladly sell his gun collection, and it might raise one hundred thousand dollars. They could also sell the family property and house. That could raise the balance, but the property had been in the family for three generations, and there were other family members to consider—that would greatly complicate the matter.

There has to be another way! He sipped a scotch and water.

Inevitably, the aging judge's thoughts turned to the missing Bolivar money. If he could just get his hands on the money, all he would take would be enough to pay for his wife's surgery. He knew the money existed and that the twins hadn't found it yet. They weren't smart enough to find it or clever enough to act like they hadn't. No, he knew the money was sitting somewhere waiting to be found, and he hoped Perry Burns knew where.

The judge walked to the window and saw his wife and daughter on the lawn below him, watching his grandson and his puppy. He sipped his drink and smiled at the scene for a brief moment. Mary Margaret waved at him and he nodded back, then exhaled deeply at the thought of his wife's situation. He needed some serious money fast.

CHAPTER 10

Jake and Virgil spent the afternoon with the members of several hunting clubs near where the doctor was attacked. The majority of them worked regular jobs and were able to hunt only on the weekends. However, one was an insurance salesman and another owned a dry cleaner's, allowing them more flexible schedules. Both had been hunting that afternoon near where the crime occurred, and neither had seen anything out of the ordinary.

They did find a local farmer who remembered seeing a pickup truck parked near where the doctor's vehicle keys had been found. But the farmer couldn't remember any details that really helped. He thought the truck was white or gray but couldn't remember what kind it was. "It was raining, and I had a cow in labor that had breached," he explained. "I was preoccupied."

The injured doctor had improved a bit but was still being kept in a coma to allow his swelling to subside. They were planning to wake him up within the next twenty-four hours.

They all agreed that if the doctor woke up soon, it could really help them understand what had happened that evening. Perhaps he could steer them in the direction of who the assailant was, or at least his race and details about height and build.

On the drive back to town, Virgil returned to the subject of placing a listening bug in the Bolivars' house. The problem was how to get the tiny recording device inside. Even if the Bolivars were gone, Jake explained, they had dogs outside.

"I have an idea," Virgil said while he checked his e-mails and Jake drove.

"I'm all ears."

"It's almost winter. It's getting cold, and I'm sure that river house has propane heat. I have a connection that works at the gas company and owes me a favor. I'm betting we can get a company truck and pretend to check the tank and hoses coming into the house. We can say that we suspect a leak or something."

Jake looked at Virgil, who was scrolling Facebook. "Are you serious?"

Virgil looked up. "Yeah. Why not? If we can recover the money, we don't have to say exactly how we did it."

"Isn't that illegal?"

Virgil sighed and smiled. "Only if you're caught."

"You ever done anything like this? Bugged a house illegally?"

"You gotta be kidding. You won't even tell me who's feeding you information. You don't trust me. Now you want me to incriminate myself to you? I'm just trying to help."

"That's not exactly true, I trust you. I was just asked to keep quiet."

Virgil grunted.

"So how are we going to do it? They might recognize us as wardens if we confront them later."

"They know me for sure. But I have a buddy in Tupelo that's a retired marine. He loves doing stuff like this. I just text-messaged him to call me," Virgil said with a smile.

Jake realized Virgil was trying to help even though his methods were a bit unorthodox. *But maybe they aren't,* he thought. He was new to fighting crime. Maybe this was how you got the upper hand. Jake smiled slyly back at Virgil and imagined what it would be like to look at a million dollars in cash. His mind wandered and considered what he would do with the money. He imagined dumping a box of cash on the bed and watching Morgan's reaction.

* * *

Rosemary sank into the antique leather chair in her father's study. The dark room crowded with books had always been a sanctuary for her, and today was no different. After a few keystrokes, her laptop connected with the wireless Internet. Her e-mail account hadn't been checked in a few days, and she had friends who had checked in on her.

After replying to her friends, she considered her extensive to-do list. Luke was scheduled to start classes at Oak Hill, the local private school, in two weeks, when the new semester started. Rosemary had graduated from the school herself and was thrilled that her son would be enjoying her old stomping grounds. Getting him set up correctly was a priority.

Her divorce was progressing at an expected slow pace, and she needed to turn some paperwork around to her attorney. Everything about the divorce was stressful, but she was through being upset.

With all that completed, she surfed Facebook and laughed briefly at a cat in a shark suit riding a Roomba. She then checked on some old friends from high school and college. Everybody's lives looked better on Facebook, and she marveled at how ordinary her friends' had turned out. For the moment she craved ordinary. She didn't get upset thinking about signing the papers that would officially end her marriage, but seeing all her friends' happiness brought tears to her eyes. Of course Rosemary was happy for them; she was just sad for herself and Luke.

Her life wasn't playing out like she'd expected, but she was about to start over. She wiped a tear and took a deep breath.

A few more keystrokes and she navigated to Jake Crosby's page. There wasn't much there. She smiled, thinking that he probably didn't even know how to use social media. His wife's page was a different story. The photos were endless. There were a lot of family pictures with her, the two kids, Jake, and a dog. Rosemary zoomed in on Morgan's pictures and tried to analyze her. She remembered her from college. Morgan was a few years younger, so they hadn't run in the same crowd, but they'd seen each other at school events. Morgan was attractive, and there were pictures of her running in a 5K. Rosemary searched for more pictures and wondered if Jake had ever told Morgan about her.

Rosemary wondered often about her decisions. The world she'd been so keen to see hadn't been all that great to her, but it had helped her realize that all she'd really ever needed was right here, and she had messed that up too.

* * *

That evening the robber tailed the dentist to his hunting camp, then pulled past the property and parked at a crossroad to think the situation through. The iPhone map app showed the property and all its internal roads and fields. There was no sign of a camp house, though it was possible one might have been built after the satellite image had been taken. Hopefully, that wasn't the case. No camp house meant that the dentist would be returning to an unlit area—a welcome advantage.

The image of the expensive watch was tantalizing, but not enough to cloud the instinct to avoid unnecessary risk. Though local sheriffs would be watching for suspicious activities, the fact that they were twenty-five miles farther south into another county offered some comfort. And there still had been no media reports of the latest robbery. Also, Noxubee County was more rural than Lowndes, which meant significantly less funding for law enforcement. Modern 911 was not an option in its rural hardwood swamps, pine plantations, and large soybean fields—land characteristics that made for incredible deer hunting.

There was every reason for confidence. The decision now made, a seldom-used logging road adjacent to the property felt right to hide a vehicle. Then there was nothing left but to strike a trail toward the entrance road and follow the dentist's tire tracks to his vehicle and wait for him, just like the others.

The tracks were easy to find, as was the dentist's vehicle parked in a cedar thicket. The truck had an empty trailer behind it, since he had ridden an electric golf cart to his stand. Studying the muddy ground, the robber determined exactly the direction he had gone. The evergreen cedar trees made an excellent thicket in which to hide and await his return.

The dentist enjoyed his afternoon in the deer stand. There were no kids biting him, no unhappy dental hygienists, no insurance forms, no medical equipment salespeople, no complaining mothers, just peace and quiet. It was where he came to think. He loved the outdoors. In the summer he frequented a beach house near Dauphin Island on the Alabama coast, where he chased speckled trout while his daughters and wife lay in the Southern sunshine and plotted their next shopping spree. His winters were spent chasing deer and ducks in the Mississippi woods when he wasn't practicing dentistry. His wife cooked everything he killed, and he felt good providing lean, healthy meat for his family. He had been raised to be a responsible hunter, and it was a large part of his lifestyle.

This afternoon he saw a few does but no bucks. He had infrared game cameras strategically placed all over his farm, and dozens of photos of a huge buck he was hunting. The buck was the largest he had ever seen, and chasing the deer consumed all his free time. His buddies at the country club would be jealous when they saw the rack. That's exactly why he was hunting solo: he didn't want anyone else to kill the buck. He couldn't stand the thought. Big whitetail bucks would do that to a hunter.

At last the dentist nestled his rifle in the foam-padded rifle rack, switched the cart to forward, and stomped the accelerator pedal to take him back to his truck. It had turned cold, and although he was dressed in the finest high-tech fabrics, the ride back in the cart brought tears to his eyes. After a few minutes of winding logging roads, the taillights of his truck reflected, and he knew he was close to warming back up.

Having anticipated the dentist's return route and hidden accordingly to avoid the cart's headlights, the robber checked the time and snuffed out a cigarette at the sound of the dentist's cart sloshing through the mud.

The dentist arrived like a NASCAR driver at a pit stop, and with only a slight speed reduction immediately drove the cart straight up onto the trailer. He then jumped down, leaving his rifle in place, to crank the truck to life and get the heater started. Rubbing his cold hands together as he walked back to raise the trailer gate, he never saw the robber approach from behind with a pistol in one hand and the voice-altering device in place.

"Don't move, and don't turn around," the evil voice said. The sound of the pistol being cocked had its usual effect.

"What the hell! Is this a prank?"

"I'll only say it once. Drop to your knees," the weirdly distorted voice demanded coldly.

The dentist remained standing in a defiant posture, wanting to turn around but staying still as he tried to comprehend what was happening. At the first slight twist of the dentist's head, the irritated robber pounded his temple with the butt of the pistol, causing the gun to fire, stunning them both. The dentist instantly fell to his knees, fully submissive. His head throbbed from the blow, and his ears rang from the pistol report next to his ear. Writhing in pain, he fell forward into the cold mud, catching himself with his hands.

Equally shocked at the pistol firing—because the pistol was cocked, it hadn't taken much impact to drop the hammer—the robber quickly recovered. "Do you have a pistol on you?"

"Huh?" the dentist answered, rubbing the side of his forehead.

"Do you have a pistol on you?"

"No, no, I don't," the dentist explained, holding a hand to his right ear.

After patting the dentist down anyway like a cop on television, the robber ripped the man's wallet free of his back pocket and tore out the obvious cash.

"Give me your watch."

The dentist groaned. The watch had been a gift from his parents when he'd opened his own practice. He slowly pulled it off his left wrist and handed it over his right shoulder.

The heavy watch was an enormous pleasure to hold. After shining a light on its face, the robber stuffed it and the cash into a fanny pack and zipped it shut.

It was time to leave. The shot could have attracted attention. No one would be suspicious, but a nosy neighbor might come to help the dentist, thinking he had killed a deer.

"Keys and cell phone," the emotionless electronic voice demanded.

The dentist groaned again. He had just bought the phone a week before. He pulled it from the zippered front pocket of his jacket. "The keys are in the truck."

When the robber took the phone from his hand and saw the dentist was shaking, euphoria bloomed at the situation's delicious power dynamic. The feeling was addictive.

"Keep staring at the ground!"

"I've got kids. Please!"

Silence only elevated the tension.

"Take whatever you want. Just don't kill me."

A quick survey of the area confirmed that no one was approaching. The truck was running, and the radio was tuned to the sports radio show. Someone was screaming about Alabama football.

The dentist's mind was bogged down. This couldn't be happening to him. He wanted to look around at his assailant but, fearing what might happen, remained focused on the mud in front of him and waited for instructions. His head was pounding, and his ears still rang. He had just started praying when the robber clubbed him again with the butt of the revolver, and the dentist fell over onto the ground. Pain pulsated through his head, and then he blacked out.

Satisfied the victim was out cold, the robber shut off the truck and plucked the keys free. Silence enveloped the scene. The Remington bolt-action .270 with a Schmidt & Bender scope retrieved from the cart was easily worth a couple grand, if not more, and the dentist's backpack was heavy with gear.

As the robber looked around, the scene was absolutely static. The truck door hung open and the cab was lit up.

Grabbing the rifle and backpack, the robber felt their weight and imagined the cash value before starting a fast walk back to the county road and the hidden vehicle.

That was easy.

* * *

Morgan and Jake sat quietly in the den of their home. She was reading a fitness magazine, since Covey was sleeping, and Jake flipped through the channels, trying to find something worth watching. He hadn't been able to get off of work and had missed Katy leaving for her first date, but he wasn't going to miss her return home. Jake constantly glanced at a clock on the wall; it would have been obvious to anyone watching that he was anxious.

"What time did the movie start again?" he asked.

"Jake, I already told you. Seven. And then they were going to get something to eat." Morgan smelled something disgusting and blamed it on Kramer, lying in the center of the room on his back.

Jake grunted as he settled on a channel with a rerun of *Modern Family*. "Where?"

"Chili's."

Jake grunted again, trying to recall his own days of dating. He didn't think he'd gotten started at fourteen. In fact, he knew he hadn't.

Morgan never looked up. "Will's mother is chaperoning them. Would you just relax? Please."

"What movie did they go see?"

"*The Fault in Our Stars,*" Morgan said, dropping the magazine to watch Jake.

"Isn't that a love story?"

"It's supposed to be a sweet story," Morgan replied emphatically.

"I would have preferred the SpongeBob movie."

"She's not eight anymore."

"I can't believe she's old enough to be on a date." Jake sighed. "They probably snuck into *Fifty Shades of Grey*."

"She's growing up, Jake, and there is nothing you can do about it."

Another sigh. "You're right."

"I know I am. And why are you still wearing your uniform and pistol? Are you planning to intimidate a fourteen-year-old boy?" Morgan said with a laugh.

"No." Jake smiled. That was exactly his plan. "Maybe."

"We've raised her right, Jake."

"I know," Jake said feebly.

When the Housels' car pulled into the driveway, Kramer immediately started barking. Morgan looked up and said, "That's them. Now don't embarrass her."

Jake resisted the urge to look through the front door glass, but based on how fast Katy came through the door, there wasn't much time for a good-night kiss, which thoroughly pleased him.

Katy came into the house smiling big and wasn't at all surprised to see her parents waiting up. "Mom, Dad, I had so much fun. The movie was so good, and we ate nachos afterward."

"I'm glad you had fun," Jake said, trying to sound excited for her.

"And Dad, I asked Mrs. Housel to stop at Krispy Kreme, since the red light was on, and I brought you four hot glazed doughnuts!"

Jake was astonished. His heart melted a little bit.

"And Mom, I got you two cream-filled doughnuts," Katy said, holding the box in front of her, very proud of herself.

Morgan looked at Jake with a *See? You had nothing to worry about* look, and he smiled back at her reluctantly. He was just considering that maybe he could handle Katy growing up after all when his smiling daughter opened the lid to show off her gifts, and Kramer launched himself at the box, sending doughnuts all over the floor. Before anyone could respond, he'd swallowed one whole and was working on the second and third.

"Dad!" Katy screamed.

"Jake, put that dog outside! He is making me crazy!"

CHAPTER 11

"Hotel California" played in the background as the twins tried to forget about the past and contemplate the future. Chase and Chance had been drinking together for several hours, which was unusual for them, since they hardly ever spent evenings or nights with each other. Chase typically had a date with a local sleazy real estate agent, and Chance drank himself to sleep most nights while playing online poker and watching ESPN. Tonight was different: they were attempting to interrogate Perry Burns about their father.

Perry knew what they were trying to do and guarded his words. He needed to earn their trust until he could get a few hours alone, even if it took a few weeks. He tried to tell them positive stories about their dad from prison, but there weren't many. Their dad stole cigarette money from the other convicts through his wild schemes, and the majority of the imprisoned men hated him. A lot of the older convicted men worked to get their lives together in an effort to live out their years with some dignity. Not Bronson. He was always planning his next con.

These stories helped validate the twins's view that their dad had seen them as just another pair of people to be scammed. Their inheritance had been withheld from them; what little they'd received had been attached to liens that made accepting it a burden.

Eventually, the stories of their dad's cons just confirmed for them that they were just like their father, even though they would never admit it. There hadn't been anything even remotely normal about their childhoods. Never once had Chance's dad come to watch him play Little League baseball, and Chase had always wanted to dance at the local dance academy like other girls but never got the opportunity. Their dad was always too busy. He would, however, engage them as actors in whatever ruse he was trying to pull when necessary. At those times they felt loved, and both craved the attention from their dad the projects created. Now their suppressed feelings had manifested into anger and hatred for him.

When Perry ran out of Bronson Bolivar stories to tell, he started telling stories of some of his friends from Louisiana who were world-class con men. When he knew them, their easiest scores came in the early '90s by purchasing web domain names before most people realized they would want a domain name. As the Internet exploded, they sold them for small fortunes, until the Justice Department ruled it illegal. They did, however, make a great deal of money prior to that, which created a need for more money, which in turn eventually led to hard-core criminal activities.

Chase was beginning to wonder if the old man actually knew anything about their dad that would be helpful. She was also beginning to doubt that they would actually ever find any money. For three days she had been listening to Perry run his mouth nonstop about all his wealthy New Orleans connections and their talents for making loads of money. The more Perry talked, the more an idea began to form in her mind that had promise. She was certain her dad would be impressed. Her slow-minded brother would be needed to pull this off. A quick glance at him convinced her he was buying everything Perry was selling. That was to be expected. She would share her idea with him tomorrow and then lay out a plan when he was sober. For now she smiled at Perry and encouraged him to tell more about his profitable criminal friends from New Orleans.

* * *

When the phone rang at 3:30 a.m., Jake sat straight up in bed. By the third ring he grabbed his iPhone and slid the button to accept the call from Virgil.

Clearing his throat, he answered, "Hello."

"Hey man, sorry to call at this hour, but we got a problem. We've had another hunter attacked. They just got him out of the woods, and they're taking him to Baptist Hospital."

"Who and where?" Jake asked, rubbing his forehead.

"Clayton Worden. At his property in Noxubee County."

Jake was wide awake now. Morgan was stirring and sighed deeply at having her sleep interrupted. She had yet to get used to Jake being on call. The stock market had never caused him to rise at awful predawn hours.

"The dentist? I know him!" Jake exclaimed. "My daughter goes to him. Is he okay?"

"They said he had a bad knot on the side of the head, and he spent several hours on the cold ground knocked out until he woke up and flagged down a passerby that called the sheriff."

"Same attacker?"

"Gotta be. Get dressed and meet me at the ER."

Jake hung up and stared in surprise.

Morgan was now awake. "What's going on?"

"Clayton Worden was involved in some sort of incident. He's on his way to the hospital."

"Oh my God! What happened?"

"I don't know yet. I gotta get to the hospital." Jake didn't want to tell too much just yet. Morgan was a worrier.

"His wife, Diane, is in my yoga class," she said, rubbing her eyes.

"I know," Jake said as he climbed out of bed to get dressed, tripped over Kramer, and pitched blindly into the dark.

* * *

In the inky black before dawn, the Baptist Hospital of Columbus was bathed in a mysterious shade of pinkish orange from the parking lot lights. Most of the cars were covered with frost, and they glistened like a million tiny diamonds in Jake's headlights as he parked. The dash thermometer read twenty-seven degrees. He placed the bag of frozen black-eyed peas he was holding into the cup holder and shouldered the door open.

The ambulance and EMTs were leaving as Jake jogged to the entrance, passing Virgil's vehicle and the sheriff's cruiser on the way. He paused for a moment and wondered what he was about to encounter. The previous victim had finally awakened from his induced coma but had no memory of the traumatic event—a tough break. No witnesses and no leads and a victim who didn't remember anything made for a tough case. He hoped the dentist had information that could help. *These crimes have to be related,* Jake thought as the automatic doors opened and he looked for Virgil.

Two deputies leaned against a wall with cups of coffee, looking concerned, and then Virgil came around the corner, wearing street clothes and carrying a giant cup of coffee of his own.

"He's in the back getting cleaned up. Big knot on the side of his head, but he's gonna be okay," Virgil said to Jake, and then added, "What's the matter with your cheek?"

"I tripped over the dog and hit the wall. Do you know any details yet?"

"Robbed him at his truck last night. Same freaky scenario as before," Virgil explained, and exhaled deeply. "I think we have someone preying on our hunters."

Both deputies nodded in agreement. Jake soaked in what had just been said. He had never considered anything like this before and was trying to work out what would be involved in catching this criminal.

"It's interesting that both victims were doctors," a deputy said, then sipped coffee loudly.

"High–net worth individuals," Virgil offered. "They have cash, expensive watches, guns, and equipment. Which makes them targets."

"What's the next step?" Jake asked.

"The county sheriffs will be lead investigators on each crime, and we'll assist."

"Yeah, but these are hunters, these are our guys!" Jake said excitedly.

The deputies shared a glance but kept quiet.

"They also fall under the jurisdiction of the counties," Virgil said, "and the sheriffs have more personnel and experience investigating crimes like these." He nodded at the deputies.

Jake was obviously frustrated. Virgil had seen the look before. The new guys always wanted to do more and push the limits.

"We're gonna assist," Virgil said, beginning to push Jake away from the deputies. "Now come on. We need to go look at the crime scene. We may see something that they don't." He called back to the deputies that they'd see them later, then leaned in tight to Jake and whispered, "We need to get outta here."

Jake was confused but moved away with Virgil, then finally stopped. "I want to see Clayton."

"Why?"

"I just think it's important that I see him. I think it will help me work on the case. I can't explain it. That's just how I feel."

Virgil understood and knew they had time. He nodded to Jake. "He's right down there on the left. I'll wait for you here. I have some e-mails to check. I may update my profile on my dating account."

Already cooled down, Jake wanted to say *Lose forty pounds and that will help your profile out more than anything,* but he didn't. He turned and walked down the hall.

The last time he was in this hospital ER was after he had been left to die in a drainpipe in a remote river swamp. He still had regular nightmares about that night and about Moon Pie Daniels, the man who had tried to kill him. This very ER had helped save his life, but he still felt uncomfortable. The smell took him right back to that night, and his breathing went shallow. He recognized the anxiety and pushed through it as he knocked softly.

An obviously aggravated nurse opened the door but, seeing Jake in full uniform, allowed him entrance. Jake saw Clayton Worden with his wife, who had been crying. He wanted to comfort them and let them know he would help find whoever had done this and make things right. This was his new career, and the idea of helping folks really appealed to him.

"Can you be brief?" the nurse asked.

"Yes, ma'am. Of course."

"Hey Jake," Clayton said, trying to sit up straight.

"You okay, Clayton?"

"It's been a long night, but he'll be okay," Diane said with a sniffle.

Another nurse was wrapping a bandage around his head, and he grunted in pain.

"I told Virgil everything I know."

"That's good. I'll get with him, then. I just wanted to stop by and let you know I would be helping out on the case. We'll find who did this."

Clearly frustrated by all the people needing to talk to her patient, the second nurse finished bandaging the head wound and then informed everyone they needed some privacy to get the patient into a gown. But then she looked at Jake and informed him he needed to put some ice on his own eye.

Jake didn't like the sudden attention or offer an explanation. "I'll be going," Jake said as he handed a card with his contact information to Clayton's wife. "We'll stay in touch, and if you think of anything else, please call."

"Thank you, Jake," she responded while reading the card.

"Be careful out there, Jake," Clayton said as the door was shutting.

Jake exhaled as he walked down the hallway. Seeing Clayton being bandaged made the crime real for him. He knew the victim, he could feel the family's suffering, and seeing the injury inflicted by a criminal helped galvanize Jake's duty to the community.

When Virgil saw Jake, he jumped up and called him away from the others in the waiting room.

"You get your morning motivation?" Virgil asked.

"Yeah, I did," Jake answered slowly while his mind processed everything.

"Okay, Dirty Harry, let's ride," Virgil said with a knowing grin.

"Why the rush?"

Once they were out of earshot of the deputies, he said, "We gotta get to Clayton's hunting property at first light."

"What's going on?"

"You're gonna love this," Virgil said as he winked at a nurse and scared her. "Clayton called me two months ago. He had a giant buck show up on one of his cameras and asked a bunch of questions about motion-sensitive trail cameras. He wanted to know what unit was the best."

Jake's good eye widened. A trail-camera photo would be a huge lead, undeniable evidence with a date and time stamp.

"Yeah, he just told me he put 'em all over his property to learn where this deer was living. He told me where to look," Virgil said with a smile. "I'm hoping his cameras got a picture, and I wanna get it before the deputies do."

"It's two hours until daybreak, though," Jake said, looking at his watch.

"Oh yeah. Well, that gives us time to go to the Waffle House and get you something cold for the black eye you got coming."

"I have some frozen peas in my truck."

"Black-eyed peas, I suppose?"

Jake chuckled. "Of course."

* * *

Chase had been considering a ruse for several months that would tap into the continuing greed for their late father's missing fortune. There were plenty of covetous people who believed the money existed, but she'd been waiting for someone who was just shy of desperate and had connections to real money. Her plan required a special person. It didn't take her long to realize that Perry Burns might be precisely qualified. Her research into the old man could only go so far, but he purely reeked of desperation: no money that she could see, no caring family, and no hope for a job that could support him. His stories of friends with shady streams of big cash had sealed his fate as a target.

It was known by all who knew Bronson Bolivar that he loved mysterious old things. He collected Civil War relics, Indian artifacts—anything that connected him to the old worlds. He had books that explained values based on 1985 dollars for much of his collection. Other books told the history of the local Chickasaw and Choctaw Indians and also included French and Spanish influences. His favorite story was of Hernando de Soto, the famed Spanish explorer, who passed through the area in the 1500s.

Chase's plan was to bait Perry Burns with a totally fabricated story. One built on local historical facts that merged with their father's interests. The grand story would be that Bronson had found a Spanish conquistador helmet while digging a septic tank for a park on a historical site. The helmet had been found on land where the Tombigbee lock and dam were being built in Columbus in the mid-'80s. It was a site rich in Indian cultural history, where the area's river and major creek intersected. The site was said to be a huge Chickasaw community, with thousands of Indians living there. As an added touch she would explain that since the artifact had been on federal property, taking it had been a felony. This had been a problem for Bronson, and even now the kids couldn't sell it easily and cash in for fear of attracting unwanted attention. The scrutiny through the years had been intense. Now that it had cooled down they needed somebody to launder it for them or to outright buy it from them to resell to a collector. She'd read online that the Smithsonian had valued a similar find in Florida at six million dollars a few years back. In Chase's plan, the twins would be willing to take a lot less in cash, allowing a middleperson to profit significantly as well.

The plan seemed promising to her. A few weak details needed to be polished, but the main points were believable, and Bronson Bolivar's pre-prison life made them completely plausible. The area was rich in history, which would also support the story, as would the obvious difficulty in selling an artifact this valuable without outside help.

Chase tried to think of any reason that Perry would be leery and back away. There were a few, but if he genuinely had wealthy connections, was in need of money, and was still a con artist himself, this plan would appeal to his greed. Of course she had to think through all the angles to her story, but if she and her brother could convince Perry to bring them a million in cash for something he thought he could sell for five to six million dollars, then they had a con that could generate her some real money. His greed would perpetuate the scam. She loved the idea and opened a bottle of water to sip while she thought it through one more time.

CHAPTER 12

Morgan awoke and played the overheard pieces of Jake's phone conversation over and over. She worried about her friend's husband and wanted to know more, but there was nothing to do about that but send Jake a quick text and hope he responded with good news.

The bed was warm, and though she could hear the heater running, she knew the wooden floors would be cold. It was almost time to get Covey up and feed her. Katy, who barely tolerated mornings, would need to get up soon as well.

Sighing, she grabbed the remote and clicked on the television to a local channel in anticipation that the story of Clayton Worden was being reported. As she turned to replace the remote on the stand, Kramer lunged up and licked her face without warning.

"Uh! Dammit, dog!" After ripping the sheets back, she hurried across the frigid floor to let the dog outside. By the time she returned, Jake had responded to her text.

Claytons OK. In the ER. Contusion on head. Robbed at his hunting lease last night. Not many details yet.

Morgan sat down on the edge of the bed, the information he'd given her immediately conjuring up bad images for her. It wasn't many years ago that Jake and Katy had had a bad run-in with some white trash rednecks at his hunting club. She thought about the awful day often, but recent news made the memories even fresher. She would call her friend later.

She texted, *How is your eye?* and despite the dread that had welled up inside her, giggled as she hit "Send."

Covey could be heard beginning to cry. Morgan's day was about to begin. But as she rose, her phone pinged, and she giggled again as she read the text.

Black.

* * *

The judge had just finished a call with the French surgeon who specialized in kidney replacement. They had been corresponding via e-mail for several weeks and took the opportunity to discuss Mary Margaret's deteriorating condition. The judge could tell she was weaker, and he worried about her more every day. The doctor's broken English was a challenge to understand, but the judge was convinced he was willing and able to help them. The judge needed to send a down payment that would start the process. Receiving a new kidney was his wife's only hope of living and seeing her grandson grow up. He would get the money somehow.

After he hung up the phone, the door to his study slowly opened, and Rosemary was standing there with a shocked look on her face. The judge realized she'd overheard the conversation.

Rosemary closed the den door and walked toward her father. "What's going on, Dad?"

The judge sighed deeply and turned to look out the window. He knew he would tear up if he looked at her. They had been trying to shield his daughter from the worry. She had so much on her mind.

"Your mother needs a kidney. Her kidneys are failing, and because she had chemotherapy for the melanoma a few years back, she can't qualify for the donor list."

Rosemary sat down on the edge of her dad's desk, and the gravity of the situation fell on her. She could witness the hurt in her dad's eyes. She was angry for not being told, but she understood why, or she guessed she knew.

"How much longer does . . . ?" Rosemary started to ask, and choked up instead.

"Without a new kidney, the doctors think she has less than a year, but they said she could battle a little longer," the judge said with a sigh. "I'm sorry, Rose. Your mother didn't want you to worry."

Rosemary bent down to hug him. "How long have you known?"

The judge paused in thought. Lately every event with Mary Margaret was a blur to him. "Let's see, it was just before the Fourth of July. We had to wait over the holiday for the results of a test."

"About the time I told you about my marriage problems," Rosemary said as she stood up straight and wiped tears from her eyes.

"Pretty close."

"Who else knows?"

"No one. You know how private she is."

Rosemary considered what her father had said. Her mother was intensely private and always worried about what others thought. This was a trait Rosemary had found frustrating in her school years, but now, as a parent, it seemed to make more sense.

"That was the doctor?"

"Yes, he's a brilliant surgical urologist from France. He has a highly respected clinic over there, and we can basically buy a kidney for your mother."

"France?"

"It's our only option."

"There's no way to get on the donor list here?"

"No. They are very strict. It's a long list. More people need kidneys than there are kidneys available, and they are trying to give the recipients the best chance for organ acceptance. I can understand, although it doesn't make it any easier."

"When?"

"This doctor has a very busy schedule. We're looking at four weeks minimum, unless someone cancels."

The judge wasn't going to tell her the cost unless she asked, and he hoped she wouldn't.

"So what will all this cost?" she asked, and watched the judge's shoulders sag.

She always gets right to the point. "Total about five hundred thousand."

Rosemary swallowed hard. That was a lot of money. "Do you have it?"

"I got about half of it. Maybe a little more. We'd be fine except for having to take care of your grandmother's medical bills a few years back. Your mother was too proud to see her on Medicaid."

"Dad, what are you gonna do?" Rosemary always asked the tough questions.

"I'm selling some guns, refinancing the house, and a few other things, but that's not gonna be enough. I'm working on something else that will help."

Rosemary looked at her father. She had never seen him so lifeless. He looked like he had been carrying this burden for a while. She touched her father's shoulder softly. "I'll help you."

"Thanks, but I'll figure it all out."

"I need to talk to Mom."

"She went to take some food to the church. There's a funeral this afternoon."

Rosemary looked at her dad lovingly while he sat in his old leather chair. His bifocals hung around his neck, and he looked as dignified as always, in his neatly starched shirt, but his eyes told a different story. She wrapped her arms around him and squeezed.

"Go easy on her. It was her idea not to tell you."

"I will," she replied, and kissed him on the forehead. "I love you, Daddy."

* * *

Jake and Virgil sat in the Waffle House and compared notes of things they needed to do. They both had a long list of landowners who required attention. Hunting season was about to go into full swing. The rifle deer season was in one whole week, and duck season was ten days away. In the fall and winter, a warden's life was chaos. Their hours were out the window, since calls came at all hours of the day and night, and everyone expected immediate attention. Landowners and hunting clubs always had trespassing issues. Groups were always shooting deer at night for sport and for meat, so the nights of wardens were frequently ruined. Once duck season started, there would be seemingly endless cold mornings in the swamps chasing hunters bent on killing too many birds or blasting away on somebody else's property. Jake became a warden to protect a sport and a heritage he treasured, but he missed the freedom to enjoy his own Saturdays with his family. His weekends now were spent checking on others; he hadn't considered that when choosing his new career. Many times he wondered what life would be like working for his father-in-law, which his wife wanted. At least he would have weekends off.

Virgil had been a warden long enough that he was an expert at both managing his time and looking busy. He knew what was important and what drew attention, and who was connected to the politicians and the brass in Jackson. Jake didn't.

The two wardens were currently responsible for three counties, which was clearly too much country for only two officers. The

Mississippi wildlife department, like many state wildlife agencies, was stressed for funds, but that didn't mean the officers didn't work hard and didn't care. The system had jaded Virgil, and he milked it for all it could provide him, but at the end of the day he was still actually concerned about the resources he protected. The heritage of hunting and fishing was an important aspect of life in the South. In fact, hunting had recently been voted a constitutional right by the people of Mississippi. Jake was proud of that.

Virgil flipped open a notebook and starting prioritizing his list.

"The bosses in Jackson don't know about the attack last night yet, but when they do, I promise they are gonna want us knee-deep in it."

"That's right where I wanna be," Jake said as he stretched. The leather holster creaked as he moved.

"Catching that guy is a top priority. By the way, have you ever made an arrest?"

Jake swallowed and looked around at the gaudy yellow interior of the Waffle House, trying to think of a way to sugarcoat his experience level. "No, not an actual arrest, but I've written lots of tickets."

"This is different. It's an investigation. It's got a chain of evidence that has to be managed so that everything holds up in court. We don't have time to investigate like the sheriff's department does. We got daily problems scattered across three counties we gotta tend to. This ain't like TV, where they spend their time chasing one criminal."

"The fact that they targeted hunters, though—doesn't that mean it falls in our jurisdiction?"

"On the surface, yes, but our best bet is to hit this quick before the issue even gets settled. Get a picture off the trail cameras and identify the perp, then go make an arrest and find the stolen property. That's how we do it."

Jake stared straight ahead, thinking about his rank in the legal system. This wasn't what he'd envisioned when he'd signed up. He didn't want to only chase trespassers. He hated the thought of letting other departments take the lead on a case that he knew should be theirs.

Virgil scratched his chin and sighed. "We need to plant a bug at the Bolivars' house too."

Jake had briefly forgotten about the judge and his request. This latest attack had seized all of his attention. He sipped coffee and looked at his watch, realizing they had another hour before sunrise.

"Hey," Jake said, "what about the other victim? He remember anything yet?"

"No, nothing. The whole event has been blacked out of his mind like it never happened. The docs say it may come back to him slowly."

Jake shook his head. "When the word gets out on this, there's gonna be a lotta nervous hunters."

"There's also gonna be a lotta guys totin' pistols and rifles and looking for someone suspicious. Someone could get hurt."

"Two doctors, both hunting alone. They most certainly were targeted."

"No doubt," Virgil agreed, "and it's someone from this area."

"So, you know where these cameras are located?"

"I know about where they are. We need to wait until daylight so we don't step on any evidence that might be out there and the cameras will be easier to find."

Jake nodded in agreement.

A waitress walked over and yawned.

"Early, ain't it?" Virgil asked with a smile.

She didn't appear to be in the mood to flirt with him, which he took as a personal challenge.

"You got any bananas?"

"For your waffle?"

"I'm trying to be healthy."

The waitress looked at Virgil stuffed into the booth and laughed. "You probably should have started a while ago."

* * *

The Noxubee County sheriff interviewed Dr. Clayton Worden for about thirty minutes. The old-school law enforcement officer was astonished that someone had, in Clayton's words, "jumped" him at his truck when he returned from hunting. He hadn't seen anything like this happen in his county and couldn't recall it happening anywhere else. Sure, there were shootings, stabbings, beatings, rapes, robberies, burglaries, and more mischief than six deputies could manage. But he could never recall a hunter being robbed. An armed hunter was a dangerous target in his mind. *Has to be drug related.* Drugs got the bulk of the blame for any crimes in his county, even a recent crime of passion where a female murdered a cheating husband. It wouldn't have happened if it hadn't been for the drugs, he'd told his constituents.

"Is there anything else about the assailant that you can remember that would help us identify him?" he asked after glancing back over his handwritten notes.

"No, the main thing I remember is that voice. It was so odd sounding, like it was mechanical or electronic. I've never heard anything like it."

"So can you say if it was male or female?"

"No, I couldn't."

"Or black or white?" the sheriff asked, already knowing the answer.

"No, sir."

The sheriff stood up and folded the brim of his cowboy hat. He glanced at his watch and then checked the radio on his hip. He had a busy day ahead. All his days were busy, busier than he'd realized when he ran for the job.

"What kinda person could do this?" the wife asked him.

The sheriff exhaled deeply. "I'm thinking this is gonna be a crazy white male. I don't see any of my people hiding in the dark woods. Now, they'll stay out at a club all night long, but not in the dark woods."

The dentist just looked at the sheriff while his concerned wife was gently rubbing his forehead. "I don't know about these things," he replied. "But I've never had any trouble out there."

"I was raised in this prairie country and been sheriff a long time. This was a crazy white boy that needed him some cash to buy meth."

"Do you think you can get his watch back, Sheriff?" the wife asked.

"I doubt it. But it may turn up in a pawn shop."

The wife and the dentist made eye contact. They knew they would probably never see it again, but neither really cared. The watch could be replaced. A husband and a father couldn't. "You never know," she said, trying to say something positive. "We might get lucky."

"Ma'am, from what I can tell, you folks already been lucky. Lucky that he wasn't hurt worse last night."

The dentist and his wife looked at each other. They had heard about the surgeon at the hospital. The wife had a tear in her eye, and she bent down to kiss her husband.

* * *

Chase had found on eBay a very old-looking fifteenth-century reproduction helmet that had been used as a prop in one of the *Lord of the Rings* movies. She really didn't know exactly what a Spanish conquistador helmet looked like, but this reproduction was old and looked real. Highly impatient, she couldn't wait for the bidding to end, so she hit the "Buy It Now" button. Overnight delivery came in handy. She hoped it looked as good in person as it did in the online photos.

"So where is he?" she asked Chance as he poured vodka in his orange juice.

"He's up in the guest room watching television. He's addicted to *True Detective*," he said with a chuckle.

"Let's go outside, where we can talk."

Once on the deck, Chase laid out her plan for her brother in great detail. She had thought everything through. The plan seemed flawless, assuming they could convince Perry Burns they had an authentic Spanish explorer artifact from the de Soto expedition. They couldn't let it be examined, though. They had to let a prospective buyer talk them into selling it to them and take the cash as quickly as they could. Then an unfortunate accident could befall the purchaser.

"So what do we ask for it?" Chance asked.

"I think we tell 'em we expect it to be worth four or five million. They can sell it to a serious collector and double their investment. We walk away with a cool million in cash."

"Can't we get more?"

"Maybe," she said, "but I don't want to get too greedy. For this to work, we need for the buyer to be greedy."

"That sounds good to me."

Chase looked up at the upstairs window. "We gotta make him think we found it and we've had it for a while and we just don't have any idea how to sell it. We're scared to sell it."

"You just tell me what to do."

"I will, and I'm gonna need you to be ready to dump the buyer in a hole somewhere once we get the money."

Chance laughed and took a big swig of beer. "I can handle that."

"When they find out it's a fake, somebody will be upset."

Chance nodded in agreement.

"I still have some details to work out, but I'll keep you in the loop. The helmet will be here tomorrow, and we'll make a plan to tell him about it."

"Maybe in the meantime he'll remember something that Dad said that might help us find the missing money," Chance said with sudden optimism.

Chase expressed her growing doubts about Perry Burns ever helping them find the money, or for that matter that it even existed. But now he was going to help them find some new money.

Chance smiled and finished his beer. Two of her three comments pleased him immensely.

CHAPTER 13

As Rosemary waited patiently for her mother to return home from the church, she walked through the finely furnished home, touching antiques as she passed by. The furnishings were from years of attending estate sales and antique shops. Rosemary didn't want the antiques; she wanted her mother.

When Mary Margaret finally arrived and took one look at her daughter, her intuition told her Rosemary knew. The knowledge was actually a relief. The two talked, cried, and even laughed for over two hours. Rosemary spent more quality time talking to her mom that morning than she had in years, and her mother found it cathartic to talk to someone other than her husband. She had longed to tell her daughters but hadn't wanted to burden them.

Rosemary learned about how her parents kept her secret from family and friends. She listened to her mother tell stories about her father, the most rational man she knew, fussing with doctors and hospitals. Mary Margaret said she'd never felt more loved than when hearing her husband beg for the doctors to help, though it hurt to see her husband in such pain. They had been together for fifty-four years and survived being apart at different colleges, the Vietnam War, raising two very active daughters, and being caregivers to Mary Margaret's parents when they couldn't take care of themselves. They took care of each other. She made certain he ate well and got exercise every day, and he monitored her medicines, making certain they didn't react with each other, and scheduled her doctor's appointments. He'd recently purchased a low-impact treadmill so she could get exercise on the cold winter days and work at her own pace.

Rosemary did her best to understand her mother's sad situation. She could see how her dad had become so frustrated with it. There had to be a loophole or a way around the system, but she also knew her dad would have looked and found it if there were. For now the Internet could answer some of her questions, and she had a nurse friend who she would call later.

Dammit! she thought as she watched her mother walk away.

* * *

Several days a week Chance would slip away to his secret hiding place. Deep on his late father's thousand acres there was an old 1950s-model school bus that had once been a squirrel-hunting camp. The bus had not been cranked in over forty years and had sweet gum trees growing out from under its wheel wells. Even if the old bus's engine could crank, it would take a chainsaw to get it out. The tires were dry-rotted, and the windows were so dirty from years of tree sap that they were mostly black. Peeking out from under the black sap, the bright-yellow paint still made its presence known. On the sides it read "Lowndes County Schools." Rust was the next most notable feature.

What had once been a vehicle that helped educate countless rural children was now Chance's refuge from society. He loved the simplicity of it. There was no electricity, he heated it with propane, and the inside was cramped with an old couch, a stove, and a homemade table. It was also packed with bottles of water, ammo, food, and supplies in case of crisis. He wasn't a prepper, but he did appreciate having a place to hide and survive if the world went crazy. He planned to purchase a generator and have limited electricity, but he didn't like the idea of the noise. Chance had allowed his son to visit the camp and hoped that one day he would enjoy it as much as he did.

The bus was not comfortable by most people's standards, but Chance preferred it that way. It was here, buried in two Igloo coolers, that Chance had hidden the portion of his father's missing money that he had already found. He'd discovered it years ago and never trusted his sister enough to tell her. He didn't know what to do with the money. When he needed some cash, he took some, but almost all of it was still there. He was scared to put it in the bank. If he told his sister, he would lose half of it, if not more. Chance didn't want to do that. He liked his life. It was simple, he had a job that took care of itself and money if he needed it, and he could basically do whatever he wanted.

His father had hidden the money in a safe in a secret basement in the old antebellum house he had been restoring. One day while tearing out a subfloor, Chance had found a secret entrance. It had been almost impossible to tell it was there. Chance figured the secret room had been built during the Civil War to hide valuables or maybe even people. The safe's combination had been impossible to crack, but a welder's torch had eventually cut it open. Later, under a full moon, he'd dumped the pieces of the safe into a deep gravel pit pond.

Some days when he knew the sleazy lawyer wasn't around, he would spread the money out in neat little stacks and re-count it. The stale smell of the old money was exhilarating. Often he would sit and think about all the things his old man did to get the money, and he would smile.

Chance was surprised that there wasn't as much money as his sister thought, but he figured he didn't find it all. There had to be more. Either way, he wasn't parting with any of it, and he enjoyed the constant chatter about the missing money. He loved that it had grown into a local legend and the fact that his sister was so obsessed. Chance just played along and enjoyed the ride.

* * *

The area that Clayton Worden hunted was very remote, and access was limited. When Virgil and Jake arrived, there were multiple sheriff's department cruisers and two unmarked vehicles. Yellow tape had been stretched to keep officers from walking inadvertently through the crime scene and destroying potential evidence.

Virgil quickly assessed the situation and explained it to Jake, who was rapid-firing questions. There were two groups of officers, one at the entrance to the property and another farther down the road about a half mile. Virgil knew the investigators were canvassing the area where the robbery had occurred and where they thought the assailants had parked a getaway vehicle. Virgil was interested in the area of hardwoods approximately three hundred yards long that he'd been told had four motion-sensitive game cameras strapped to trees. Clayton had felt like the robber would have walked through some part of the area.

Using his GPS map app, Virgil located the property and where they were within it. He knew approximately where the cameras were, but they still would have to find them, and that wouldn't necessarily be easy.

Everybody knew Virgil, and he took the opportunity to introduce Jake. Several recognized Jake's name from his past. The deputies had searched the site around the vehicle and had found only a couple of chewed cigarette butts. Now that it was daylight, they also found boot tracks and had a good line on where the robber traveled, though none had ventured into the woods just yet.

"We need to see the travel area of the perp," Virgil explained. "We may find something that will help."

The lead investigator immediately agreed. He snapped his fingers and caught a deputy's attention. "Take these men to the crime scene and let them look around, and be sure and show them the boot tracks so they can study the route."

"Yes, sir," the deputy responded. "This way, guys."

The deputy introduced them to an investigator that Virgil already knew, who started giving them the tour.

Beyond the addition of a trailer and electric cart, this crime scene had the same abandoned feel to it as the first one. "We found the cigarette butts over there," the investigator said. "We think that's where the perp hid until the hunter approached his vehicle. Based on the tire tracks, we think he attacked him just after he loaded up the cart. The trailer ramps haven't been loaded yet."

"That's consistent with what Clayton told us," Virgil answered. "Can I see the cigarette butts?"

"Yeah, here they are," the investigator said as he pulled a Ziploc baggie out of his coat pocket.

Jake stepped forward to look alongside Virgil. "Chewed just like the others."

"They sure are," Virgil said. "I expected that."

"What's that?" the investigator asked.

"The incident we had in Lowndes County, the perp chewed on his cigarettes. Gotta be the same guy," Virgil explained.

"I need to see those reports."

"I'm sure they'll share."

"Hey," Jake said, "how did Clayton get out of here?"

"He couldn't find his keys, so he walked to the road and flagged down a carload of high school kids out joyriding," Virgil offered. "They loaned him a cell phone, and he called his brother-in-law, who came and got him."

"I don't think he was going to call us, from what I understand," the investigator interjected.

"Yeah, his wife made him." Virgil squatted down to look at the boot prints. Based on his initial look, they appeared to belong to a rubber slip-on boot. By the size of them, Virgil guessed they weren't dealing with a large man.

"Makes me wonder if it's happened before and was not reported," the investigator said.

Virgil looked at him and nodded. "It's quite possible. Some men don't want the hassle and might even be embarrassed."

"If we put it on the news, we may have some others come forward," Jake said quickly.

"That's a good idea, Jake," Virgil said, back to studying the boot tracks.

"That electric cart's worth a lot of money," Jake said. "I'm surprised that he didn't take it."

Virgil looked up at the accessorized cart. "Timing. It would have been time-consuming to drive in and deal with the trailer and all. But yeah, you're right, Jake. He could sell it to some hunter who didn't ask questions. Would've been risky, though."

"He did get about two hundred in cash, a Rolex watch, an expensive scoped rifle, and expensive binoculars," the investigator explained.

Another deputy nodded. "All easy to sell."

"No doubt. Hey, show us where the tracks leading in and out are. That's what I'm interested in."

"Right over here." The investigator walked them over and pointed them out. "We heard y'all were coming, and we thought we'd let y'all do the woods work, since we got our hands full here."

Virgil thanked him. "Come on, Jake, let's go. Don't step on any tracks."

Jake went to work with enthusiasm; if there were cameras, he was determined to find them.

"Keep an eye on the tracks so we don't lose him," Virgil barked as he started scanning the woods ahead.

After a hundred yards of searching, no cameras had revealed themselves. The wardens moved slowly on, continuing to look for anything out of the ordinary. Another fifty or so yards on their efforts earned them a mixed reward: the sight of a camera that had been removed. There were boot prints at the base of the tree, and the bark of the red oak was scuffed where the camera belt had been strapped. Jake had found it and whistled for his partner. Virgil cussed their luck. The robber must have seen the red flash and taken the whole unit. He hadn't anticipated that.

"Dammit," Jake mumbled.

"I know," Virgil said. "Well, let's keep looking."

After the two wardens had followed the trail like bloodhounds for another twenty minutes, Virgil suddenly straightened and stared in a direction off the trail.

"Bingo."

"What do you see?"

"There's a camera," Virgil said as he started huffing the thirty yards to the unit, which was sitting like a silent sentry strapped to a tree. "With any luck we'll have a picture."

"That's a long way from the trail," Jake noted, shaking his head.

"Yeah, so the perp may not have seen the red flash on this one. Everybody makes mistakes, and let's hope our attacker may have made one."

* * *

Chase Bolivar planned to meet Perry Burns for supper at Harvey's, a local fashionable eatery and watering hole. Her plan included loosening the old man up with some good food and drinks, then telling him about the Spanish conquistador's helmet. The perceived value of the rare artifact should get his mind racing for a way to turn it into a profit for himself. The story had a few holes, but she was confident she could fill them in as needed on the fly. Chase could be creative and was always known to think fast on her feet. After ordering a bourbon and water at the bar, she checked her watch. The drink would suppress her excitement and hopefully dilute her growing frustration. Chance was supposed to bring Perry, and as usual he was late.

Halfway through the drink, she ordered an appetizer of firecracker shrimp. Chance was dependable but insisted that everything move at his speed and time. He resented being told what to do. So when she asked him to bring Perry and meet her at 6:30, she already knew he would be late. Slave to her own nature, though, she still had to be on time, which left her nothing to do but seethe and stew.

When her brother and Perry rolled in at 7:20, she'd had time to think through her story and even consider what she intended to do with the money. She was weary from the stress of having to be the glue that held their struggling business together. Payroll, inventory, taxes, office rent, maintaining their fleet of work trucks, and insurance for all the above kept her tense all the time. She worried about it all, and her brother never gave any of the issues a second thought. The business wasn't making her any real money. Her salary didn't begin to make up for the stress it inflicted on her. Chase was tired of looking for money she would never find, bored of the septic tank business, and resentful of taking care of her lazy brother.

"Hello, Chase," Perry Burns said as he walked into the bar area with Chance following slowly, staring at his phone.

Chase swallowed the urge to comment on the time. "Let's sit over there," she instructed, and moved toward an isolated corner booth.

"Have you ordered?" Chance asked, looking up from Instagram for a moment.

"No," Chase replied coldly. "I was waiting on you guys."

"So what's good here?" Perry Burns inquired as the ex-con slid into the booth across from her.

"It's all good," Chase offered.

A waitress took their orders, and Perry Burns sat back in anticipation.

"How is the search going?" Chase asked the two of them, already knowing the answer.

"We looked at the old furniture factory this morning," Chance said. "Tomorrow we'll search around the shop warehouse. I just want him to see the place. Maybe he'll see something that sparks a memory."

Chase nodded in agreement.

"Y'all sure he never went to Brazil?" Perry asked without removing his gaze from the television in the corner, on which a news reporter was talking about a band of rain expected to hit the area the next day.

"Not to my knowledge," Chase said.

"He talked about it all the time."

"We are not going to Brazil, Perry," she said emphatically.

"I'm just saying he talked about the Confederados a bunch."

Chase rolled her eyes. "I know it. He was infatuated with the idea that it was like the Old South."

"Dad loved everything old," Chance added. "We've told you that."

"Yeah, I know."

Anxious to get the plan rolled out while he was clearheaded and then lubricate the conversation with alcohol, Chase saw an opportunity to start the dialogue.

"Did you tell him about the old Spanish mask that Dad found?" she asked her brother demurely.

"No, I hadn't thought about it. I really didn't think he could help us sell it," Chance explained according to the script.

Chase nodded as the old man's brow furrowed with curiosity. *Greedy people are so freakin' predictable.* The ex-con had taken the bait.

She sighed and said, "Yeah, I don't know what we are gonna do with it."

Struggling to appear only mildly interested, Perry took a big swallow of bourbon and water. "What are y'all talking about? I might be able to help you kids."

The twins looked at each other for several long seconds. Chance shrugged as if to say he didn't care. Chase sighed.

"We haven't told anyone."

"What?"

"Mainly because we don't know what to do."

"What? Just tell me."

"You can't tell anyone about this."

"Who am I gonna tell? I've been in prison. Nobody wants to talk to me," Perry said with a laugh.

"Well," she said, "right before Dad had all the legal problems, the septic company was building some bathrooms at the park on the river. It was federal land, which means all sorts of agencies have jurisdiction. Anyway, they dug up a very well-preserved Spanish conquistador helmet that's thought to be over five hundred years old."

Perry blinked a few times and took another sip. "That's old. Those things are rare, aren't they?"

"That's right. And what makes it even more special is it's thought to be from the de Soto expedition that came through this area."

Chance was trying hard not to smile and had to look up at the television to distract himself. If he blew this, she'd kill him. Literally kill him and dump him down his own damn hole.

Perry hadn't noticed a thing. His face said he was very interested in what she was saying.

"He never said anything about it."

"He didn't tell you about his hidden money either," Chase pointed out.

"Why can't y'all sell it?"

"It's complicated. The Smithsonian had an archeologist on site because they knew of the area's historical significance, but he had gotten the shits after eating some boiled crawfish the night before and was late getting to the jobsite, and Dad had already found it and left. He knew they found something from the way the dirt had been carefully brushed away and the helmet left an indention in the dirt. So they have been watching ever since to see if it ever popped up somewhere. The good news is we think it's cooled off now."

"That's something," Perry said, soaking it all in and nodding. "I remember my junior high history class talking about de Soto and that expedition."

"It's a felony to dig artifacts on federal land," Chance added.

"I see. And you have it, you say?"

"Yes," Chase said.

"Were there any other workers present who might have seen it?"

"One, but he was killed in an accident not too long after," Chase replied, pleased with herself at this bit of embroidery.

Perry's eyebrows arched. "What happened?"

"Septic tank caved in on him."

"That happen much?"

"Not really," Chase said.

Perry was visibly jumping to conclusions.

"We need to sell it to a discreet private collector," Chance said, breaking his silence and pleased to add to the conversation.

"A well-heeled, discreet private collector," Chase added. "They're not easy to come by."

Perry held up his empty glass to the waitress across the room and glanced around to see if anyone was listening to their conversation. "So what's this thing worth?"

Chase rolled her eyes. "It's hard to say. But a similar find on private land in Florida sold for just over five million."

Their food arrived then, and it took two waitresses to bring it all. Perry observed the rare prime rib as it was slid in front of him while his mind was overloaded with gluttony and greed. He watched everyone's food as it was placed on the table and waited for the waitresses to leave before speaking.

"Let me think about this," he said with exaggerated casualness. "I may have a way to help."

Chase and Chance smiled.

CHAPTER 14

From the outside, you could not see into Virgil's state-issued Ford truck. The vehicle was dark green with black tinted windows. Inside, Virgil and Jake had inserted the memory card from the game camera into his laptop and were nervously searching it. Jake watched as Virgil skimmed through pictures to reach the time frame that might hold the huge clue they were after.

"Nice deer," Jake said as they went past a series of pictures of a big buck walking down a trail.

"That's probably the buck that Clayton has been hunting so hard," Virgil offered without taking his eyes off the pictures.

Soon the images changed, and Virgil slowed down the scroll. "Here we go," he said excitedly. "This should be it." The pictures were coming up slowly, and the men were hanging on every click.

Outside the truck the investigator and a deputy had gathered after hearing that the wardens had found a camera. None of them had ever seen a trail camera, and they were happy Virgil knew how to work it. This case was unusual for them, and they needed a direction to start.

The radio cracked and the dispatcher asked for Virgil or Jake. They both sighed, hating the interruption. This was their lives, though. Rarely did they have a thirty-minute stretch in which someone didn't have an issue requiring their urgent attention. That's why they tried not to work at the same times, so they could spread their hours over a larger time period. This case, though, had the attention of both of them.

Jake grabbed the handheld microphone. "One-nine-five-oh to base, over."

A ten-second pause followed, and then the radio crackled with a female voice.

"One-nine-five-oh, you have a Clay County landowner that wants you to call him and needs immediate attention."

Jake wrote the name and number down while he watched the screen of Virgil's computer.

"One-nine-five-oh, copy that, over," Jake replied.

"There is something in the corner of this image," Virgil said, squinting at the image. "How can I zoom in?"

"Let's see." Jake leaned in. "Click that," he offered, pointing at the screen. "Yeah, that's it." He was surprised he knew, but he didn't let on.

"Well, there is something, but it's getting darker as we zoom in."

"Dammit."

"Is there a way to lighten up the image?"

"Not that I'm aware of." Jake was not known for his computer talents.

Virgil opened his truck door, noticing the small crowd of law enforcement gathering. He loved being the center of attention. "We got an image, boys. It's of the perp coming out and it's dark. No details," he said with a deep sigh.

"Do you think you can take it somewhere and get it enhanced?" the lead investigator asked.

"Where?"

"The Columbus Police Department?"

"I can ask, but I don't think they can do anything special."

Jake had an idea. "Hey Virgil, listen. I know a guy who works on campus at the Mississippi State photography lab. He has access to all kinds of equipment. I bet he can help!"

Virgil looked at Jake and then the other officers, who were nodding their heads in agreement.

"Jake, that's a great idea and probably our best bet. You take the card to him, and I'll go on that landowner call."

Jake loved the idea. He went to church with the photo lab director, and he knew the guy would try to help. He was a digital photography expert.

"Jake, when you get to his lab, the first thing you do is make a copy of this card. Then seal the original in an envelope. You guys work off the copy. That way we can't be accused of manipulating the image."

Understanding the protocols of evidence from his recent training, Jake nodded his head in agreement.

Everybody was looking at Jake, who looked back at Virgil.

"Go! I gotcha covered."

* * *

Perry Burns arrived back at the river house and couldn't quit thinking about the enigmatic expedition helmet. He didn't care about the artifact, but he sensed a chance to at the very least distract the twins while he searched for the missing money. Maybe he could talk one of his old buddies in New Orleans with serious assets and connections into fronting the cash and helping him broker a discreet deal. Perry could negotiate a commission on the front and back end, or he could steal it from the twins somehow and capitalize completely on his newfound project.

He hadn't asked to see the valuable helmet because the thought never crossed his mind that it didn't exist. His self-indulgent mind had purchased their story completely. The ex-con's head hurt from all the alcohol, but he was thinking clearly enough to grab his little black book and search for his old friend's phone number.

Finding the name, he ran his finger over the number and hoped it was still active. Fabian Antoinette was a proud Cajun, completely in touch with his French heritage. His people had lived in New Orleans since Napoleon sold Louisiana to the United States in 1803. He was always interested in making large sums of money fast, or at least he had been when Perry had been introduced to him before he was imprisoned. They'd met at the Port of Call restaurant and bar in the Garden District of New Orleans, where Fabian ate a gourmet hamburger and drank cocktails several nights a week. His house was close, allowing him to stumble home with certainty. A pair of DUIs made walking seem like a good idea.

Perry knew that Chase had not followed them home, and he heard Chance outside feeding his dogs. He picked up the phone in his room and heard the dial tone purr. Energized by the ideas flying through his mind, he slowly dialed the number.

On the fourth ring he heard a voice with a familiar Cajun accent answer the phone. "Haylo."

"Fabian, this is Perry Burns. How are you doing?"

"Perry! I'm doing good. Tell me, has the great state of Mississippi finally let your sorry ass out?"

"That's right. I paid my debt to society and I'm a free man."

"Good for you, but I don't think my debt got paid, though."

"That's 'cause I didn't owe you anything," Perry said with a laugh.

"Maybe you're right."

"You got a minute, Fabian?"

"Yeah, I was just sitting here watching the replay of the LSU game and drinking my toddy."

"Are you still interested in making money?"

"Is a green frog waterproof?"

Perry laughed out loud. "Yeah, you haven't changed a bit. Look here, I have a chance for us to make some serious money."

"Is it legal?"

"Probably not. But ain't nobody gonna be watching this. It'll be easy."

"Is this a secure line?"

Perry had to think about it. He didn't know and finally muttered, "Uh, yeah. I wouldn't call you if it wasn't."

Fabian didn't sound particularly convinced. "Perry, I'm always interested in making some money, but I don't want to talk business on the phone. You know what I mean?"

Perry nodded. He hadn't thought about someone listening. He wasn't thinking at full capacity. "Yeah, you're probably right."

"Can you get down here?"

"It may be hard for me to get to New Orleans. I just got out, and I don't have real dependable transportation yet." Perry tried to think how he could get there. Maybe Chance would let him borrow a vehicle or drive him.

"I tell you what there, Perry. I am going to Jackson day after tomorrow to buy a vintage Mercedes. I collect them now, you know. Can you meet me there, and we'll discuss it someplace private?"

"Hell yeah I can do that," Perry answered, though in fact he had no idea how he would get there. Maybe Chance and Chase would go with him.

"Meet me for breakfast at the Jackson Hilton about nine. They got a wonderful breakfast. We'll eat, catch up on old times, and maybe talk some business."

"The Hilton. Got it. Thank you, Fabian. I think you'll really like this."

* * *

After Virgil closed his computer down and watched Jake race off toward the Mississippi State University campus twenty minutes away to enhance the camera images, he sat and tried to think through the recent events. The other officers had all begun to walk back to their vehicles. The attitude among everybody was confusion. They had never had a crime quite like this occur, and they knew they needed a lucky break to narrow their focus down. In most crimes people brag about what they got away with to others, who prove eager to provide the information to the police in exchange for leniency for some crime they themselves committed. It took time for the word to permeate the local criminal underworld.

Breaking the top off a bright-yellow banana, Virgil thought about the crime. The perp would have a good fence it would be easy to sell the stolen goods to in order to turn them into cash. Guns and scopes all had serial numbers, and that was a problem. Professional fences were careful because serial numbers inevitably came back to haunt them at the most inopportune times. Virgil knew a few fences he could pressure and see what turned up. They would stiff-arm him, but he needed them to know the law was paying attention.

The crimes bounced around in Virgil's mind as he tried to make sense of them. They were difficult to understand. Did the perp know his victims? Was he following them until they presented an opportunity? Most hunters hunted with a partner, making a crime like this more difficult. Both victims had been hunting alone. That wasn't the only thing they had in common. They were both doctors who lived in Columbus, Mississippi. *That could be crucial.* They didn't work together, but they might hang out at some of the same places. Virgil made a note to ask them if they had any seedy patients that might have expressed an interest in their hunting habits.

As he finished his thirty-eighth banana in thirty-six days, he had the sensation that this perp was not a normal opportunistic robber. There had to be more of a common thread, and Virgil needed to figure it out. He would share his thoughts with the other investigators, and they could collaborate.

He was about to call the landowner who needed assistance when his phone rang. The number was familiar, and he shut the door before he answered. He was excited to learn what the caller had to say. The caller was his buddy, a retired Navy SEAL, and literally capable of anything.

"Tell me you got some good news," Virgil said.

"I'm going to get that digital recorder inside the Bolivars' house today."

"Same plan?"

"Affirmative. I borrowed the propane gas truck and uniform from your cousin, and I'm going to tell whoever's there that it's time for a routine line check for leaks. I can't imagine anyone not letting me crawl around and look, and that will give me a chance to place the recorders and a transmitter."

Virgil smiled as he cranked his truck. "You be careful now. They got dogs."

"Yeah, I will. Look, if something goes wrong, I need you to back me up with the sheriff."

"If something goes wrong, I can't imagine you not being able to handle it right when it happens."

"Seriously, I can't do that anymore. This ain't a Third World country."

"I got your back," Virgil assured him. "Just let me know when you're out." But his mind was already wandering back to the missing money and what he might do with it. Would he turn all of it in or keep some? Would he split it with Gunner and Jake? Gunner would take some, but he didn't know about Jake.

* * *

Morgan sat down to pay bills but grew frustrated after only a few minutes over the money they were losing each month. Jake wasn't making near what he had been, and she was going to have to get a job if they were to keep up their lifestyle. She wasn't excited about that idea, but she was willing to do whatever it took to help the family. She had never realized that kids were so expensive.

She decided to do the math on what a day care for Covey would cost and think about getting a job. There were several accounting firms in the area, and she could get back into the swing of keeping books. It had been a while, but she hoped it would come back to her. It had been ten years since Katy had spent time at the church day care, and Morgan knew that monthly costs had risen. Unless she found a really good-paying job, the costs of day care would negate what she made, or at least a large chunk of it. Morgan didn't really want a forty-hour workweek while raising two daughters. She didn't want to miss anything. Deciding to try to trim some costs from their life, she made a list of items to discuss with Jake that included their gym membership, horse-riding lessons for Katy, Jake's hunting club membership, and their social membership at the Old Waverly Golf Club.

They were also planning to pay four hundred dollars a month to have Kramer finished. It was a term she didn't understand. He had already been at the dog trainer for a three-month session. Shouldn't he already be finished? But there was no doubt he did need more training, and one month probably wouldn't do it. Morgan looked at the dog sprawled at her feet and knew he would take the maximum amount of time, whatever that might prove to be.

Why couldn't we have gotten a smarter dog?

She'd known he wasn't a wonder dog, but she'd still been shocked when he'd recently burned his tongue on a hot iron. As a joke, Katy had used the iron to warm up a grilled cheese sandwich that had gotten cold. The dog smelled the cheese on the iron, and one lick had him whimpering. Morgan had tried applying an aloe lotion, but the dog liked the taste and just licked it off.

She sighed and ran her fingers through her hair. She desperately needed a haircut, but she had no choice except to wait.

Something had to give.

CHAPTER 15

Dwayne "Gunner" Benson had retired from the marines three years before. Having grown up in Columbus, he knew his way around the area and the people. He knew the ones with money and without. He knew the good folks and he knew the bad. Twenty years of military service had taken him around the world and taught him skills that he rarely got to employ these days.

Since retiring, he had been trying to start a private investigations company, but it had been a slow go. He didn't enjoy following cheating husbands and wives, and that was what most of the calls concerned. To supplement his income, he had been trying to diversify into a beaver control business that would allow him to utilize his knowledge of explosives. Area swamps were full of beavers, which constantly posed problems for local farmers and landowners. When the problems finally got bad, they would call Gunner and his box of explosives. He was one of only two licensed local explosives experts since the events of September 11 had dramatically changed how explosives could be purchased.

When Virgil called and explained the need to learn what was being said inside the Bolivar river house, Gunner got excited. It wasn't exactly what he wanted to do with his skills, but it beat hiding behind the dumpster at the Ramada Inn. Besides, he and Virgil had been lifelong friends, and he enjoyed helping him. Virgil was paying his expenses out of his own pocket, so Gunner knew it had to be important, as his friend was a notorious tightwad.

The borrowed gas company shirt was a little tight, but otherwise Gunner looked the part. He hung an old radio on his belt to help him look more official. The truck had to be returned by the end of the day, so he had only a few hours.

Gunner was fearless. He had always been, but the marines training had cemented that trait in him. He knew how to protect himself, though if you looked at him, you would never suspect his past career. He wasn't the normal chiseled marine but had the appearance of someone who stayed in reasonable shape but enjoyed eating fried chicken also.

He knew of the Bolivars but had never met them, so decided the best bet to get into the house was to just drive right up and ask. He'd studied the house from his desktop the night before. Google Earth didn't have a street view, but the aerial helped him understand the basic layout.

When he drove up, the dogs in the pen were barking incessantly but appeared to be contained in the enclosure. Another dog was loose and barked, but not with the same rabid enthusiasm. Gunner exited the truck and bent down with a beef jerky snack. It took only twenty seconds for the dog to stop barking, relinquish her control of the area, and take the snack from his hand.

There was only one vehicle to be seen, and Gunner walked up to the front door and knocked loudly.

When an old man answered the door, Gunner wasn't surprised. His intel from Virgil had said he could potentially be there. Gunner wasn't as worried about him as he was the Bolivar twins. He needed to watch out for them.

"Can I help you?" Perry Burns asked through a half-opened door.

"I'm with the gas company, and we are doing a winter gas leak inspection. I just need to check the lines."

"Well, I'm not the owner. They didn't say anything about you coming out."

"Yeah, I'm sorry about that," Gunner said. "I was working this side of the county and got finished early with some other jobs this morning."

Perry stood there, confused. He wasn't paranoid, like most criminals, and he really didn't have a reason to suspect anything out of the ordinary. And the fact was the house really didn't seem that warm to him. He would probably be doing the twins a favor to let the serviceman check.

Gunner could tell Perry was considering compliance. "Where are the owners?" he asked.

"They just left."

Gunner looked at his watch as though he were in a hurry. "Well, I don't know when I can get back, but tell them I came by."

"Hang on there. What do you need to do?"

"I just need to look at the propane tank around back and then look inside, where the lines are coming into the house. Ten minutes tops."

"I don't know where the unit is. I'm just staying here with 'em for a few days."

Gunner gave a comforting smile. "No problem. I can find it easy. I do it every day."

"Well, I guess it will be okay," Perry said. "You want to get the inside part done first?" He opened the door.

"Thanks. Let me grab my bag. I won't be long."

Perry let Gunner inside and then wandered away into the kitchen, leaving Gunner to walk slowly into the main room and look around. He heard the refrigerator door open and knew that the old man wasn't watching him closely. Just outside the large den there was a small half door that had to be the heating and air-conditioning unit. He cracked the door open and set his bag down in front of it. Listening for the old man, he grabbed his electronic bug and walked back into the den, acting as if he were looking at the vents.

Hearing the old man fumbling with a drawer of utensils, he silently placed the unit on the top of an old velvet Elvis painting that had probably held its place since the King was still on two feet. Satisfied that it couldn't be seen, he smiled, thinking that Elvis himself would love to be playing a part in catching a criminal. Virgil had once explained that President Richard Nixon had made Elvis an honorary federal agent at large, complete with an official identification badge that Elvis treasured.

The listening unit was state-of-the-art digital recording equipment. It sat idle until it heard conversation, and then it recorded. Nine seconds of silence would render it back into sleep mode, and the range was more than adequate. The memory card was massive, and since it was recording audio and not video the capacity was incredible, perfect for this kind of work.

Gunner backed up and looked around the room. After confirming that it was clearly the best place to hide it, he zipped up his bag and loudly shut the thin door to the heating unit.

"This looks fine to me," he called out to the old man. "I'll check the unit outside and be outta your way."

"That's fine," Perry called back. "You want some coffee?"

"No, sir. Thank you, though," he said as he walked to the door. "I'm not much of a coffee drinker."

"All right then. Take care."

Gunner bounced down the steps, looking for anyone approaching. He was relieved to see nothing had changed. All he had to do now was give the appearance of checking the propane tank while hiding the transmitter that would send the audio recordings to Gunner's waiting receiver. The pitbulls in the pen had gone out of their murderous heads again the moment he stepped outside, but the loyalty of the other waiting dog was easily purchased with another treat.

He knew from the computer images where the tank was located, and walked to the north side of the river house and bent down to examine the big silver gas tank. Out of view from the inside of the house, he hid the transmitter in a waterproof plastic box and covered it with dirt and leaves. The unit itself was the size of a pack of cigarettes and easy to conceal.

Gunner made a show of walking around the tank and, content he had been convincing to anyone watching, strolled back to his work truck. Perry Burns wandered out onto the porch just as he reached the vehicle, and the two exchanged waves, and Gunner cranked up and let out a sigh as he dropped the gearshift into drive. He loved covert operations and the adrenaline rush that each provided.

The gas truck was out of sight of the river house when Gunner noticed a vehicle approaching. The gravel road was not wide enough for two vehicles to pass without one pulling over. Staying in character, Gunner pulled his gas truck over next to a huge old concrete silo and rolled his window down. A white diesel Chevrolet truck slowed down next to him, and he recognized the unsmiling face of Chance Bolivar behind the wheel. Gunner touched the butt of the pistol in his holster and unsnapped the protective strap holding it in place.

"Can I help you?" Chance asked, looking Gunner dead in the eye, then down at the logo on the side of the truck.

"Just needed to check your propane lines. We're doing that more often now, just to make double certain there aren't any leaks."

"Where's our usual guy?"

"He's delivering gas," Gunner said with a reassuring smile. "It's all hands on deck with this new safety program on top of regular deliveries, especially with this cold front that's coming."

"Everything okay with our tank?"

"Yeah, man, it's fine. Y'all got a pretty place out here."

"Thanks," Chance said, slowly nodding his head.

Chance's diesel roared as he accelerated away without looking back at him. The ex-marine swallowed and smiled. He looked in his rearview mirror at the truck getting smaller, and he knew he was out. Then he stepped on the gas, and the company truck slung gravel as he left.

* * *

The judge was assessing his options for funding his wife's surgery. He was beginning to think the idea of the twins finding the money might be a pie-in-the-sky fantasy. The money had been missing so long, it was crazy to think it would now suddenly be found just in time to help him save his wife. He cussed aloud at his stupidity for thinking it was a viable option. Even if they found the money, he'd still have to somehow steal it from them.

And yet his desperation kept the notion alive.

Jake reported in to him every day. He had been by the river house numerous times and followed Chance and Perry as much as he could but had yet to gather any useful information. It had been a long shot engaging Jake, but the judge didn't have another option. He was also aware that Jake didn't have finely honed law enforcement skills yet, but that was actually what he was counting on to help him get his hands on the money. Jake's naïveté and loyalty could be useful.

At some point in his life, he had heard that if money can solve your problems, you don't have a problem. Well, he had one. His wife needed a kidney, and money was the only way he was going to be able to help her. The local bank wouldn't loan him the money after he explained what he wanted it for; another was willing, but the judge would have to sign over his family's land as collateral. He really couldn't do that, since his brother and sister each owned a third. The judge had a stock portfolio that he was certainly willing to cash in, but that and his gun collection would yield only 40 percent of what he needed. He had considered selling his wife's Blue Willow china collection, but he didn't think it was worth much and he didn't want to stress her out. He hadn't told her what the operation would cost, only that he had it handled. His marriage style had always been to keep her out of larger financial matters. He handled the money, and so far it had worked just fine.

So far.

He was expecting a call or text from Jake with an update. Maybe something had occurred that would help him get the money needed without turning his personal life upside down.

CHAPTER 16

Virgil sensed that this morning was going to be busy. He was surprised so many people hunted on Sundays. When he was growing up, his mother would rarely let him and his brothers hunt on the Lord's Day. On Sundays she made them listen to the Gospel Singing Jubilee on television while they got ready for Sunday school and church. If he had made good grades, when the weather was right and the hunting at its best she would allow him to skip church. Those days were special, and he did well in school just for that reason. Today, Sundays seemed to be just another Saturday for a lot of folks. He explained his thoughts to Jake, who was checking his e-mails from the bosses in Jackson and texts from landowners who thought they had trespassers.

Jake never looked up from his screen. "My wife's pretty cool about it," he explained. "She says she'd rather have me in the woods thinking about God than in church thinking about hunting."

Jake looked at Virgil and smiled, remembering his own mother, until the crackle of his patrol radio interrupted his thoughts.

"That damn radio never stops," Virgil said as he looked down at it.

Virgil and Jake listened as the dispatcher explained about a convenience store robbery. They were asked to be on the lookout for a lone black male in a red late-model Ford Mustang.

Virgil wrote the information down and shook his head. "It really starts in December."

"What starts?" Jake asked.

"Robbing gets bad. I think it's folks trying to buy Christmas presents."

"This will be my first December on patrol."

"You'll see."

"Do you think the two hunters that got robbed are Christmas related?"

Virgil considered the idea for a moment. He thought about the timing and what the robber had stolen. It could all be turned into cash easy enough. "Maybe," he said. "There's no way of knowing right now. But honestly I don't think so."

Jake had his own opinion about the incidents with the two hunters. He felt someone knew these men and their habits. It was a crime that was well planned and thought out. Maybe even two or more people participated. One drove and another did the actual robbery? Whoever it was robbing the hunters was clearly comfortable in the woods, especially after dark.

"It's so different than any other robberies," Virgil said as he peeled a banana. "Our local criminals just don't fit the profile to me."

"You think it's someone from out of town?"

"No, I think it's someone local that we would normally never suspect."

"It's a shame that game camera picture quality wasn't better," Jake said. "I hope he can enhance it."

"When did he say he could let you know?"

"He was in Memphis and left a wedding at the Peabody to come back and work on it. I should know something tonight."

Virgil grunted in frustration. "I just hope it can be enlarged and enhanced."

"Speaking of enhance, did you update your online profile?"

"I'm thinking about it." He shook his head. "It's been three months since I've had a date."

"Are you too picky?"

"No, they just don't make women like they used to."

Jake smiled. "Like your mama?"

"Yeah, is that too much to ask?" He took a bite of his banana and shook his head again. "None of these women today know anything about canning vegetables and making jellies."

"Maybe not," Jake said, "but they don't have to—as long as you do."

Virgil looked at Jake and then out the window. "You may be right."

* * *

Perry Burns explained his big idea to Chance and Chase. The idea was to get his old buddy Fabian to purchase the Spanish helmet artifact, and then he would resell it to a private collector. He didn't know for certain that Fabian would buy it, but he felt that if there was enough profit potential in it for him that he would buy and sell anything.

Concerned her smile would make Perry suspicious, Chase decided at the moment she needed a beer and walked quickly into the kitchen. Chance kept a stoic look and spit into an empty Mountain Dew bottle.

"Here's the thing," Perry said confidently, loud enough for Chase to hear. "Y'all set the price, but just remember that my guy has got to be motivated, and he only gets motivated by money."

"What did he say?" Chase asked as she walked back into the den.

"He didn't want to talk about it over the phone, but he's meeting me at the Jackson Hilton on County Line to discuss the opportunity."

"And you think he has the money to front this?"

"He had plenty last time we did some business together."

"What did y'all do?"

"It involved the Hurricane Katrina cleanup, and let's just say that Fabian cleaned up."

Chance and Chase both nodded in approval.

"So you could say he owes you?" Chance asked.

"He does," Perry said with a glimmer in his eyes they had never seen. "I showed him how to bill the government for work that he hadn't done."

"But didn't you go to prison for that?" Chase asked.

"I did, but I learned from my mistakes, and Fabian's family was bulletproof in Louisiana. They were old money from New Orleans."

Chance and Chase were excited. Chase more than her brother, but he was enjoying the idea of conning someone out of a pile of money.

"So what do we need to do?" Chance asked.

"Y'all need to determine your bottom dollar, and we need to make a plan to see Fabian in Jackson."

Chase took a swig of beer and thought. "Chance can drive you to the meeting. I'll take some pictures of the helmet tomorrow, and you can take them to show him."

"We can't take it?"

"No. Not until he has money in his hand. I can't risk losing it."

"Fair enough," Perry responded.

Chase didn't even bother to ask Perry what he wanted for his part of setting up the sale. She had no intentions of paying him anything anyway.

"So," Perry said, "how much are you thinking?"

Chase and Chance looked at each other, but Chase always made the financial decisions.

"It's worth several million," she said. "We know that. Probably more than five million to the right buyer. It's a rare one-of-a-kind artifact dating back to the 1500s."

Perry took a pull from his beer. He loved talking about so much money, and he would have a chance to steal it from these kids soon.

"I would—I mean, we would—be happy with one point five million," Chase said boldly.

"In cash," Chance added quickly with a nod. That would be seven hundred fifty thousand dollars for him. That sounded good.

Perry was quickly running numbers in his head. He could make this work, he figured. It all depended on what Fabian could sell it for and if he knew someone that would buy it. New Orleans and Louisiana were filled with crazy wealthy people who collected all sorts of strange things.

Chase said, "That way your friend Fabian can sell it to whoever he wants and make a nice profit for all his risk and effort."

"I'll drink to that," Perry said excitedly, extending his drink in front of him.

The Bolivar twins stepped forward, and they all clicked their beverages. Smiles glowed from their faces.

* * *

Fabian Antoinette had been pleasantly surprised to hear from Perry Burns. Their relationship went back quite a few years. Fabian had respect for Perry and had been disappointed to hear he had been convicted and sent to prison. Now that he was out, they could catch up on old times, and Fabian could learn about Perry's new project, which no doubt involved his favorite subject: making money.

Fabian had lived a life of crime. It was in his family's DNA, and it was the only lifestyle he had ever known. His father had taught him to respect the past and those who had helped him build a life of financial independence. He had a younger brother, and they hid the fortunes behind a lawn care business and a printing shop. Ironically, their businesses did very well on their own, but their string of illegal activities made more cash than they could spend—though, in classic Louisiana style, they tried.

The New Orleans police and local Louisiana State police had never been able to bust the Antoinettes for any illegal activities, but Fabian's history of DUIs had compromised his driver's license. Still, the old man continued to collect vintage cars. In a few days his driver would take him to Jackson, Mississippi, to purchase an old restored Mercedes two-door convertible coupe. It would be the crown jewel of his car collection.

The printing business had opened unique doors for the Antoinette brothers. Modern digital technology had inspired them to try their hand at counterfeiting a few years back, and they had nearly perfected both the twenty- and the one-hundred-dollar bill. They were proud of their product and sold it to trusted associates across the South. They were careful, and so far they had not had any issues. Each lived in constant fear that he would be raided, but they'd invested heavily in security cameras as well as in a highly talented printer who could reproduce anything, given time. Their ace printer's talent wasn't limited to the reproduction of the difficult currency itself; it was also in replicating the perfect wear and tear on the money so it didn't feel brand-new. He would not allow anyone to see his technique, though Fabian knew it involved a Maytag front-load dryer.

The Antoinette brothers and their hired specialty printer had no idea that agents from the United States Secret Service and the Treasury Department were watching them.

* * *

Jake stood at his friend's desk in the photo lab. Virgil was slowly eating a banana and studying the high-tech equipment. He was fascinated with the process and had no clue how any of it worked.

"The image is pretty low quality," Jake's friend said. "I mean, some of these cameras have pretty sophisticated lenses, but this one was pretty basic. Combine that with the photo being taken in low light and at a distance. That's why you're here."

"So can you do it, Professor?" Virgil asked as he studied a lens that looked to be two feet long.

"Yes, I think I can make it better," the man said as he grabbed his mouse and isolated the part of the image he wanted to enhance. "And by the way, I'm not a professor." He tapped on his keyboard, and the image doubled and got grainier quickly.

"Is that a glow on the person's right hand?" Jake asked.

"That would be the reflection from a watch," Virgil said, leaning in. "Right, Professor?"

"Yeah, I think so," the man said with growing frustration.

"But the perp's outline. It's still a silhouette with no detail."

"Is that a ponytail?" Jake said, disbelieving his eyes.

They all moved closer to study the photo. The lab technician tried enlarging it more and, with no success, dropped it back to a smaller size.

"I think that's a rifle barrel," Virgil said. "He's carrying it on his shoulder and that's what you're seeing."

"Heck, I can't tell," the technician admitted.

"I don't think he's wearing camo. The pants look lighter than the jacket. He doesn't look like a really big person, but we can't tell age or race from the image," Jake said in frustration.

"That's the best we can get, I'm afraid," the lab technician explained to Jake.

"There is nothing else that can be done?" Virgil asked.

"I don't think so, guys. Sorry."

Virgil tossed away a banana peel, still thinking. "If we have a chance," he said, "we could recreate the image and determine some height information that could be helpful."

"True," Jake said. "Just stand in the same place, hang the camera at the same height, and you could."

Jake and Virgil thanked Jake's friend and took the copy with them as they walked silently down the halls of the college building. Virgil was looking for coeds.

"You hungry, Jake?" Virgil asked just before his phone rang. He sighed and reached in his pocket, but when he saw the number he smiled. "This could be interesting."

CHAPTER 17

Chance and Perry arrived in the capital city of Mississippi in time to eat supper and check into the Hilton. It was an unusually towering building for the Jackson area, and they shared a room halfway to the top. Perry insisted on separate rooms and sold the argument by reminding Chance of his lack of privacy at Parchman for the last ten years. He now craved the quiet created by solitude.

The drive north had been uneventful. Perry wanted to talk about things that occurred in the world in the last decade, and Chance just wanted to listen to sports talk radio. His Mississippi State Bulldogs football team was having a great season, and each game was more important than the last.

Chase had provided them with four digital photographs of the helmet and an iPad to show the images. Upon examination, the helmet was perfect for the ruse. She'd spent time rubbing mud in the cracks and drying it with a hair dryer in an attempt to make it even more believable in the photographs. The helmet itself was remarkably real looking. Chase briefly wondered what time period *The Lord of the Rings* was set in and vowed to watch the movie if the helmet fooled the buyer.

Perry had asked again to take the helmet to show Fabian, and Chase had told him flat out that wasn't happening. She explained that they kept it in a box similar to a cigar humidor inside a safe. It would only be transported when the sale was occurring. She gave strict instructions that if Fabian Antoinette had any questions, she would be available to talk via her cell phone.

Perry once again agreed to her terms, since he really didn't have any choice, and made her feel confident that he could pull this sale off.

* * *

Gunner listened to the recording twice and could not believe the audio they had captured. It wasn't unusual to hear criminal activity spoken of in the dwelling of such clearly criminally inclined characters, but this crime was especially interesting due to its federal implications. He immediately called Virgil and requested that they meet at once at Virgil's place.

Arriving first, Gunner stared at the tapes on the truck seat and sipped his coffee while he waited. He knew Virgil was about to be very busy and sincerely hoped he could be involved in his upcoming activities. Since Gunner had retired from the military, his life had not been nearly as exciting. He lit a cigarette and glanced at his watch.

When Virgil and Jake arrived, Gunner snubbed out his cigarette and opened his truck door.

Virgil knew something good was about to happen and was all smiles. "Gunner, meet my partner, Jake Crosby."

The two exchanged greetings and shook hands.

Jake took quick stock of Gunner. He was a stout guy, and Jake figured him to be deceptively strong. He also figured he was carrying a pistol under the bulky coat he was wearing and probably had all the permits.

"Gunner is my go-to guy when I need something done," Virgil explained.

"You boys are gonna want to hear what's on these tapes. There are a bunch of hours of nothing and then a conversation that will be very interesting to you."

"Well, let's hear the conversation," Virgil said, and leaned against the side of the truck. With his nearest neighbor a half mile away, there was no chance of anyone overhearing the recording. He rarely let anyone inside his trailer.

"It's cued up." Gunner set the tape recorder on the hood and pushed "Play."

Jake anxiously leaned against the truck hood. Virgil had explained to him on the ride over that Gunner's recording tactics with the Bolivars had produced instant results. Everybody was excited.

The three men stood silently listening to Chase, Perry Burns, and occasionally Chance Bolivar. Virgil was stunned to learn that Bronson Bolivar had found a Spanish conquistador helmet. He hadn't heard of one ever being found in the area, but he knew all about Hernando de Soto's visit to the region, so it was quite possible. However, it would be so old, Virgil couldn't imagine it would be in good shape.

Jake listened without saying anything, trying to understand how they could use the illegally obtained information. He wasn't good at lying. He listened but stared at Virgil, watching his reaction.

Gunner listened while watching the clouds in the sky, and when the conversation ended he mashed the "Stop" button.

"That it?" Virgil asked.

"Yep."

"Holy shit!" Virgil said, and rubbed his face. "This is federal. That's a stolen artifact that came from federal land."

"What are we gonna do, Virgil?" Jake asked.

"We're gonna bust 'em. I just don't know how yet. I need to think of a way we could line this up that works, that sticks, and we don't have to drag Gunner into it."

"Yeah, I'd appreciate that," Gunner said with a chuckle.

"There's a way. I just have to think it through. We need to find out when and where it's going down and bust 'em as they are selling it." He turned to Gunner. "Would you be willing to drive to Jackson tonight and see what you can do to listen and observe what they are doing?"

"You know I will do whatever you need me to," Gunner replied, "but Chance saw me when I installed the bugs. The Perry guy too. They're likely to recognize me."

"You're right. That's too big a risk."

Jake was glued to the conversation. "I can go. They don't know me."

Both guys looked at Jake for a moment, and then Virgil said, "You look too clean-cut. They are gonna smell you a mile away."

Jake was disappointed but kept at it. "It's at the Hilton, right? There will be lots of businessmen there. I'll look like a salesman there on business."

Jake was right and saw that Virgil was considering it.

"Look, I can be there in a few hours. The meeting isn't until tomorrow morning."

"Okay," Virgil said, "here's the deal. You go. Gunner will go and be backup for you. He can hide and listen. He has the equipment."

"I can do this by myself."

"The only way I am gonna agree to this is with Gunner going and watching your back. It's not negotiable. Chance is capable of anything."

Jake nodded and agreed. No point in arguing with Virgil. Jake was excited about the possibilities of this criminal investigation. It was going to attract attention, maybe even from the governor. He also appreciated Virgil's genuine concern for his safety.

"I'll get organized here," Virgil went on. "You keep an eye on Chase and keep our bosses off your back."

Jake nodded.

Virgil exhaled deeply. "It sounds like this is just a meet and greet to see if the buyer is interested."

"That's my take too," Gunner agreed.

"Y'all stay in touch with me. Gunner, you'll be on the clock, and I'll die owing you before I beat you out of the money. I promise to pay you when I can, but I need you to keep an eye on him. If the sale goes down and Jake has to arrest 'em, he may need some Good Samaritan assistance with Chance."

"You got it. I trust you."

Jake leaned into Virgil. "Is there somebody we should call?"

"I probably should call in some help, but I'd have to explain how we know," Virgil said, shaking his head. He really wanted to see the money. He remembered hearing Chance's voice insist on cash. *That is gonna be a lot of green,* he thought. "Let's see what happens at this meeting."

* * *

Jake decided not to tell Morgan exactly what he was going to do. Only that he had a last-minute meeting in Jackson that he had to attend. He didn't want her to worry about him. She was surprised that he didn't have to take a uniform and packed his suit, but she believed him when he explained that it was a meeting in the department offices. He kissed Morgan, Katy, and Covey good-bye and hurried out the door.

As Jake was driving to pick up Gunner, the judge called. Jake reluctantly told him something was going down, but he didn't have to explain. Fortunately, the cell service was poor, and Jake was able to disconnect as the judge was beginning to ask a bunch of questions Jake didn't want to answer. He felt secure in telling the judge if it came to it, but he also knew he needed to be careful. Jake explained just enough to keep him content that he was doing his job. He was a federal judge, after all.

Gunner met him at the new Hampton Inn in West Point, where Gunner left his truck. They both agreed it should be safe parked overnight there.

Gunner loaded a standard overnight bag and two gear bags that rattled when he set them down on Jake's backseat.

"What's in those bags?" Jake asked.

"Everything we might need to keep you outta trouble."

"That's reassuring. Is there anything in that bag you have to have permits for?"

"Most everything in the bag," Gunner said with a laugh.

"I have no idea what we're getting into," Jake said as he pulled out of the parking lot.

"If we do end up needing something in there, believe me, you'll be really pleased that you brought me along."

Jake pointed his truck toward Jackson and set the cruise control. "So what's your story, Gunner? How did you and Virgil become such buddies?"

"We went to high school together. We were the guys that didn't play sports and spent our time either in the woods or on the river. We really didn't fit in and spent a lot of time hanging out. I guess you could say we were best friends. He went to community college, and I went into the marines, but we stayed in touch. We have a lot in common. We both love the outdoors and Mississippi, and we're both not very good at keeping wives."

"What happened with Virgil and his ex? He doesn't ever talk about it."

Gunner chuckled. "It's a crazy story. He had been married a few years and his wife somehow made it on the television show *Who Wants to Be a Millionaire*. You know how Virgil has an answer for everything whether he knows about it or not?"

"Yeah."

"His wife navigated through two episodes of tough questions and got all the way to the five-hundred-thousand-dollar question. She only had one lifeline left, the Phone-a-Friend. Believe me, it was a lot of drama."

"Five hundred thousand dollars? Wait, so if she got it right she could potentially win a million dollars?"

"That's exactly right, or she could choose to not play anymore and walk away with half a million."

"What was the question? What did she do?"

Gunner laughed again. "She went for it. The question was tailor-made for Virgil. 'What is it called when it's raining while the sun is shining?'"

"Oh, Virgil had to be all over that one," Jake said.

"That's what she thought too. She asked for a Phone-a-Friend and called Virgil, her know-it-all husband, who was back in Mississippi trying to reintroduce some kinda endangered frogs in a refuge. She was pissed about that already, by the way."

"What, he didn't know the answer?" Jake asked, looking at Virgil in disbelief.

"Oh, he thought he did. She hurriedly asked the question and he immediately answered, 'The devil's beating his wife.' She asked, 'Are you sure?' Virgil calmly said he was one hundred percent certain. Then the call went dead."

"So what happened?"

"I can't remember all the answers. One was sun-showers. One was a real long meteorological term. But I clearly remembered she smiled really big and said, 'B. The devil is beating his wife. Final answer.'"

"That's right! I have always heard that. It's an old Southern saying."

"Well, it may be, but the answer was sun-showers. It's a weather phenomenon."

"No way! Hell, I would have missed that too!"

"She missed the question, and she only ended up with like thirty-five thousand after all that, and Virgil couldn't take her constant reminders. She blamed him, he blamed the network, and their marriage just completely deteriorated."

"Wow. I never heard about that."

"I felt sorry for him. She was pretty upset, and he doesn't speak of it very often."

Jake smiled at the thought of Virgil confidently answering the question. Then he shook his head at the thought of losing that much money. Anybody in the South would have said the same answer, unless they were a meteorologist.

"Anyway," Gunner said, "my story is much simpler. I just never found a woman that would put up with my crap."

"Women don't like crap," Jake noted. "I learned that early on."

"Wake me in an hour. I'm gonna get some rest. It's a marine thing. Always rest when you can. Who knows what tonight might bring?"

"It's gonna bring me a restful night with no baby crying to be fed," Jake said.

"I hope you're right. But just in case," Gunner said as he reclined in the front passenger seat.

Jake exhaled and drove steady while he thought about the Bolivars and their illegal activities. Virgil had explained to him that they had already violated the Archeological Resource Protection Act, probably the Native American Graves Protection and Repatriation Act, and the Antiquities Act, and were in possession of a stolen government-owned artifact. It totaled over forty years of prison time and huge fines. It was much more of a crime than most game wardens get a chance to crack. Jake glanced at Gunner and his bag of tricks and smiled as he cruised through the black night toward the towering Hilton, the nicest hotel in Jackson.

CHAPTER 18

The darkness of the night made Virgil think about how the robber hid in the shadows, waiting on a targeted, unsuspecting hunter to return to his vehicle.

It was a unique crime for sure. The brass in Jackson had e-mailed him and wanted updates whenever there was any new information. The local news had generated a lot of interest, and Virgil's cell phone vibrated with calls, although so far none had been at all helpful.

He'd continued to monitor the bug at the Bolivars' river house, but so far all he had listened to was the sound of the television. He was pretty sure Chase was there, since *The Bachelor* could be heard. Virgil sipped whiskey while he watched the Weather Channel on mute and listened live to the Bolivar house.

Based on the conversation they'd heard, he knew the helmet hadn't made the trip to Jackson tonight, and that meant it was probably in the river house. He had to get the artifact. It was invaluable and belonged in a museum, maybe the Smithsonian, or at least the Chickasaw Nation's collection. He had no idea what it would actually be worth in terms of dollars, but it would be one of the finest cultural artifacts ever found in the Deep South.

Virgil drained his whiskey and imagined the accolades that would follow if he and Jake could make an arrest and take possession of the conquistador's helmet. He might finally get a promotion. He had been slow to move up in rank since joining the Mississippi wildlife department.

Virgil poured another glassful as his phone vibrated. He wanted the world to slow down. He had the Bolivar case and a robber attacking rich hunters, and deer season was in full swing, with duck season about to start. There weren't enough hours in the day. Virgil clicked a button on his phone and answered.

"Hello."

A man introduced himself and quickly told Virgil that the police gave him his number and that he had been robbed just like the doctors. This information caused Virgil to set the whiskey drink down and grab a notebook.

"When did this occur?"

"Last year about this time."

Virgil exhaled. "Tell me the whole story."

* * *

Chase spent the night alone at the river house watching television and thinking through the con. It had come together so fast she felt as if she were walking a wire with no safety net. She was expecting it to pay off, but she knew eventually the buyer would realize the helmet was a fake. That's where she was counting on Chance to earn his keep.

She wanted to make the sale or just steal the cash—it didn't matter to her which. She was tired of looking for her dad's missing money. She'd been born into a family that was supposed to be well-off. Her family was old money, old Mississippi money, but her father had ruined them.

Chase had been angry at her father when he was alive, and she hated him now that he was dead. The man left her more bills than assets, he made a mess of her inheritance, and her family name was a joke, with everyone looking for the missing Bolivar fortune. She was a Bolivar, dammit. It was her fortune. But Chase had begun to realize she wouldn't find it, and that's why this con was so important to her. Maybe somebody had already found it, but the money from the con of the helmet would be hers. It would be real money and she would enjoy it.

Chance had called when they were checked into the hotel. She knew they were probably at the bar in the hotel now. She reminded him how important this meeting was and that they could call her if there were questions. She liked the anonymity and mysteriousness her not being there created for the situation. They were her mouthpieces and her puppets.

The misting November rain had made her skip her run. She hated to miss a run and would double up tomorrow if it was clear. For the time being she sat cross-legged on the couch with her laptop and searched for Eva Marie Mitchell. She'd always wondered why she left so suddenly.

Her father had loved Eva Marie. They'd met at the Princess Theater in Columbus, where she'd been playing Stella in a version of *Cat on a Hot Tin Roof* during a Tennessee Williams festival. She was tall and thin with dark skin, dark eyes, and mysterious ways. She looked like Cher in her younger days, and her dad fell hard. Chase knew Eva Marie was one of the few people who had ever conned her father. They lived together off and on for five drama-filled years. Chase remembered them well.

It seemed odd to Chase that someone who was an actress and survived by her public notoriety had seemingly vanished after she'd left her father. There was nothing on the Internet, not a trace.

Chase burned with curiosity but didn't know what to do to track down a person with no digital footprints. The idea that maybe she was dead occurred to her. Then the thought crossed her mind that maybe Eva Marie Mitchell didn't want to be found. She turned the computer off and leaned back on the couch. Not much about Eva seemed to make sense, but that thought—the idea that maybe she didn't want to be found—suddenly did.

* * *

Jake and Gunner slept in separate queen beds in a room close to the elevator on the tenth floor. Jake checked into the hotel, and Gunner, wearing Ray-Bans and a State cap to conceal his identity, later walked up and joined him. Virgil was a bundle of nerves and texted them both with instructions. They ordered two pizzas and watched a college football rankings show on ESPN. For the first time either could remember, both Mississippi State and Ole Miss were ranked in the top ten, and they discussed it for an hour until they both fell asleep. The night of restful sleep didn't occur for Jake, since Gunner snored all night and a bachelor party had the elevator active into the wee hours.

Since they didn't know exactly what time the meeting was occurring, they rose early. They did know it was happening at breakfast at the Hilton. The restaurant had a grand buffet that featured everything you could think of, including the creamiest cheese grits in Jackson.

Gunner brought a small parabolic microphone that could record from a distance, like from across a room. He planned to use an open briefcase to support, aim, and conceal the microphone and spent the early morning eating cold pizza and showing Jake how to set it up. Gunner had a ten-power zoom attachment for his iPhone that would allow him to take close-up pictures more discreetly than with a typical camera. He also had a mini-microphone and tiny earpieces that would allow him and Jake to talk without fear of detection.

Jake sat in the large booth and spread a newspaper, briefcase, and folders on the table while he paced himself at the breakfast buffet, waiting on the criminals to arrive. Caffeine helped temporarily replace the lost sleep. Jake exhaled deeply and felt the pistol under his coat. The coffee wasn't really necessary. Never had he felt so alive.

Gunner sat in a corner of the spacious lobby with a view of the doors to the restaurant. He had cut a small hole in a *Sports Illustrated* issue to allow his zoom lens to operate undetected. He liked everything about their setup, except that the smell of the breakfast buffet was making him hungry.

"You ready?" Jake asked discreetly over his microphone.

"Roger that. As soon as I see them, I'll give you a heads-up."

"Virgil keeps texting me," Jake said with a slight laugh.

"Me too. I put my phone on silent."

"Good idea."

"How is the breakfast?"

"Delicious."

Gunner grunted loudly. The smell of the food was making him hungry, and he intended to get a plate when the operation was over. Suddenly, the elevator doors opened, and he saw Chance and Perry step out. "Heads up." Recognizing them both from his encounters at the river house, he whispered, "We got company."

Jake sat up straight and tried to act natural. "Talk to me."

"You got Chance and Perry walking toward the restaurant," Gunner said as he checked his watch. He then scribbled "8:44" into his notepad.

The two of them waited to be seated, and Jake tried to read body language. Neither seemed nervous, but Perry Burns was obviously looking around the restaurant for someone. The maître d' led them to the opposite side of Jake's section. He heard them ask for a table instead of a booth, and they were seated only two tables away from him. A slight adjustment to the briefcase, and the microphone was in perfect position to pick up their conversation.

Jake tried to observe them with his peripheral vision and glanced over when he felt safe. The two of them were talking rapidly, and Perry anxiously watched the door.

Nervous to be seen talking alone in the booth, Jake grabbed his cell phone and texted Gunner and Virgil: *Chance and Perry r25 ft away. Perry looking for someone.*

Jake watched the phone until the text string displayed "Delivered."

Over the next fifteen minutes Jake observed Chance visit the buffet as soon as he ordered a beverage, while Perry drank orange juice and waited. At precisely 9:00 a.m. an older well-dressed man walked into the restaurant as though he owned the hotel. Perry stood up and waved to the man, who obviously recognized him. Jake noticed that the man had either a bodyguard or an assistant.

The buyer carried himself with the air of a wealthy man accustomed to the finer things in life. His overcoat looked like something from a New York fashion house, and the maître d' helped him with it. Perry Burns hugged him, and they slapped each other on the back like old friends.

Jake studied the unfolding scenario. As the two men talked, he observed Chance checking out the man and the second man Jake had pegged as a bodyguard. The bodyguard, big and bulky like Gunner, took the coat from the maître d' and sat two booths away, where he could see the room and the man who was undoubtedly his boss.

Jake took a deep breath. *This is it. This man is the buyer.*

"We got company," Jake whispered into his microphone, and then nonchalantly crumbled some bacon into his grits, acting interested in breakfast while discreetly listening to the conversation.

The restaurant was half-full of patrons. Chance and Perry were making introductions. In the lobby outside the restaurant, Gunner was watching the door and making notes of who he had just seen go inside. He knew the last guy was hired muscle, and that concerned him. No one had noticed him, however, and that gave him some comfort.

* * *

Perry Burns was glad to see his old friend, and Fabian Antoinette acted as though he was also pleased to see Perry. Chance overheard a sly comment about missing the easy money they had made together years ago. This gave Chance an optimistic feeling.

The conversation excluded Chance as the two men caught up on old times. While Perry didn't have much to add except that he had been incarcerated and now was out, Fabian had become much richer and wiser. He explained that business was good and laughed as if that were the understatement of the year. He was careful about what he said in front of Chance. Fabian motioned toward the buffet. Together the two friends went and built breakfast plates while continuing to talk. Chance watched briefly and then decided to go for a second trip.

After another twenty minutes of talking and a nod from his security, Fabian felt comfortable enough to allow the conversation to turn to their business.

"Tell me about this opportunity you have, my friend."

"It's pretty simple and straightforward. It's either going to make sense or it's not. But you being so connected—well, I figured you probably know somebody that would love to have what this young man and his sister are holding."

"And what is that?"

Chance smiled. He found Fabian's Cajun accent humorous. He knew it was authentic, but it still made him smile.

Perry started the discussion with a story of being in prison with Chase and Chance's father and how they shared cells, secrets, and many years of their lives. He explained about the many interests of Bronson Bolivar and his talent for hiding things. He was certain Fabian would have liked him.

He went on to explain how in the mid-1980s the Tombigbee River had undergone a massive change when they channelized the river and installed a series of locks and dams. In the process many federal parks were constructed, and Bronson Bolivar had been part of building a big restroom at a park right on the river. While digging out an area for a septic tank, he'd found a rare valuable artifact, and Perry went on to describe it.

"Hernando de Soto went right through the area in the 1500s," Chance added as he tried to read Fabian's face and gauge his interest. "It's in all the history books."

"So you have in your possession a Spanish conquistador helmet?"

"It's either from the Spanish during that period or French a little later," Chance said. "We don't know for sure."

Hearing that it might be a French artifact intrigued Fabian immensely. He was very proud of his French heritage. "What are you fellas wanting to do with it?" he asked as he sliced a sausage.

"The feds have long suspected that his daddy found it," Perry explained, "but Bronson hid it, and we figure after over twenty years the heat's died down and the value has gone up. We want some help selling it to a private collector."

"A discreet private collector," Chance added.

Fabian leaned in. He looked around the restaurant. There were only a few people left in the dining room. Nobody was within earshot, and that relaxed him.

He said, "There are a lot of collectors that would like to have something like that in their collections, but it's going to be a dangerous sale. I mean, whoever buys it really can't share it with the world. Maybe their close friends and that's about it."

"We think it's over five hundred years old," Perry said. "One was found and sold in Florida a few years ago, and we're told it went for over five million. But look, we realize we can't get the full price. We want to sell it for a modest price to someone that can sell it to a collector and make a nice profit also."

Fabian never looked up as he finished his eggs. "So what do you want for it?"

Perry Burns lifted himself into his salesman's role. Establishing value and price would be a very delicate part of this sale. "There are two owners, as I explained—Chance and Chase. It's been hard to get them to agree on a price, or even to sell for that matter, but they both agree on two million."

"That's too much," Fabian said, shaking his head.

"You haven't even seen it," Chance objected as if insulted, though he'd known that would be Fabian's response to any price quoted.

"Do you have it here?"

Chance pulled out his iPad and pressed the power button. "No, but we have pictures."

"The actual helmet is in a climate-controlled safe," Perry added.

Chance opened the photos app to the folder holding the images and slid the iPad across to Fabian. When Chance had demonstrated how to slide between photos, the man appeared immediately transfixed, seeming to soak in every detail of the pictures.

"It is absolutely fantastic," Fabian said with awe.

"So do you think you can sell it?" Perry asked.

Fabian looked back through the pictures. He wanted the artifact for his own. He could almost feel the connection to Europe and his ancestors. He believed this had a connection to France. If he could get a deal on it, he would buy it with counterfeit cash. No one in front of him scared him in the least.

"It's quite possible," he said, finally looking up, "but I will need a few days to consider. I have questions I need to find answers to. If I do decide to help you, I will make you a nonnegotiable offer in cash. I will do the math and treat you fair."

"I told them that, Fabian," Perry said with a smile. "You've always been a very fair man."

"Who is this other owner?"

"It's my twin sister. She'll be the one you negotiate with."

"I don't negotiate."

"Yeah, well, she does," Chance said. "Unless she likes your math."

"Where is she?"

"She prefers to be in the background," Chance explained with a sly smile.

"Does this mysterious sister look like you?"

"Not really. We're fraternal twins, not identical."

Fabian considered this quite fortunate for the sister but didn't say as much. He looked forward to meeting her, as he had met few women he couldn't charm. Fabian looked around the room while he considered his options. He took notice of Jake, but he didn't get suspicious. He asked Chance to e-mail him the images so he could study them and asked for a few days.

Chance was prepared and handed him a black thumb drive with the images loaded on it.

After a few seconds of silence, Fabian asked, "Have you offered this to anyone else?"

"No," Perry answered. "When I found out about it, I immediately thought of you."

"Don't offer this to anyone else until you hear back from me."

"We won't, Fabian. You have my word." Perry handed him a sheet with his contact information on it.

Fabian stood, and immediately the man in the far booth arrived and helped him put on his overcoat. Fabian placed the note in his pocket and smiled at Perry Burns, who hugged him. Chance rose quickly and shook his hand, and after that the two men from New Orleans left.

Perry glanced at Chance. A slight nod from Chance indicated he was pleased, and Perry smiled.

"It does sound promising," Chance said as he watched the men pass through the lobby's main doors.

Both men sat back down and exhaled. Smiling after refilling coffee cups, the waitress then placed the bill for all four men in front of Perry. "I'll take that when you're ready," she said, and walked off.

Perry Burns looked at Chance and slid it across the table to him with a smile.

CHAPTER 19

Jake watched the entire meeting through his peripheral vision, taking quick glances in their direction when he could. Though he could hear only muffled words from his booth, he felt confident he had recorded it all.

Their plan had been simple: don't attract any attention, monitor the meeting, and try to learn what they could. When the meeting was over, they would meet in their room to review the tape before calling Virgil.

From the very beginning Jake had been fascinated by the man that he assumed to be the buyer. He was larger than life, carefree, giving the impression of serene confidence. His bodyguard probably gave him some of his confidence. The guy looked plenty tough to Jake.

Jake's perspective was that the meeting went as Perry and Chance had hoped. Jake had watched the man study something on an iPad screen, and even he could tell that the man was enthralled. After viewing the images, Chance had smiled and handed the man a small black thumb drive.

Jake had been so preoccupied with watching the meeting, he hadn't realized that Gunner was texting him until the meeting was obviously concluding. In a string of texts, Gunner complained of something interfering with the recordings. Jake had no idea what would have caused the interference but could tell from the texts it was frustrating Gunner immensely.

Panic hit Jake as he wondered what could be done to salvage the audio of the meeting. He glanced out the door of the restaurant, and he could see Gunner in the lobby, holding out his arms as though he didn't know what was going on.

At the moment Fabian stood up to leave, Jake dialed Gunner's number.

He answered on the first ring. "I got nothing. Someone is running an interference field."

"Hell, it's over now. They're moving toward you," Jake said quietly as they both watched the man and his bodyguard leave the restaurant.

"It's gotta be the buyer. He must have some mic-scrambling device on him. I've heard of them but never encountered one. This guy has serious protection."

"So you didn't get anything?" Jake whispered.

"No, nothing. But I did get the tag number from their car, and you ain't going to believe what else I saw!"

＊ ＊ ＊

Virgil was beside himself with worry and curiosity. He had spent the morning on the phone in his house trying to pacify landowners without having to visit their properties. The last thing he wanted to do was go to a remote location and lose cell service and not be able to communicate with Jake and Gunner.

When Jake called, he was relieved to hear that the meeting had occurred and that everyone was safe. Clicking his cell phone to speaker, he leaned back to listen to the guys tell him the story.

"We didn't get squat from the recordings" was the first thing out of Gunner's mouth.

"What?"

"They were pros and prepared. They brought an interference field."

"Bolivar?" Virgil asked with surprise.

"No, the client. I got their tag number. It's a Louisiana plate."

"That's good. Text it to me and I'll run it."

"That's not all of it, Virgil," Jake added.

Virgil leaned forward. "What else?"

"The Louisiana guys, they were under surveillance, according to Gunner."

"What?"

"I'm pretty sure they were FBI. They definitely were feds of some stripe. One came in the lobby to observe, and another waited in a car."

After absorbing the details for a moment, Virgil said, "We gotta learn who this guy is."

"Chance and Perry just checked out of the hotel," Gunner said. "I overheard them say something about going by the Bass Pro Shops before heading home."

"FBI, huh? That's interesting."

"Who else could they have been?" Jake asked.

"CIA, maybe Homeland Security," Gunner said.

"And they didn't pick up on you guys?" Virgil asked.

"I don't think so. Your boy Jake looked just like a salesman killing time on his expense account, and I stayed hid behind some fake plants most of the time."

"Did you get the good guys' tag number?"

Gunner hung his head before he answered, "No. Dammit."

Virgil rubbed his head in frustration while he tried to think. "Y'all get on back. You did real good. With a little luck they'll discuss the meeting with Chase in the river house and we'll get some more info," he said as he picked up the phone. "And text me the buyer's tag number."

* * *

Morgan called Jake three times before he finally answered his cell phone. That wasn't unusual when he was working; however, it made her slightly suspicious, since he was in Jackson and not a remote part of the county with no cell service.

Jake finally answered and explained he had been in a meeting but he was about to start the drive home. She instructed him to be careful on the road; the weather was turning nasty, and Mississippi was under a rare threat of snow. Morgan had already been to the grocery store to stock up on milk and bread, a Southern tradition when snow or ice threatens.

Jake wanted to tell her that he had just conducted his first semi-undercover covert operation, but he knew she would worry. Maybe he wouldn't even tell her at all. But he sure wanted to. Jake wished he could tell her things without her worrying. He realized his recent track record for getting into unhealthy situations was probably the reason she worried so much.

As Jake drove, he and Gunner discussed the events of the morning. They were both certain that the buyer was a big fish, and that excited them both. If he was being watched by the feds, he had to be involved in some serious crimes. Jake was still energized from being so close to the criminals and observing them. He wondered what the mysterious man and his bodyguard were involved in besides purchasing the stolen artifact.

"Could it be drugs?"

"I don't think so," Gunner said as he leaned back in the passenger seat. "I didn't get that feeling from what I saw."

"What about Mafia?"

Gunner thought for a few seconds. "He could be part of the Dixie Mafia. Yeah, I could believe that."

Jake thought about some of the Mafia movies he had seen. He didn't want to tangle with them at this stage of his career. He had a lot to learn, and after all, he was just a game warden. He didn't have the training to tackle the Mafia, and he didn't think that Virgil did either.

"Does that still exist?"

"Yeah, I think so. The dark suits following 'em could have been ATF. You know, Alcohol, Tobacco, and Firearms. I could see that guy running illegal whiskey."

Jake stared straight ahead as he drove, deep in thought. A Johnny Cash song played in the background.

"Did you know," Gunner said, "many years ago Johnny Cash was arrested in Starkville, Mississippi, for picking some flowers after a concert?"

Jake looked at Gunner and shook his head. "You sound just like Virgil."

Gunner pulled his cap down over his eyes and laughed. "Yeah. Dammit."

After a long stretch of quiet driving, Jake said, "Gunner, this is bigger than we thought."

"I agree. This guy that's buying the artifact, you can bet that he is a bigger catch than the local rednecks you and Virgil bust for shooting rabbits at night."

Jake looked at Gunner and smiled. He knew he was telling the truth.

* * *

Fabian Antoinette had always been a fan of European history in America. He could trace his roots back to when Bienville had helped settle the territory for France. He had old paintings, silverware, coins, furniture, and even a candelabra chandelier, all of them hundreds of years old. The helmet of unknown origin intrigued him. He knew about

Spanish history, and he knew La Salle and Bienville were rumored to have explored the area. He rode in the silence of the backseat while his driver sped him home. He wanted the helmet.

His first call was to a friend who owned an antique store in the heart of old New Orleans. The dealer traveled Europe and brought back the finest antiques to sell to his customers. The dealer changed phones and had Fabian explain the piece one more time. He exhaled deeply and told Fabian it could fetch upward of eight to ten million. He had three buyers he knew would buy it immediately if it were authentic.

That thought hadn't crossed Fabian's mind. Was it authentic? He could find a way to verify it beyond question once he had it in his possession. The dealer had confirmed what he strongly suspected. It was a rare find that was extremely valuable. It could be his best investment ever. Having it authenticated ahead of time could attract unwanted attention and ruin his chances to purchase it.

He did go so far as to call an LSU history professor who he knew from football games. They tailgated next to each other and shared a love of old things. Fabian was careful not to tell him exactly what he had but to simply ask how such a piece could be discreetly authenticated. He was relieved to know the professor could do it from sight and a simple acid test to confirm what it was made from. He was familiar with the metals they worked with in the old days. He explained that the older metals were free from impurities that had been added in more modern times. Fabian paid close attention and grew more excited during the conversation. Though he almost told the professor about the helmet, he was more worried about someone else getting it than having it verified. Greed had permeated his mind and clouded his judgment.

His final call was to his younger brother at his office in the French Quarter. They were close from years of working side by side to enhance the family's financial situation first and keep their family together second. They had 100 percent trust in each other and went to great lengths to take care of one another. He explained to him what he wanted to purchase and the amount of money he needed in their best one-hundred-dollar bills.

He smiled when his brother assured him this would be no problem. By the time they passed Magnolia, Mississippi, on Interstate 55, he had formulated his plan and forgotten his Mercedes.

* * *

Chase waited on Chance and Perry to return. She had gotten the condensed version of the events from a call as they left the Hilton in Jackson, and had already started planning how to spend the money. She hadn't decided how she was going to cheat her twin brother out of his half yet. She needed his talents for later, and he would give her an alibi. That was critical. *Chance can't even spell "alibi,"* she thought.

By the time Chance and Perry arrived back at the river house, she was primed to hear them recount in detail the events of the morning's meeting. Chance came up the stairs two at a time and swung open the door with enthusiasm she hadn't seen in a long time.

"Well, sister, we got a fish on the line," Chance bragged as he dropped his duffel bag. "A big one."

"So Perry's guy feels good?"

"Oh yeah."

Perry pushed open the door. "Whew! It's getting cold out there!"

Both Perry and Chance were wild-eyed with excitement.

Perry dropped his suitcase and walked straight to the fridge. "I'm starving."

Chase walked across the room and sat on a barstool. She watched Perry help himself to some cold Popeyes chicken. Chance plopped on the couch and changed the television channel to local news.

"Did he ask to see the helmet?" she asked, looking at Chance and then Perry.

Chance laughed. "No, he never asked. He loved the photos."

"He trusts me," Perry said as he chewed the meat off a chicken leg.

"Tell me exactly what he said when you told him two million."

"'That's too much,'" Chance said.

"He's gonna make us an offer, though," Perry said. "I know he is."

"When?"

"I'd say within a few days."

"He asked us not to offer it to anyone else," Chance said with a laugh, and that made his sister smile. "He had a bodyguard," he added. "Big guy."

Chase considered what this might mean. On the surface it meant they were dealing with a very cautious guy who had plenty of money and reasons to be cautious.

"This guy had the feeling of a rich, well-to-do guy that could buy anything he wanted," Chance said. "He had some fancy clothes, and when he drank his coffee his pinky finger poked out."

"What does that mean?"

"I don't know, but I think the guy is loaded."

"I told you," Perry said. "He has the correct change."

"I Googled Fabian Antoinette while y'all were gone," Chase said, "and it shows he's involved in everything in New Orleans from politics to Mardi Gras."

"He's well connected."

"Perry Burns, I'm impressed and glad you came to visit us," Chase said.

The older man peeled the skin off a chicken breast and nodded. "This is gonna work out for all of us."

Chase stood up to leave. "Dinner is on me tonight," she said.

"It may snow soon," Chance responded.

Chase rolled her eyes. Snow and ice were such a pain in the ass in the unprepared South. "If it does, we'll go someplace close. I hope we have enough propane in the tank to keep the house warm if we have a storm."

Perry looked up from the chicken. "Oh, you should. The gas company was out here the other day checking it."

Chase looked at him with curiosity.

"Yeah, I saw 'em too," Chance said without looking away from the television, then quickly added, "Oh shit! Shh."

"What?" Chase asked.

"The news is talking about some hunters getting robbed!" he said with a snort.

Chase walked closer to the television while Perry looked for more food.

* * *

Jake and Virgil met to discuss the situation as soon as Jake returned to the area. Gunner had to go check on his elderly mother, since the threat of snow had her worried. It was nothing a loaf of bread, some milk, and a few cans of soup couldn't cure.

They met at the Jubilations Coffee House and drank coffee and ate Oreo cheesecake. The owner allowed them a private table to discuss their matters.

"This place okay with you?" Jake asked, knowing Virgil might consider this too fancy for his tastes.

"We shoulda gone to the gas station. They got a helluva chicken basket on special."

Jake rolled his eyes. "Next time."

"Is your wife worried about the storm?" Virgil asked as he slurped loudly.

"Of course. She always worries."

"We got a lot going on with the Bolivars, the robber, deer season, and now this storm. You haven't ever been through one; we'll probably get a bunch of calls to help the sheriffs."

Jake hadn't considered their involvement in helping the community stay safe in a snowstorm. He'd been hoping they would get a few inches and he could play in the snow with Katy. A plastic swimming pool would make a good improvised sled, he'd figured. Now he wondered if he would get the chance.

"No problem. I can do what needs to be done."

Virgil slid a piece of paper with two photos attached across the table. "I ran the tags and found the car belonged to Antoinette Holdings, a New Orleans company. I figured it was one of these two guys. Am I right?"

"That's him right here," Jake said, pointing to a picture.

"That's Fabian Antoinette. He's sixty-five years old. He's had several run-ins with the law for racketeering. He's been accused of extortion, money laundering, obstruction of justice, and bribery, but he's never been convicted of anything other than two DUIs. I'm unsure who the other guys watching him are, and frankly, I'm scared to open that can of worms. I know we'll be told to back off."

Jake studied the paper. He'd seen enough movies to know the federal boys always trumped local law enforcement.

"What's the latest on the robber?"

Virgil snorted. "We got no leads and at this point no real chance. The guy is gonna be harder to catch than my ex-wife's boyfriend."

Jake laughed and looked over his call reports. He had at least a half day of paperwork that needed to be done.

"I did get an interesting call from a man in Columbus that got robbed the same way last year," Virgil said. "Everything is the same. He didn't report because he was embarrassed."

"Where?"

"Down near Macon."

"That makes three."

"I'm betting there is more."

"What made him call you?"

"He saw it on the news and realized he might have some info that could help."

"Was he a doctor?" Jake asked.

"No, but he is wealthy," Virgil said as he stood up to leave.

Jake got to his feet too. "We need a break in the case."

"We gotta be patient. By the way, I'm hoping when I get back to the house that I'll have a fresh conversation with the Bolivars on tape. Maybe that will help us know exactly when the sale is gonna occur."

Jake and Virgil walked to their trucks, which looked identical, except Jake's was newer. Virgil waved good-bye after reminding Jake to get his paperwork done.

As Jake was climbing into his truck, his cell phone rang. The judge was calling. He shut the door and answered the phone.

"Yes, sir?"

"Jake, I just wanted an update on the Bolivar twins."

CHAPTER 2Ø

The judge soaked in every word Jake said like a sponge. He tried to remember any mention of the rare artifact during the trial and couldn't. His aging mind was normally razor sharp, but he couldn't even remember any rumors. The de Soto part made sense, though; there was a state marker in downtown Aberdeen that described how he and a group of explorers had marched right through the area. He had noticed it many times but never really paid much attention to it. He didn't have much time to appreciate history when he had so many modern issues pressing.

The idea that the heathen Bolivar twins were expecting a briefcase of cash revived his waning hopes. The money was involved in an illegal activity. The Bolivars were white trash, and he needed the money for his wife's operation. He had already justified it in his mind. All that was left was to determine how to get it, and Jake was the judge's means to that end.

His dear wife had a doctor's appointment tomorrow, but he knew without the doctor telling him that she was deteriorating. Her breath was shortening and she had grown even more lethargic. Her kidneys weren't filtering the waste from her system, and the buildup was slowly killing her. Yesterday she had grown confused in the afternoon, a symptom he had been warned to watch for.

The doctor from France had tentatively set a range for the date of her procedure that was four to eight weeks away. The judge was expected to wire a twenty-thousand-dollar deposit tomorrow, and he had already made the necessary arrangements. He hoped to God she could make it that long.

The judge planned to stay very close to Jake over the next few days.

* * *

When Virgil arrived at his modest double-wide, he rushed through his evening bachelor routine. There were hours of data recordings to sit through.

When he sat down to listen, the Bolivars' television was activating the microphone and they were watching *The Walking Dead*. Virgil had never watched the show, and after having to listen to it decided he would check it out. He had a lot of flaws, but he prided himself on being current with popular entertainment. He carefully rewound the digital recorder back to when Chance and Perry had arrived.

As the three criminals discussed the meeting in Jackson, Virgil really didn't learn anything he didn't already know, except that an offer was forthcoming and that the price would be around two million bucks. He shook his head at the thought. They didn't know when but expected a counteroffer soon. He had to make sure they found out when and where. If he could, he'd also like to learn where they were keeping the artifact. That would be very valuable information.

Virgil's career had stalled years ago, and he hadn't done anything to change its course. This case—this missing valuable artifact that was an antiquity of the great state of Mississippi—could be exactly what he needed to set a new direction. He could visualize himself getting a major promotion. Jake's career would be set on a different course too, if they could catch the Bolivars and Fabian Antoinette.

Virgil checked his cell phone, and he had received no calls. Considering the weather, that surprised him. It also suddenly surprised him that he cared. Tomorrow would be a crazy snow day in Mississippi, and he hoped he got the chance to help people in need. The thought of people stranded in the snow reminded him that the heating unit of his double-wide hadn't shut off since he had been home. He looked out the window and admired the beauty of the snow falling under the security light in his front yard. Everybody else had stocked up on staples; Virgil had purchased bananas and whiskey.

With much on his mind to consider, he poured another drink and, sticking his pinky out as he sipped, settled in to think about the two million dollars. Soon after that he fell asleep watching the Weather Channel.

* * *

The time had come for Fabian to call Perry Burns and make an offer on the artifact. There was no need to play games and act uninterested, since he was going to pay for it with fake money. He found the paper they gave him and carefully unfolded his bifocals so he could read the number.

Chance was prone on the couch, watching the drizzling snow illuminated by the spotlights outside their house. He couldn't remember the last time it had snowed. When his cell phone rang and displayed a 504 area code, he instantly knew it was Fabian. He yelled for Chase and Perry Burns, then confidently answered on the fourth ring.

"Hello."

"Is this Chance?"

"Yeah, it is," he said, and then burped.

"I was expecting Perry. Is he where I may speak with him?"

"Yeah, hang on," Chance said, then handed the phone to Perry while smiling at Chase.

The two siblings looked intently at Perry as he took the phone.

"Fabian, my friend, thanks for calling."

"Perry, it was so good to see you, and I appreciate your bringing me this opportunity."

"It's my pleasure, friend. Do you think you can move it for us?"

Fabian smiled. He had no desire to sell it just yet. He wanted it for himself.

"Yes, Perry," he said. "I think I can find a home for it."

"So what do we need to do to consummate this deal?"

"Can you tell me with a hundred percent certainty that it's real?"

Perry was a bit stunned by the question, but he recovered. "What are you saying, Fabian?"

"How well do you know these people?"

For the first time since he had heard about the artifact, Perry remembered that they were children of a world-class con man, and that in fact their dad didn't even trust them. His next thought, though, was of money. At the very least he was going to earn a commission for arranging the sale.

He took a deep breath and looked Chase in the eyes before saying, "I knew their dad a long time. It's real. This area up here is a hotbed for artifacts. History tells us the de Soto expedition came through the area. That's a fact."

Fabian didn't immediately respond. Finally he answered, "Okay, I want it, but I won't pay asking price."

Perry looked at Chance and back at Chase. "So what will you pay?"

"I've researched it. One point two in cash is the price."

"One point two in cash," Perry said for the benefit of Chase. She immediately shook her head no. Perry exhaled. "Fabian, let me talk to them. Can I call you back?"

"Yes, Perry, my friend, call me at this number. It's my cell."

"Thanks, Fabian."

CHAPTER 21

Jake helped Morgan clear the dishes after a supper of shrimp and ched-dar cheese grits. It had been a banner day: he'd had grits for breakfast and supper.

Morgan had been unusually quiet during the meal. Jake had decided to let her open up on her own. If he brought it up, it would probably taint the evening. He had learned that much. When she was ready to talk, the floodgates would open.

Katy bounced around the house from window to window, watching the snow fly. She had seen snow only once before. School had already been canceled, and her friends were planning a day of constructing snowmen and sliding down hills with reckless abandon.

Kramer—who had been kicked out of PetSmart yesterday and banned from ever returning—had followed her for a while but had eventually given up and was now enjoying lying on the cushions of the couch until Morgan discovered him.

When the last plate was put away, Morgan left to bathe Covey and put her down for the night. Outside the night air was cold and damp, but inside the house was warm.

As the evening wound down, Jake's mind went back to recent events, specifically the idea that Bronson Bolivar had found a Spanish conquistador's helmet. While Morgan read an article in *Southern Living*, Jake opened Morgan's laptop and sat next to the fire in the den. The quiet of the snow and the crackle of the fire invited his mind to consider the possibilities.

Jake looked at an image on the Internet of a conquistador's helmet from the time period. *How in the world did Bronson Bolivar find one? The odds have gotta be astronomical.*

Jake searched further. There had been buttons, uniform ornaments, axes, rings, and coins found, but only one helmet had been found in Mississippi or Alabama, according to his search. It was uncovered near Camden, Alabama, on the Alabama River.

So it's possible, he thought. *Just not probable.*

Jake threw another log on the fire and tried to consider more possibilities. Morgan was still avoiding talking to him; she continued reading and appeared to be enjoying her hot chocolate. On an impulse he searched for medieval helmets for sale and found three that were replicas. The one that looked best to him had recently sold on eBay for a thousand dollars. He studied the helmet images and finally decided to e-mail the seller and see what he could learn.

Afterward he logged on to Facebook and scrolled through the status updates of friends and family. Some were interesting and noteworthy; others were mundane updates that were a waste of time. He and Virgil had actually used Facebook and Instagram to solve a few wildlife crimes. Some people couldn't help posting pictures with too many doves or turkeys, never considering that the photos could be used against them.

It seemed like everyone was on Facebook, he thought, and that gave him an idea.

Jake moved the cursor to the search bar and looked up at his wife. Morgan was quietly reading, and Kramer lay at her feet in a ball. He typed in "Rosemary Rothbone" and hit "Enter." A face he hadn't seen in a long time appeared on the screen.

* * *

Chase wanted to get as much for the imitation artifact as she possibly could. Truth be told, she would take the offer; however, if he was willing to pay one point two, maybe she could get him to pay one point five. A million and a half dollars had a nice ring to it, especially since she had paid only a thousand dollars for the helmet less than a week ago.

She decided her time was best spent determining where and how the sale would go down. So far the prospective buyer hadn't expressed much concern that the artifact was genuine. That was a good thing. It probably helped that Fabian knew Perry and trusted him. It would take an examination by an expert to tell it wasn't. The helmet was carefully weathered with mud and looked fantastic. It was very believable to the untrained eye.

Chase had purchased a wooden cigar humidor and lined it with red flannel. The helmet fit snug inside, and she'd dropped a few packets of silica gel in with the helmet to make it look as if she were trying to protect it. The whole unit looked museum ready while it was waiting in her closet for its new owner.

After some thought, she realized she didn't want the buyers to know exactly where she lived or the property she owned, so meeting at the river house or their office weren't viable options. She wanted a place that wouldn't give the buyer a comfortable place to study and evaluate the product. A perfect scenario would be for her to open the box, show the artifact, and collect the money, and then for both groups to leave.

She finally decided the boat ramp parking area at Columbus Lake would be an ideal place. In the winter there would be few boats, and she could point across the lake to the lock and dam area, where she'd claimed her late father had found the valuable artifact. That would be a convincing touch to their scam that she felt certain the buyer would appreciate.

* * *

The three men sat at their usual table in the corner of the Port of Call restaurant in the French Quarter. They met most evenings to down a hamburger or steak along with a few drinks before they went home to the healthy meals their wives were cooking. They'd discovered it to be an excellent way to help keep peace in their households.

Fabian finished his steak and pushed his chair back to check the room, then his smartphone.

His brother stabbed a big piece of steak and pointed it at him. "You sure you want to buy this old thing, this—what's it called?" he asked, waving the meat at him.

"It's a very rare, very valuable artifact. They think it's a Spanish conquistador helmet, but it could be French."

The steak-wielding brother smiled and turned his attention to the third guest, a longtime family friend. "My brother and his collections. When he was a small boy, I remember him collecting baseball cards and pocketknives. Then it was cartoon animation cells. After that muscle cars, which turned to old vintage cars a few years back. Now he is into old European headwear!"

The three men chuckled. There was no reason Fabian Antoinette couldn't have anything he wanted. He was what locals referred to as "well heeled."

"It's our heritage, Brother," Fabian explained with a laugh and a shrug. "It fascinates me, plus I think I can sell it later and maybe triple my investment in real money."

"I may want some of that action," the brother replied.

Fabian didn't say a word; he only smiled to show his amusement.

The brother leaned in close so the next table couldn't hear. "So what happens when the buyer finds out that the money is funny?"

"I'm still thinking that through. It's only Perry. I know I can handle him. The other man, though, Chance Bolivar—he makes me a bit nervous."

"Nobody can get to you," the brother said, looking up at their protection sitting near the door working on his second massive hamburger.

"This Chance, he looks unstable. He is either crazy or fearless. It's making me pause."

"You've always been a good judge of people."

"I'm too old to be looking over my shoulder, but I do still enjoy the thrill of the game," Fabian said with a smile as he wiped his face. "I'm just much more careful than I was when we were younger. I'm not as greedy."

"Greed is bad?" the third man whispered with a sly grin.

Fabian slid his chair up to the table and leaned in. "They haven't agreed to a price yet, but they will."

"You really want this helmet?" his younger sibling asked again.

"I do, Brother."

His brother stabbed his last piece of steak and looked up. "Then the old helmet will be yours."

In another moment the three men pushed back from the table, and two checked their watches.

"When do you expect to hear from them again?" the brother asked.

"Soon. They are considering my offer, but I'm confident they will either take it or counter."

"My brother, he also loves to barter like an old woman at a flea market."

All three men laughed out loud again, looking forward to drinking their dessert before heading home.

"Monsoons all around?" Fabian asked.

"Of course," they both replied in unison.

* * *

Before dawn Virgil was patrolling rural roads and checking for iced bridges. Listening to the patrol radio, he realized this part of the state had fortunately missed the heaviest snow of the big storm. There were only two inches of accumulation. The countryside was beautiful in the headlights of his vehicle. He was anxious for daylight and the winter wonderland it would expose, even though he knew the weather would create excess work for him.

Jake woke at 6:00 a.m. and carefully stepped over the sleeping dog to look out the bedroom window and see if the snow had stuck. He could see a beautiful white blanket covering everything. When he went to the back door and cracked it open, the silence created by the insulation of snow was obvious. Kramer streaked by him and dove into the white powder, and Jake laughed quietly at his antics. Snow was a new experience for the young dog, and he ran around the yard as if a monster were chasing him.

Jake stood enjoying the view and the sunrise. He wished he could call in sick today and spend the time with the family, but while the powdered accumulation had the outside world silenced, inside he could hear his cell phone ringing.

"So it begins," he said aloud, and hurried inside.

Virgil's name was displayed on the screen, and Jake quickly answered it and moved back outside so he wouldn't wake the family.

"You seen the snow?" Virgil asked.

"Yeah, it's beautiful."

"That's the difference between you and me. You see it as a beautiful event, and I see it as a day when somebody could get killed in an icy road accident or an old lady who can't pay her electric bill will freeze to death."

"That's a little morbid, isn't it?"

"It's reality."

"I would think most people know to be careful today," Jake said. "It's been all over the news."

"People can't be trusted. That's why they have to install automatic flushing toilets in public places. People can't even be trusted to flush the toilet."

"Did you need something?" It was too early in the morning to listen to a Virgil rant.

"Can you meet me at my house this morning? One of us ought to always be monitoring the Bolivars live. They probably won't work today and may discuss the sale. It could happen soon. We need to know when and don't want to miss it."

* * *

After their recent road trip, Perry Burns and Chance Bolivar had started to enjoy each other's company. Chance liked to hear the prison stories and cons the old man had pulled that eventually got him sent away, and Perry enjoyed listening to Chance's hunting stories and his tastes in country cooking. Chance knew the best places to get real authentic soul food. Perry had spent too many years eating bland prison food, and now he appreciated quality cooking.

With the anticipated snow on the ground closing the septic tank business, Chase had predetermined she was going to sleep late. During her late night of drinking, she'd drunkenly told Chance she wanted Perry to call Fabian midafternoon. She was ready to make a deal, she'd explained, before she'd stumbled to the master bedroom.

Chance had killed two deer in the snow before anyone else at the river house had even thought to get out of bed. When he returned, he told Perry the story and showed off his prizes. He was exactly one buck over the daily limit, but such a care never crossed his mind. Finding the snow to be no hindrance, Perry and Chance decided to eat an early lunch at an old restaurant in Columbus. The fried chicken reminded Perry of his mama's cooking.

Full as ticks, the two criminals pulled back into the river house by two o'clock and found Chase sipping coffee in the den, dressed as if she were going to a Colorado ski resort.

"Where have y'all been?"

"We went for some soul food."

"I don't know how you eat all that greasy crap," Chase said, shaking her head.

"It's damn good," Chance assured her.

"Oh, I agree. I love it, but I would be as big as . . . well, I guess you," she said with a condescending laugh.

"I love it too," Perry added.

"Y'all ready to call the man?" she said, handing Perry her cell phone and a torn corner of paper with the phone number.

Perry smiled. "What do I tell him?"

"Tell him we'll take one point five."

Perry looked serious and sighed. "He said he wouldn't negotiate. He said one point two was the price."

"I know what he offered. This is our counter," she said as Chance nodded his head in agreement.

"Okay, okay, but you're gonna have to show me how to dial this phone, though," he said, handing the phone back to her.

Chase dialed and handed it back to Perry. Chance was already on the couch with a beer.

For the next twenty minutes Perry was in the middle of Chase and Fabian's negotiations. He went from nervous to frustrated. In the end they finally agreed on $1.3 million for the artifact. Both sides were pleased, as both felt like they had won. Chase got an extra one hundred grand, and Fabian was buying the rare artifact for less than asking price.

After the price was determined, Chase finally spoke to Fabian directly. She'd wanted to stay mysterious during the negotiations, but now she would talk to him. She had strict meeting instructions and insisted the deal occur in Columbus. Fabian, a consummate ladies' man, was smitten with her strong, dusky voice and listened intently as she explained the meeting site. After she finished, he immediately agreed and explained he would fly to Columbus on a private plane and personally hand her a Louis Vuitton suitcase full of money. The vintage case was a last-minute idea he had after hearing her voice and already knowing her age. Fabian thought she would appreciate the touch.

Everyone's eyes grew wide, until the phones disconnected, and then they all yelled in excitement.

CHAPTER 22

Jake took the first shift listening to the Bolivars' live conversations. The only information he gathered was that Chance had killed two of something—he suspected deer, but it could have been wild hogs, which had no limit. Chance didn't go into enough detail for the warden to determine. It did pique Jake's interest, though, and he wished he were observing the river house from the edge of the woods again. It would have been more interesting than Virgil's boring double-wide. The décor was so basic, and he doubted the trailer had ever been vacuumed, much less dusted.

Virgil showed up at twelve thirty after pulling a truck out of a ditch near the paper mill and issuing trespassing tickets to two distant relatives of Elvis Presley he'd been trying to catch poaching for years.

It had actually been a relatively slow snowstorm from Virgil's perspective. Knowing his partner would be hungry, he'd brought two Arby's roast beef sandwiches.

"Have you heard anything useful?" he asked as he dropped the bag of food.

Jake pulled his headphones off. "Not yet. One of those for me?"

"Yeah, you eat and I'll listen," Virgil said as he reached for the headphones.

"Thanks. I was scared I was going to have to eat a banana. Oh, and Chance killed two animals this morning in the snow. I don't know whether they were deer or pigs."

"Just file it away. We don't want them to get their guard up just yet, you know?"

Jake was hungry and glad to see the food. As he chewed his sandwich, he checked his smartphone. Morgan had texted that the dishwasher was making a funny noise and Katy had outgrown her insulated rubber boots. When he checked his e-mail, there was one that caught his eye.

"Mr. Crosby, I am sorry to inform you the replica helmet sold last week to a collector in Mississippi. It was a classic piece that you would have appreciated. If I locate another, I will e-mail you."

Jake read it again. *Mississippi? It had to be the Bolivars,* he thought. Jake ran his hands across his face and studied the screen. A jolt of excitement shot through him. "Virgil, check this out!" he said excitedly, handing him his phone.

Virgil slowly read the message, then looked up. "How? Where did you find this?"

"Last night I just thought about the chances of Bronson Bolivar finding a real helmet. Then I began searching on the net and ran across a page on eBay where this replica recently sold. So I e-mailed the buyer. That's the response."

Virgil sat perfectly still. "So it's a con! There's no real Spanish helmet."

"Looks like," Jake said as he took another bite of sandwich.

"That actually makes more sense. This is impressive detective work, Jake Crosby."

Jake nodded his head in appreciation for the compliment.

"We gotta think this through and make sure we aren't missing something," Virgil continued, "'cause it's not a crime to sell a replica. I mean, they are misrepresenting it. Dammit! This changes everything."

Virgil stood up and started pacing the room. "I would really like to know exactly who that helmet got sold to, but they might alert their customer if we ask too many questions. Some people don't want to help the law at all."

"I could e-mail them back and say I wanted to try and buy it from the person in Mississippi. They might give me the e-mail address. That could help confirm."

Virgil thought for a minute. "Did you use a personal e-mail address?"

"Of course."

"Then let's do it. Blind-copy me. It's a good idea, and it could confirm what we suspect. Just act anxious to buy that exact one. Say you're an independent filmmaker and you're in a bind."

"You're pretty good at this lying thing," Jake said.

"It's not hard. My ex-wife said I had a talent."

* * *

Rosemary Rothbone had been at the First Baptist Church in West Point several times the past week talking to the preacher. He had been at the church since she was a child and he knew as much about her family as anyone. Her parents were secretive and led quiet lives, but the preacher had kept up with the stances that the judge had taken in his trials and knew he was a one-man force for justice and Christian beliefs. The Rothbones quietly and dependably tithed every week. If there was ever a spoken need for money for a church member, local family, or mission, the money always showed up anonymously, but the preacher knew the Rothbones were the source. They tried to go unnoticed, but the church's new security cameras captured them and silently explained years of anonymous cash donations. If the preacher needed help, Judge Rothbone was his first call, and he had never turned him down. To now learn that Mary Margaret Rothbone had a medical need hurt him deeply. He wanted to help them.

Rosemary also met with Samantha Owens, a meticulous young attorney who had quickly learned her way around divorce court and settlements, developing a reputation for getting her clients more than their fair share. She and Rosemary hit it off immediately. Samantha knew her father well, having appeared in his federal court a few times and early on struck a friendship. The judge had also known her late father, who had been his high school football coach and had encouraged him to stay in college and get a law degree. The man was a very important figure in the judge's early life. Though he was careful not to show her any partiality, when the big high-dollar attorneys jetted in to appear in his court against her, the judge had her back. Samantha too absorbed all that the judge was now facing and knew she had to do something to help.

Finally, Rosemary took an overnight trip to visit her mother's closest friend, who lived in Jackson. They were sorority sisters who had met during their freshman year of college. Her family was old Mississippi money. The two ladies and sometimes their children got together every year at the Peabody Hotel in Memphis. Rosemary had watched the ducks march the red carpet many times growing up with her mother and her friend.

Rosemary felt guilty for exposing her parents' pain and problems, but she only told people she knew loved them. One of the beautiful things about Southerners was that, while they were prone to gossip, they were also eager to help someone they loved. Favors were remembered and handed down through generations.

* * *

Jake stood at the den windows of Virgil's trailer and watched the snow melt. He was disappointed it hadn't lasted longer. Katy had texted him earlier that she and her friends built a snowman but Kramer destroyed it. She was not happy.

When Virgil heard the whole gang gather in the room to call Fabian Antoinette, he snapped his fingers rapidly to get Jake's attention.

Jake turned around and was confused by the crazy hand gestures his partner was making. "They can't hear us, can they?" he whispered.

Virgil blinked his eyes twice. "No. Hell no they can't." Then he laughed out loud.

"What are they saying?"

"They're calling the buyer!"

Virgil turned the headset inside out so they both had an earpiece, and the two wardens sat silently, hanging on every word, Jake watching the audio equipment meters bounce while Virgil smiled and doodled on a legal pad.

After approximately twenty minutes they heard the group yelling and screaming in excitement. The men had heard everything, including where the meeting would occur the day after tomorrow.

Virgil set the headphones down and whistled. "One point three million dollars!"

"Damn, that's a lot of cash."

"We got a lot to think about," Virgil said somberly. "A lot to do and some decisions to make."

"You mean calling in some reinforcements?"

"Yes. And the fact the fed guys were watching Fabian at the meeting in Jackson still worries me."

Virgil tried to imagine what a briefcase full of the money would look like. He had seen it on television but never in person. He'd come close to a million-dollar check once with his wife and a goofy game show question, although that seemed like another life now. He wished the money were his, all one point three million dollars. He laughed to himself when he realized he had an answer for the damn TV show that had helped sink his marriage. Yes, thank you, he actually did want to be a millionaire.

"Virgil. Virgil?"

Virgil shook his head. "Sorry, I kinda zoned out there for a second."

"I think we should call Jackson and tell 'em what we have stumbled into," Jake said frankly.

"We can't tell 'em about the bugs, and without the bugs, how do we explain all this?"

Jake stared at a mounted deer that looked twenty-five years old and shook his head with frustration. "I don't know."

"Have you heard back from that e-mail to the eBay seller?"

"Not yet," Jake said, and sighed.

Looking at the same deer head, Virgil calmly explained, "Until we confirm, I think we have to act and conduct ourselves like we think it's authentic."

"I bet they'll get back to me soon, probably in the morning. They responded overnight to my first question."

"I really hope that the helmet is real," Virgil said, "because if it's a fake, I'm not sure any laws have been broken, at least none serious enough to justify all this attention."

"The whole thing still feels wrong, though."

"If it's a replica, about all they are guilty of is misrepresenting the facts. False pretense—that one happens every day."

Jake sighed. "Look, I'm the low man on the totem pole here. I will do whatever you think we need to."

"Let's just keep it between us for now. We may never, ever be able to talk about the way we intercepted the information," Virgil said as he held up the headphones. "I'll get Gunner to help us at the sale. Then we can decide."

* * *

Morgan was worried about her husband and her marriage. Jake had gone to Jackson without any warning and taken his sport coat and tie. It didn't make sense to her that he wouldn't take his warden uniform. She had checked their credit card account online and was surprised that he had indeed stayed at the Hilton—and had ordered enough pizza for two people, she figured, plus two breakfast buffets the next morning. It was all very suspicious.

Lately Jake hadn't been himself, and with the demands of his new job, Morgan had been forced to deal with everything around the house. Taking care of Katy and Covey consumed her day, and that didn't even take into account all she did to take care of Jake's damned dog. No matter how hard she tried to make the new finances work, they just didn't. She had all the pressure of their world on her. Jake never saw the bills. So Morgan had been aggravated for a good while, and now she was worried he was seeing another woman. That was the only explanation. So much of the time she never knew where he was or what he was doing. Whenever she asked, he'd just say he couldn't talk about it. That was his standard answer. She wasn't buying it anymore.

She wanted Jake to go to work for her father in Tupelo. He had a steady business selling grave monuments. It wasn't as exciting as Jake liked, but her father did very well and would have welcomed Jake into the company. Eventually, Jake could have taken it over. It was eight to five, forty hours a week, and twice a year they would go to conventions in Orlando and Vegas. She couldn't get Jake to even consider it. He said the whole business gave him the creeps.

So now he had given up his career as a stockbroker and had become a game warden. He was totally starting over. The job didn't pay great and the hours seemed awful. He had promised it was only forty hours a week and he would set his own hours, but lately he was working a lot more.

There had to be another woman. Now she just needed to determine how to handle it. She wanted to know for sure before she talked to him. She wanted to be in control of the situation.

Her mind exhausted, with coffee in hand she sat down in a bay window to check Facebook. There was always a post to distract her mind. After a few minutes of boring shared videos and posts, her mind drifted back to the situation with her husband and she found herself looking up "Rosemary Rothbone," Jake's old girlfriend. After scrolling down a few posts, Morgan noticed that Rosemary had recently moved back home. Not only that, she'd been to Jackson—and on the same day as Jake.

Morgan leaned back in her seat, feeling sick to her stomach and hot in the face. Then she got angry at Jake, but that emotion was soon replaced with sadness. A tear formed in her eye, and then there was Kramer's head in her lap. His tail wagged gently, and she rubbed his head and sighed. *Dammit,* she thought.

* * *

The Bolivar twins met at their septic tank business office to discuss the swap of their artifact for Fabian's money and what would occur afterward. Her office door was shut, and the old wood-paneled offices looked even older than they usually did to Chase. The building was filled with filing cabinets stuffed with folders dating back to the day the business began. Chase hated every one of them. Chance didn't care either way.

Chance liked Chase's idea to rendezvous at the boat launch. It was a large, wide-open area, capable of holding hundreds of trucks and boat trailers. There were two concrete ramps and a long man-made peninsula between them. There were a few trees, but nothing large enough to hide behind. The only obstruction of vision or place that anyone could hide behind was a concrete-block restroom. Chance was very familiar with the location. Growing up, he'd fished and water-skied on the Columbus Lake every weekend he could. During his younger years he'd placed a four-foot bull shark he'd caught off the Mississippi coast on the bank next to the ramps. Prior to that, dozens of locals sat on buckets and fished off the bank at the spot each day during the summer. It was a month before any of them would return. Rumors swirled all over the community for weeks that the shark had swum up from the gulf and been caught at the ramps. When the story made the Sunday edition of the *Commercial Dispatch*, Chance considered this prank his pièce de résistance.

Chase had known that her brother would approve and had at first determined that he should arrive at the site by boat. She might need a quick escape plan, and the Tombigbee River would be perfect. The river would be practically abandoned that time of the year. Her brother was a river rat, and he could navigate and outrun anyone. But could she trust him with the money? No, she couldn't, and that accounted for her decision to stick with vehicles. She would leave with the money herself.

"Here's what I want to do," Chase said as she poured coffee into a stained mug. "We're gonna do this Monday. I want you and Perry to be in your truck, and we'll all approach at the same time. I'll be in my vehicle. They'll be taking a rental car from the airport."

"We gonna kill 'em?"

Chase thought about it as she sipped coffee. "I haven't figured it all out yet. But I can't see any other way, can you?"

"They're eventually gonna figure out it's not real," Chance said. "And they'll be pissed."

"Yeah, but it may be days or weeks. That'll give us some time."

"Time? Time for what?"

"To figure out our next move," Chase said.

* * *

Jake and Virgil were getting lots of calls that needed attention, both from the county dispatch and their cell phones. Their list of calls was two pages long, and both knew they had to get out of the trailer and be seen and see landowners. If they didn't soon, someone would call their bosses. They always did. Give a few bucks to a politician's campaign, and you feel they owe you a favor. Virgil had received a message that originated with a call to the governor himself, who'd called the head of the department, who'd called a supervisor, who'd then called Virgil. Jake didn't have a clue yet.

Gunner walked into the trailer without knocking, sat down at the only barstool that wasn't covered in dirty clothes, opened a beer, and asked for an update. Virgil explained everything to him in great detail. Jake grew more excited just listening to the story.

"Here's the deal, Gunner," Virgil said when he was done. "We need your skills. We have less than forty-eight hours to get ready, and we have to be waiting at the boat ramp, hidden from view, when they make the sale."

Jake was curious. "Are we going to bust them before or after the sale?"

"Right after," Virgil said. "As soon as we see or think the money changes hands." He turned back to Gunner. "Gunner, I need you to go and scope out the location and give us some ideas. Jake and I need to get caught up on our warden jobs today before we lose 'em. You know the area?"

"Yeah, I do."

"Okay, good. It's wide open. Not many places to hide. We need video, and I want pictures."

Gunner swigged his beer. "I can do that. I'm guessing that we aren't calling in the reinforcements."

Virgil stood and looked out the window. The sky now was bright blue, and an airplane could be seen racing across it, leaving a long vapor trail in its path like a line drawn in the sand.

"Nope, we are gonna do this by ourselves."

"Is that a good idea?" Jake asked.

"Jake," Virgil said, "you see that plane?"

Jake joined him at the window. Very high in the sky was a long white plume of vapor trailing behind an airplane. "I see it."

"Some people believe our government is spraying something to control the weather or us. They call it a chemtrail."

"What?"

"I'm serious. I see 'em almost every day. They are like giant atmospheric crop dusters dispersing some kinda chemical."

Jake had no idea what the trail was, but he'd never considered that it might be some government conspiracy. He still didn't believe it.

Gunner began laughing.

"You're crazy, Virgil," Jake said.

"I didn't say I believed, Jake. But just like I can't explain that phenomenon in the sky, I can't really explain why I don't want to call in support," Virgil said with all sincerity. "This bust, the money, the artifact—I don't know what to think of it all just yet. I don't even know if it is a serious crime. But whatever it is, it's ours."

Jake looked at him. He knew Virgil was different. He had a history of marching to his own drumbeat. But he was Jake's first partner, and Jake didn't intend to betray him. At the end of the day, he trusted Virgil, and he would trust him on this arrest as well. After all, Virgil always seemed to have Jake's back.

Virgil started pulling on his duty jacket. "Let's get busy with our calls and meet back here tomorrow morning at eight o'clock."

CHAPTER 23

The judge's mind dissected all that Jake had explained about the Bolivars and their million-dollar scheme. The two dim-witted twins would soon have enough cash to solve his problems or get themselves into trouble. He wasn't sure if he was jealous or angry. He needed only about a third of the money. He wasn't greedy. He just needed some of it.

Jake had kept him informed. The new game warden and family friend had responded exactly like the judge had hoped, with loyalty. The inside information was paramount to his plan. He now knew the deal was going down Monday afternoon. What he didn't know was how he was going to get the money. Every idea he came up with pointed to him stealing it. Ideas that no one, much less a sixty-plus-year-old federal judge, needed to be considering.

Monday morning he would cancel court and find a believable reason to be gone all day. He wanted to be nearby when the money changed hands. He had considered various ways to steal it from the twins but had decided it would be easier to take it from Jake and Virgil. He knew Virgil well enough to know he couldn't trick him, but he knew Jake would do whatever he told him to.

In the last two days the judge had sold several expensive shotguns, mortgaged what he could of their home, dipped into savings, and sold his stock portfolio, and a man was coming to buy his two best bird dogs. By his calculation he was almost halfway to his total. But halfway wouldn't get his wife a new kidney and a new lease on life.

He was crossing the line to desperation. It was the only way he could be considering what he was considering.

The snow caused court to be canceled Friday, allowing the judge to focus on raising capital and spending a little time with Luke. Rosemary had been gone for two days, tending to her personal business. He and his grandson deer-hunted Friday afternoon, and the judge thoroughly enjoyed watching Luke see his first white-tailed deer. That night he cooked Luke and Rosemary bacon-wrapped quail, and he smiled as he watched them discuss the afternoon hunt. Luke explained in great detail each deer they saw. He correctly explained that his grandfather wanted him to experience an afternoon in the woods, enjoy watching the deer, and later he could decide if he wanted to shoot one.

"He didn't want me to rush into it. He said he still has lots to teach me first," Luke explained as he petted his puppy to stop him from whining.

"That's smart. It's a big responsibility," she responded with a smile.

"I know," he spouted back with pride. "I want to learn it all."

Luke held Shadow tight, and the pup tried to lick his face. The judge watched the two of them interacting, and his heart felt both full and heavy. Luke was such a blessing to have in their home. His wife looked so happy and content. She loved being a grandmother, and that made the judge want the night to last forever.

* * *

Chance spent the afternoon at his old school bus taking inventory of his ammo. He had been stocking up on .22 shells and several other calibers.

The bus had two small gun safes that were full of nothing but ammo. Chance stocked up every Tuesday when the local Walmart received a delivery. He didn't know why he was stocking up, but it made him feel prepared for something.

He also knew that no matter what his sister desired, he didn't want to kill Perry Burns. The man was helping them, and Chance liked him. He deserved a commission for bringing Fabian to the table. That was just good business.

It concerned him that Fabian would discover the artifact was a fraud and demand more than just his money to be returned. He had done some research into the Antoinette brothers and knew they were capable of anything rivaling his worst fears.

Fabian would certainly bring a bodyguard to the meeting. That would mean he would have to deal with both of them and then live with the worry that the rest of the family would want revenge. The only way he could think to keep them at bay was to somehow impress upon them that he was as crazy as a shithouse rat.

He didn't think he was crazy at all, but his sister Chase was another story. He'd done some research online, and it had taken him maybe five minutes to flush out her diagnosis as a narcissist. Every classic symptom was there in full flame. She felt she was entitled to everything and had a need for admiration, and he could never remember her displaying an iota of empathy for others. Chance wanted the money and had decided he would take the risks required. He would look out for his sister to a point, but he wouldn't risk his life for hers. She was utterly self-absorbed and unconcerned about his well-being or safety. Their relationship had always been centered on what he could do for her.

If he could add half the money to his hidden pile, he wouldn't ever worry about working again. With a portion of his cash, he'd build his own cabin with a basement and spend the rest of his life doing exactly what he wanted.

∗ ∗ ∗

When the phone rang and Jake recognized the number was from Starkville, he felt a surge of hope that this might be some good news about the image they had recently analyzed.

"Jake Crosby," he answered.

"Hey Jake, I know I said nothing else could be done to enhance that photo. But I sent that image to an associate of mine in Washington that works for the FBI digital media enhancement lab."

"Go on."

"She e-mailed me a few minutes ago and was pretty excited that she was able to improve the image."

"Can you tell who it is?"

"The person, whoever it is, has a very distinct feature."

"Hang on for a second," Jake said as he pulled his truck over to the side of the road. "Okay, tell me."

"Your guy—he has a ponytail."

"The ponytail is real? Virgil thought it was a gun barrel."

"Yes, it's clearly a ponytail. I can't tell you with one hundred percent certainty that it's real, but it's a ponytail all right. I thought that might help you. Maybe you could match it with another lead and narrow down the list. You know?"

"We don't really have any other leads. But I'll admit the ponytail is very interesting." Jake had already started processing the information. He knew there were guys around who wore ponytails. You didn't see them everywhere, but he had seen some. It wasn't uncommon. His friend was right: the ponytail could be a significant find. "I really appreciate this information," he said.

"I'll forward you the e-mail she sent me."

"Thanks, you've been a big help," Jake said, only then realizing that his friend, ironically, had long hair and often wore it in a ponytail. He was an old hippie who was still trying to live in the past.

Once off the phone, Jake found he couldn't think of one other man who had a ponytail. Mississippi was still a very conservative place, and most men didn't have long hair. This was a good lead, and he needed to call Virgil.

Jake dialed his partner and explained what he had learned. Virgil listened intently and was silent for a few seconds.

"That does narrow our list of possible candidates down considerably, and does confirm what the sheriff said."

"What's that, Virgil?"

"It ain't a black man."

"Yeah, I didn't think so either."

"Have you gotten an e-mail from the artifact seller?"

"No, I haven't yet," Jake said as he watched a barge pushing downriver.

"Let me know as soon as you do. And Jake? You've got good instincts. You thought that was a ponytail the moment you saw it. You're gonna make a good investigator."

Jake smiled. He wanted to tell Morgan.

CHAPTER 24

When Rosemary called her new confidant, Samantha, to discuss her parents' situation, as she'd promised she would, Samantha was painting the sleeping porch that her contractors had just completed renovating.

Samantha was in the perpetual process of renovating her antebellum home in Columbus. She loved the annual spring pilgrimage and enjoyed her part of showcasing history. Screened-in sleeping porches were popular in old Southern homes as comfortable, healthy places to sleep during warmer months. She loved the idea of sleeping on the screened porch this upcoming spring.

Samantha wiped paint off her fingers before picking up her phone. "Hello."

"Samantha, this is Rosemary. Can you talk?"

"Sure, I was just painting, and I need an excuse to take a break."

"I have some good news to report. Mom's friend from Jackson pledged to give her seventy-five thousand dollars, and the preacher at their church did a love offering this morning, since Mom and Dad weren't there, and raised thirty-seven thousand dollars!"

"Oh, Rosemary, that's so encouraging. That's a testimony to how your parents have lived their lives. Have you told your father yet?"

"Not yet. I don't know where he is."

"Well, I had a good day as well."

"Tell me."

"There are some big industries in the area that have constantly found their legal counsel standing in front of your father through the years. He hasn't done them any special favors, mind you, but they have always appreciated the way he handled his courtroom and looked after his home state. You could say they are fans. Anyway, they can't just give money to your father—ethics and all that. But we decided they're going to funnel some money to me, and I'll give it to you. I'll also excuse myself from any trials up there until he retires. I don't mind."

Rosemary sat down in astonishment. "I can't believe that!"

"It may not stand up under the closest scrutiny, but I'll be able to deflect everything through our attorney-client privilege. Everybody in the circle is my client. There are a lot of people that appreciate what your father has done for the community and want to help him. They are willing to do it very discreetly."

Tears were welling up in Rosemary's eyes. "I . . . I don't know what to say."

"Altogether, I feel confident that I raised a hundred grand, so add that with your good news and what you said your father already had, and that should about do it."

"Yes. Yes, but what will we tell him?"

"Oh, that's easy. He'll understand the friend and church, and we'll tell him my clients are prepaying for some bird-dog training."

Rosemary giggled and blew her nose quietly. "That's a lot of training."

* * *

Early winter in Northeast Mississippi can run the spectrum from beautiful, mild sunshine to gloomy and bitter cold. The cold can be especially intense when it's compounded by the high humidity. Many people say that thirty degrees in Mississippi is colder feeling than eighteen degrees in Minnesota. Winter was only a few days old, and the area was already recovering from an unusual snow event. As the temperature rose above freezing, the snow slowly disappeared.

Chase dined alone at a window table at Huck's Place while watching her local world quietly spin. She was on her second Fat Tire and waiting on a plate of blackened redfish. Mentally tired, she was within twenty-four hours of having $1.3 million in cash handed to her. She had issues to resolve in her mind: what she would give Perry Burns, if anything, and what she would give her brother. These were big decisions for her.

She sensed that her brother and Perry had become friendly, and that could become problematic or it could be an asset. Chase was trying to look at both sides before she made a decision. It was her attempt to be strategic.

There was comfort in knowing that they weren't breaking any serious laws by selling the replica artifact. They were misleading Fabian, and an investigation could uncover that she had recently purchased the item, but she didn't think anyone in law enforcement would really care. They had so much more to worry about these days.

The big issue was what would occur when Fabian realized the artifact was a fraud. She didn't want to spend her life on the run or hiding from him. That's the one that demanded a solid plan. Glancing at her watch, she saw she had only a few minutes until Chance and Perry arrived if they were on time. Slowly she peeled the label off the bottle while she thought.

Her food arrived at the same time Chance flopped down in the chair across from her. They may have been twins, but they were two total opposites. Chase was dressed in expensive skinny jeans and a low-cut sweater. Chance was wearing red-tag Levi's, a flannel shirt, and a camouflage jacket. Both were happier than they had been in years. For once good things were lining up for them, and they both knew it.

Chase looked her brother over, then sipped her drink and asked, "Where's your new friend?"

"He wasn't feeling too good and stayed at the house."

"He sick?"

"I don't think so. He ate a bowl of turnip greens from the gas station this afternoon that probably didn't agree with him."

"So you left him unsupervised?"

"Well, yeah," Chance said as he pointed at the bartender and ordered a beer. "He's harmless."

Chase took a bite of her redfish and considered the situation. Perry Burns had arrived less than a week ago. While it was now obvious to her that he didn't know where their father's money was hidden, he had proven extremely helpful. Chance was right: the old man was harmless.

* * *

Fabian didn't have his own airplane, but he did enjoy flying a private charter whenever he traveled farther than a few-hour car ride. He made arrangements to travel to Columbus, Mississippi, and planned to return late afternoon. In preparation for the purchase he packed two cases: one Louis Vuitton bag filled with $1.3 million of counterfeit money, and a black military-grade backpack filled with exactly the same amount.

Satisfied with his negotiations and excited about owning the priceless artifact, Fabian looked forward to the meeting with a childlike anticipation. His plan was simple. At the meeting, if he felt good about the product after seeing it, he would signal his assistant to bring the money. He was confident the money would look too good for the sellers to have any immediate problems.

His assistant, Rook, had worked for him for six years now and had earned Fabian's trust. He had been terminated from the New Orleans Police Department after being caught taking a bribe. It took a while for Fabian to trust him completely, but since his company had caused Rook to lose his job, he felt the least he could do was show him a new career opportunity. As far as Fabian knew, he was dependable and would do whatever was asked of him. Fabian had no idea that the agents for the US Treasury Department had gotten to him and compromised him. Six weeks ago they had swarmed his house and threatened him with imprisonment unless he helped them build a case against the Antoinette brothers. Not seeing any viable options and not wanting his ex-wife's new husband to raise his young son, Rook had cooperated completely. That cooperation included explaining that Fabian was about to purchase a rare, possibly stolen antique in the state of Mississippi with counterfeit money. The agents were ecstatic and waiting on details. Rook was a nervous wreck.

* * *

The New Orleans office of the Secret Service contacted the Jackson, Mississippi, office to assist in taking down the counterfeiters at the sale. After a few minutes of grumbling about schedules, the lead Mississippi agent agreed to help out when he learned that they were going after Fabian Antoinette. It was also a perfect excuse to travel to Starkville. He had gone to school at Mississippi State and always looked for a reason to go back and revisit his old college haunts. It brought back lots of good memories, and if he could do it on Uncle Sam's dime, that was even better.

The Jackson agents were very aware of the quality of counterfeiting the Antoinette brothers produced. It was a superior product that was very difficult to detect—the best the state branch had ever encountered. The bills were passed all over the South, and though they couldn't prove it in a court of law, the men knew the product was coming somehow from the Antoinettes. The agents wanted the brothers, their printing press and plates, and everything they could learn about their technology. Authentic currency paper has tiny blue-and-red fibers embedded that had rarely been reproduced with any accuracy. The Antoinette brothers had somehow perfected a way to simulate these fibers by printing tiny blue-and-red lines. It took a trained eye to reveal that these were printed on the surface and not embedded in the actual paper.

The lead Mississippi agent had been back in the state only a year. Four moves over a lackluster eighteen-year career had finally brought him back to his home state. He knew assisting on an arrest of a counterfeiter of this caliber would bring respect and attention from Washington.

He and the New Orleans agent talked for another hour and made a plan. Everyone was making plans.

Before they hung up, the Jackson agent asked a simple question. "Are we involving the local law enforcement agencies?"

"No. Let's keep it quiet."

* * *

Once Chance left the river house, Perry Burns finally made his move. He had spent the past week trying to earn the trust of the twins and buy some time alone. He had finally succeeded.

It had been difficult, since they didn't trust anyone and rarely left him unsupervised, but Perry knew patience. Prison had taught him that. Time marched on, and he knew the day and time would come when he could properly look for the money. Now the time had arrived and he was prepared to act. Before Perry left the river house, he couldn't help but notice the floodlights shining through the blue bottles that dangled in the old tree. The silhouettes they created were ominous, like lifeless men hanging from a tree. Perry was familiar with all the superstitions associated with the trees and wondered just how many evil spirits were captured in these particular bottles. A broken bottle he hadn't noticed before caught his eye and a chill went up his spine. Anxious to move on with his plan, he exhaled deeply and pushed the thought out of his mind.

When Bronson Bolivar realized death was inevitable and before he was taken to a prison hospital, he shared with Perry, his only friend, where he had hidden two stores of cash, one much larger than the other. The smaller one had been hidden at the antebellum house and didn't interest Perry for multiple reasons, but the second, larger stash—that was the one that keenly interested Perry. He knew where it was, and he had already seen the structure it was concealed within. He had ridden by it numerous times and could hardly contain his excitement each time. Silently the structure stood protecting its secret, while every day his friend's children passed by after having dismissed it.

Perry figured he had two hours to retrieve the money. Thanks to pre-planning, he had everything he needed. In the toolbox of his truck were a pair of leather gloves, a pickax, and a sledgehammer. The old concrete silo was located halfway into the property on some high ground that had never flooded. Bronson had talked about the structure with something bordering on reverence. It was constructed in the mid-1940s and built to last. No matter what happened to it, it just stood tall and stayed the same.

When Perry parked, the truck's headlights illuminated the huge structure. He had seen dozens of them scattered across the farms in Mississippi. They were all exactly the same. If you saw one, you had seen them all.

The silo was surrounded by dead briars and weeds. Perry shined his flashlight around the base of the silo until he found the oval opening at the bottom, then fought his way inside through the briars. The interior floor was partially covered in dead leaves in various stages of decay. A puddle of stagnant rainwater proved the floor wasn't level, and years of buzzard feces painted the walls. Perry shined his light straight up. There was no roof. The silo was approximately forty-five feet tall, thirty feet in diameter, and symmetrically round.

Perry remembered what Bronson had said about the structure. Nobody ever tore one down. They lived forever. Even if a neighborhood developed on a farm, the silo remained as a landmark. He had chosen this one since it was on his property, and even if the kids figured out a way to sell it, nobody would tear the silo down. "You were right, Bronson," Perry said as he grabbed the pickax and attacked the center of the floor. He was too old to be doing this manual labor, but Bronson had explained the concrete subfloor wasn't thick.

Sure enough, after the third strike the floor splintered a bit. He concentrated his efforts in the very center, just like Bronson had instructed him. Little by little the floor crumbled and broke apart. Each strike of the pick excited Perry more.

Kneeling down, he shined the light and started pulling out chunks of concrete that revealed what Bronson had done. Somehow he had chiseled out a cavity in the center of the silo foundation that was two feet deep and three feet in diameter. When he'd finished hiding his loot, he filled the hole in with sand and then poured a three-inch layer of concrete over the whole floor. No one could tell by looking at it. It was genius.

When Perry saw the sand, he knew he was close. Checking his watch, he figured he had an hour. With his hands he quickly dug the sand out and revealed four metal military ammo boxes. Perry was breathing hard now and sat back to soak in what he was seeing. The boxes were rusty but still very much intact.

After catching his breath, he reached down and wiggled the first one out. It wasn't as heavy as it appeared but was definitely full of something. Once it was next to him, he wiped the sweat off his brow and worked the buckle on the edge of the can. It was tightly sealed but released easily. As the top folded over, his flashlight illuminated stacks of cash.

Perry laughed out loud. "Holy shit!" He grabbed a stack and flipped through it like a blackjack dealer. "Thank you, Bronson."

Perry quickly opened the other three and found them identically packed with money. He grunted with pleasure as he grabbed the ammo cases and loaded each one into his truck. Next he pushed all the concrete chunks into the hole and covered them with dead leaves until it almost looked like it had when he'd arrived, though there was now a depression in the floor, which he didn't have time to remedy. Now in a rush, he grabbed his tools and checked his watch. Perry figured he had about thirty minutes and took a deep breath to calm himself. The night air was cold, and the ex-con didn't mind at all. The fresh air felt good, and he was invigorated by the feeling that he was suddenly back in the game.

* * *

Jake sat and listened to Virgil lay out the plan to arrest the Bolivars. It sounded simple enough. This was the first arrest Jake had been a part of, though, and really he didn't know what to expect.

Gunner had several pistols laid on a table in various states of disrepair. After he finished cleaning each one, they were loaded and set to the side.

Jake had only one pistol and a service-issue AR-15. He had never carried the AR. It was still right where he'd placed it on his truck rack on the day he'd started.

Virgil was slowly eating a banana as if he were losing interest in the fruit while he studied an aerial map of the boat landing.

"You okay?" Jake asked him. "You look like you're about to throw up."

"I'm fine, but I think I've about hit the wall on bananas. I'll never make my goal."

Jake shook his head and smiled.

Virgil kept chewing. "See how there is only one road into this place, and it's half surrounded by water? It's a smart place to meet," he said with annoyance. "It'll be difficult for us to hide our vehicles, and we can't get close."

"It seems to me that just having one way in would be dangerous for them, wouldn't it?" Jake asked.

Gunner never looked up as he dropped 9mm shells in a magazine. "I think you're right. But there is another way in and out, you know."

Jake cocked his head and finally asked, "What's that?"

"Boat," Virgil chimed in before Gunner could respond.

"It's pretty cold to be on the river," Jake said. "That would be miserable."

"True," Virgil said, "but the point is we need to think and anticipate everything."

"Good point."

"Okay, gang," Virgil said. "Here's what I am thinking. Jake and I will be here by the ramp in street clothes. We'll look like we're studying the lake or my boat. Gunner, you'll hide in these trees over here, where you can move the length of the parking area. I need you to make certain there are no surprises that we can't see coming. I probably can't keep you outta trouble if you shoot somebody unless something bad is happening to us, so bear that in mind. I'll have my truck parked near us, and once the deal starts going down we'll get in and act like we are starting to leave and then turn and swarm them. I'll have the police ready back up the road to seal it off in case they run."

It made sense to Jake, and Gunner nodded his head in agreement. Jake was relieved to know the police would be involved in some capacity.

"Can I have some sorta identification to wear for when the police show up?" Gunner asked. "I don't want 'em to think I am one of the bad guys with a rifle."

"Relax. I have an extra vest you can wear that says 'Warden' on the front. They'll know you're with us," Virgil explained. "Just be sure you're hidden."

"You got anything to eat that's not a banana?" Jake asked, realizing he hadn't eaten in a while.

"Look in that basket."

Jake opened a pack of peanut M&M's and loudly crunched. Virgil glanced up and couldn't resist: "Did you know that Jack Nicholson and Meryl Streep are two of the voices of the M&M's in the commercial?"

"No, I didn't," Jake said, not believing him.

"I swear it's true. Jack's red and Meryl's green."

"Who's the yellow one?"

"J. K. Simmons. The guy from the Farmers Insurance commercials."

Jake and Gunner shook their heads. Virgil started making a list of things they needed to do.

CHAPTER 25

The Secret Service agents sat at the table at the Starkville Café and ate supper. After introductions and a few questions, all four agents concentrated for a while on the Southern cooking. It was just like the Jackson agent remembered from his days in college. Two agents were from the New Orleans offices and two were from Jackson. They all had a great deal in common, including a desire to nail Fabian Antoinette and his brother.

Like it always did, when the conversation picked up again it eventually turned to trophies. Law enforcement officers can't resist an opportunity to tell their stories. Each agent recalled previous busts, exciting stakeouts, and close calls. One even had a story of being on a presidential detail for George W. Bush. They all listened with envy to that story. The federal agents were no different than any other people trying to work the system and advance their careers. They knew results would get them noticed, and tomorrow they had a chance to get noticed if they could bust Fabian Antoinette.

"How dependable is your informant?" the lead Jackson agent asked.

"How dependable are any of them? I mean, they're all trying to get their butt out of a bind, and they all leave out details that could incriminate themselves. However, our guy Rook, he has a little boy and an ex-wife; therefore, he is highly motivated to stay on the outside so he can raise his son. That's about as good a motivation as you can get."

"Is Fabian gonna be armed?"

"Our info says that's a negative. He's a classic crime boss that never gets his hands dirty, and that's why this is such a rare opportunity. He's an older man, in his upper sixties, and Fabian depends on our guy Rook to protect him."

"I hope your boy isn't too loyal or changes his mind late in the game."

"I don't think that will be a problem. We have a good understanding with him. He's lined all this up for us."

"That's good."

"We gave him a cell phone that he can contact us with and we can track him. It's solid."

Everybody believed him, and it gave them confidence they were close to a big bust.

"Anybody wanna go get a drink?" the youngest New Orleans agent asked as he surfed on his iPhone for nearby bars. "TripAdvisor says there are several places close."

"This is Sunday night in Mississippi, not New Orleans," the older Jackson agent said. "You can probably buy beer, but not liquor."

The two younger agents wanted to try, and the two older wanted to get back to their hotel rooms.

"Y'all go. We don't have to be at the boat launch until after lunch."

The younger agents made an effort to reach for their wallets, hoping the senior New Orleans agent would put the meal on his expense account. The senior agent knew this and did what he could to extend their suffering before finally pulling his wallet out and waving his credit card.

"I got it, guys."

"Thanks, boss."

"Thank you, sir."

The senior New Orleans agent cleared his throat. "Hey fellas, do y'all know who Haym Salomon is? No? I'll give you a hint. He made a very visible impression on the very dollars we protect."

No one had a clue except for the guy's partner, who rolled his eyes as the senior agent pulled out a crisp one-dollar bill. He had told this story many times before.

"During the Revolutionary War, Haym Salomon somehow provided the Continental Army—at a time when we were losing the war—what would be millions, maybe billions of today's dollars to fight and win independence. That money was vital to our success. You see here, on the right-hand side, the thirteen stars arranged as a Star of David? This was ordered by George Washington himself. It seems that after the war, he asked Mr. Salomon what he would like for his personal reward for helping the Continental Army. The Jewish fella from Philadelphia wanted nothing for himself but something for his people. Very few people know that it was Salomon who saved the army through his contributions—and even fewer know that even though he gave all that money, he died bankrupt."

The two younger agents looked at the dollar bill, then at each other. Neither wanted to be obviously rude, so they feigned interest.

"That's fascinating, sir."

"I have plenty more facts if you're interested."

Nobody wanted to hear more, and the guy's partner quickly spoke up. "We really need to get going. You ready?"

"Yeah, we'll see y'all back at the hotel. Oh, and don't wait up for us."

* * *

Perry Burns had four .30-caliber ammo cans full of cash and no idea how much it all totaled. Bronson hadn't given him a number. Perry hadn't even been certain it existed, since his cellmate was prone to telling highly exaggerated stories. All week he'd driven by the silo every time they went anywhere. He'd been briefly tempted to tell the twins what he knew but nixed that idea. He didn't trust them, and he wanted all the money. Even now he had no desire to count the money until he was safely tucked into a hotel a safe distance away from the Bolivars.

After uncovering the money, he hurried the mile back to the river house. Grabbing the bag he had already packed, he looked around the guest room one last time. As he walked down the staircase, he decided the event needed one final touch. On an envelope he penned a note to the twins and left it in an obvious place. He thanked them for their generous hospitality, but a family emergency had developed. He would be back in touch to get his sales commission. He hoped that would explain his sudden disappearance just hours before their big sale to his friend.

If there was one thing Perry Burns learned in prison from listening to the other convicts tell their stories, it was that incarcerated men fell into three groups: the just plain dumb, the greedy, and lastly, the ones who just had bad luck. Perry wasn't dumb, and greed was what had landed him in prison the first time. Today he was making his own luck and leaving while he could. The greedy side of him wanted to stay and get his cut of the sale, but over time he'd grown reasonably certain that Fabian was going to pay for the artifact with counterfeit money anyway, since that was his style.

The ex-con's truck cranked on the third try. As he started the two-mile drive out of the property, he found himself growing more nervous with each turn. An encounter with either Bolivar could be managed, unless Chance got out and looked inside his truck, where he would see the ammo boxes. He hadn't taken the time to hide them. Hopefully, he could make a clean escape. Perry punched the gas and was almost to the silo when he saw the glimmer of headlights coming into the property.

Immediately, he cut his headlights and pressed the gas harder to get to the silo and park behind it, where he couldn't be seen.

The winding road into the property kept the oncoming vehicle from seeing Perry's vehicle as he slid it to a stop behind the silo and took his foot off the brake to kill the brake lights.

The woods illuminated, and then he could see Chase's vehicle as it came into view and passed the silo. Where was Chance? Was he behind her? Should he wait? Should he go? Perry knew he did not want to encounter Chance under the circumstances.

As he sat still, he pulled his travel bag closer and reached for his hidden pistol. When he didn't immediately feel the gun, he began to panic. Quickly he searched the pocket again and eventually felt the cold metal of the weapon. It wasn't exactly where he'd left it, and that forced a bubble of concern to float through his mind. *Maybe it shifted to the other end of the pocket while I carried the bag.*

In the darkness of the Mississippi swamp, Perry watched Chase's taillights disappear from view. Still he hesitated. He had no idea where Chance was, and that scared him. Finally, the old convict made a decision.

"Hell, I got to go!" he said aloud as he punched the gas pedal and sent rooster tails of mud spraying from the rear tires.

* * *

On the spur of the moment, the judge decided to sequester himself in Columbus at the Fairfield Inn to prepare a way to get his hands on the money. It was ideally located next to Walmart, Office Depot, and Lowe's if there was anything he needed to help his cause. It would also be quiet, and he could talk to Jake and plan his moves. He planned to call his assistant and cancel court Monday.

It was easy for him to explain to his wife. He often needed privacy to review a case and would get out of his office to clear his head. A fresh environment without distractions often gave him a better approach on the facts. He simply told her he had a case that was heavy on his mind and he needed to prepare.

The judge had received several texts and a missed call from Rosemary. She'd left a message indicating that she had some good news to share with him, but she wanted to tell him face-to-face. When he texted and asked her to tell him by phone or text, she refused and said it needed to be done in person, so they promised to make time for each other tomorrow night. He texted back that he would be home late tomorrow afternoon and went back to making plans, without telling her where he was.

The judge then called Jake. "Son, tell me what the hell's going on with the Bolivars," he said, excited.

Jake was driving home in the dark from his meeting with Gunner and Virgil. He was both tired and keyed up. He explained everything he knew about the situation, even their belief that the artifact wasn't real and how he'd gone about arriving at that conclusion. The judge congratulated him on a fine piece of detective work.

"Do you know where and when the buyer arrives in the area?"

"He's flying in on a private plane," Jake said as he turned into his neighborhood. "We don't have a firm ETA, sir."

The judge cussed under his breath. He needed to know exactly what was happening to have any hope of getting his hands on the money. He needed to arrive before the last handcuff was locked into place. He felt like he had only one viable option. That was to bluff and bully Jake and Virgil into letting him take the money into custody and deliver it to the federal offices in Aberdeen for safekeeping. It might end up being his word against a criminal's regarding how much money was actually in the bag, but no one would doubt a long-tenured federal judge. Though he had serious doubts that he had it in him to point-blank rob anyone, that was the judge's backup plan if things went sideways and either the Bolivars or the buyer somehow ended up with the cash. He would do whatever he had to, to ensure he left with the money. His chest tightened each time he thought about what he was about to do to the career that he had developed through years of making good choices.

"Jake," the judge said, "I don't want to get in your way. But I want to be there when this goes down. Actually, well before it goes down. I can be close and not threaten the security. Can you radio me as soon as you know when the buyer is due to arrive? Do you have a handheld radio I can use?"

Jake pulled into his driveway and left the truck running. He flipped open the console of the truck, revealing a pair of handheld radios at the ready.

"Yes, sir."

"Let's meet for breakfast in the morning," the judge said.

Jake knew the judge wasn't asking; he was telling Jake to meet him.

* * *

When Chance arrived at the river house at about midnight, he had already decided not to tell his sister that he had run into Perry Burns trying to leave their property with four ammo cans full of cash. When he walked inside, she was up drinking beer and handed him Perry's note about his family emergency, never asking where he had been or why he was so late coming home.

As Chance had encountered the vehicle leaving, he didn't know who it was at first and blocked the road. As Perry's truck rolled to a stop in Chance's headlights, he recognized the vehicle and slid his .357 Magnum revolver into the rear of his pants as he exited the truck. Approaching Perry's vehicle, he instantly knew what Perry was looking for as he bent over to reach something. Calmly standing at the driver's window, he commented on the beads of sweat on the old man's forehead. Like a policeman during a traffic stop, he shined a flashlight into the truck and illuminated the old ammo boxes.

Perry had a distinct lack of words and even looked guilty. Ironically, even then Chance would have made a deal with him, maybe allowing him to keep one box. He had actually grown to like the old man. But Perry sealed his own fate when he pulled his pistol and pointed it at Chance's face. The pistol clicked, not firing, and Perry panicked, pulling the trigger again and again. Each time it didn't fire, the fear in Perry's eyes grew. Chance smiled at the old man and shook the shells in his pants pocket.

He knew exactly where to dump Perry's body and his vehicle so they would never be found. The gravel companies never, ever drained old gravel pits.

He hid the four ammo boxes with the other cash that had originally belonged to his father.

Perry told him everything before he killed him, and Chance took satisfaction knowing that he had all of it but couldn't really believe that he had driven by the silo containing its hidden treasure every day of his life. It was the perfect place for his old man to hide the stash.

Watching his sister drink her beer now, he tried to gauge her mood. He could tell she was nervous after reading Perry's note and knew he needed to calm her.

"A family emergency?" Chance asked.

"I suspect it's bullshit."

"It'll be fine," he assured her. "Fabian knows where and when to meet us, and now you don't have to pay Perry a full cut."

"I was never going to pay that old fool a full cut," Chase said with venom in her voice as she held up a bundle of EpiPens. "You didn't think I was, did you?"

"No." Chance smiled at his sister's harshness and tough demeanor. He knew exactly how she thought.

"But I will cut him deep and wide if this damn deal doesn't go through," Chase said as she threw an empty beer bottle into the fire-place. "The septic business is hemorrhaging money, the IRS is breathing down our necks, and we've burned through what little cash we had. I hate to tell you, but if we don't get some money soon—"

Chance finished the sentence: "We gotta sell some shit." *Maybe* you *do*, he thought, suppressing a sly grin.

* * *

The Secret Service agents spent a restful night at the Hotel Chester in Starkville. The two younger agents slept off a beer buzz, one older agent got in the bed an hour earlier than usual, and the final agent got a peaceful night's sleep away from his wife's restless leg syndrome.

In the morning the Jackson agents brought up an old white Chevy van that appeared on the outside to be a plumber's work vehicle but on the inside held sophisticated surveillance equipment. They planned to have two agents at the boat ramp in the van and two agents preparing to pounce from their waiting position. They each had different opinions about how close the agents needed to be to the sale site. They finally decided they would start waiting at a shopping center at the entrance to the park and move closer as the sale progressed.

Because of Rook's cooperation, the New Orleans agents assumed this was going to be an easy bust. Fabian Antoinette was too old to put up a fight, he was unarmed, and his bodyguard was on their side. Rook would resist and act as if he were surprised. Fabian and his brother wouldn't know that their security guard had betrayed them. It wasn't until much later they would learn he had a much-reduced sentence for his role.

By 10:00 a.m. Monday morning the agents were all in place and already complaining about the wait. Stakeouts were the most boring assignments for 95 percent of the time. However, the remaining 5 percent was an adrenaline overload and what they enjoyed most about their jobs.

* * *

Fabian Antoinette's chartered plane arrived at the local airport and tax-ied to a private hangar. The King Air had made the trip from New Orleans to Columbus in exactly one hour and four minutes. There was a full-sized rental car waiting for Fabian and Rook.

"We'll be back by four o'clock at the latest," Fabian told the pilot.

"No problem, sir. If you want to give me a call as you're approach-ing, I'll have everything ready for you."

"Thank you," Fabian said as he watched Rook sign the rental car forms. Once he had the keys, the two men walked silently to the car. Rook carried the bags, while Fabian checked messages on his smartphone.

"Do you have the map of where we are going, Rook?" Fabian asked.

"Huh? Oh. Yes, sir."

"Rook, you seem distracted. Is everything okay?"

"Yes, sir. Sorry. I'm just worried about my kid."

"Well, get your head out of your ass and in the game, son. This is a business trip. You'll be home by six tonight, and you can worry then."

Rook bit his tongue and placed the bags in the truck before open-ing Fabian's door.

"Let's go get a bite of lunch," Fabian suggested. "And there are some old houses I want to drive by, since we have a few hours to kill. What are you hungry for?"

"Whatever you want, boss."

"Let's eat light. I have a dinner at the Commander's Palace tonight."

Fabian was seated in the backseat and had a clear view of Rook as he fastened his seat belt. His persona would not allow him to let Rook know he cared. He was trying to train Rook to be a tough officer in the Antoinette organization. To be worthy in their eyes, Rook needed to focus on business and not be constantly distracted by personal issues. Fabian was trying to show him the way.

"We need to be at the boat launch at 2:00 p.m.," Rook reminded him.

"That's right. Plenty of time." Fabian watched as Rook put the car in gear and pulled away. As Rook turned off of the airport frontage road onto the highway, Fabian remembered what he was going to ask him. "Rook, have you always had two cell phones?"

"Uh-uh." Rook looked down and could see the top of his Secret Service–issued phone protruding from the top of his coat pocket. His heart skipped a beat. "No, sir, I just got it. I didn't want to get personal calls on your phone."

"That's ridiculous. Nobody needs two phones."

* * *

Chase was incensed that Perry Burns had left them just prior to the big sale. She might need Perry to help keep Fabian motivated if he started crawfishing about something. She had to admit he was a convincing con man.

Chase left her office to drive to the meeting place with time to spare. She wasn't nervous; she was anxious to get her hands on the money. In the trunk of her old Mercedes was the replica helmet, her ticket to financial freedom. She wished she had been born into money, but her dad had ruined that for her. Later she had been denied the fortune he stole, and she had wasted a significant portion of her adult life looking for something that might not even exist. If it did exist, the fact that her dad had not left the money to her would be a cruel torture. The continuation of the legend of the missing money only angered her more. *At least I found a way to use my old man's reputation to generate cash.*

Shaking her hair as she looked in the rearview mirror, Chase realized she was proud of herself. Pride was something she hadn't felt in a long time. Her mind had created this opportunity, and there would be more, now that she had stumbled upon a formula that worked.

Chance had promised he wouldn't be late for the meeting. She needed him in attendance, especially since Perry Burns couldn't be there. If Chase had learned anything in her years it was to have options whenever you could. Her dad had forced her into a life with no visible options, a life that had included taking over the family business, working day and night to make ends meet, and bearing the burden of taking care of her brother, who if not for her would be gathering shopping carts at Walmart every day.

Chase was tired of everything, but after today she could buy a new lease on life.

Today I'm gonna get ahead.

* * *

When Jake and Virgil arrived at the stakeout in Jake's personal truck, the only other vehicle in the parking lot was an ancient plumber's van parked near the restrooms across the lot from them. Jake studied it with his binoculars, knowing it was a possibility that the feds could be following the buyer. Virgil agreed with him that the van looked abandoned, though.

Each warden was wearing plainclothes, though Virgil had confirmed that Jake was wearing his protective vest under his flannel shirt. Behind Jake's truck was Virgil's aluminum bass boat. It looked to be ten years old and was not in very good condition. Jake doubted it would even crank.

"I got it right before my divorce," Virgil explained to him after seeing Jake looking back at it. "In fact, you could say that's what pushed her over the edge. Apparently, you're supposed to ask before you make a purchase like that."

"Well, yeah, everybody knows that."

"I didn't. I've always had a boat. Just decided to upgrade." He shook his head. "That ended up being one expensive boat."

"I had heard she left because of the television show *Who Wants to Be a Millionaire*."

Virgil eyed him, then sighed. "That certainly didn't help, and that started our spiral down. I swear, all my life I had heard that when the sun's shining while it's raining, that means the devil's beating his wife. I still think it was a trick question and a good attorney coulda got us a settlement, but she wouldn't hear of it. Said I embarrassed her on national TV. It was a mess, Jake."

Jake stretched, and his holster groaned with its familiar sound. The vest wasn't uncomfortable, and he couldn't understand why Virgil didn't wear one. Their bosses in Jackson required all Mississippi wildlife officers to wear them at all times. Jake always wore his while on duty, but Virgil did only when a supervisor was in the area, claiming it was uncomfortable. That was just plain stupid, Jake thought. He and Virgil had argued about it many times, though Jake wasn't surprised that Virgil had asked if Jake was wearing his.

"We just need to look natural," Virgil said. "We can be looking at my boat or the lake. Just don't stare at them when they arrive, got it?"

"Yeah, I think I can handle that. So can you see Gunner?"

"He's in those trees," Virgil said, pointing across the street. "Probably under that big oak, if I had to guess." The winter woods were bare, but there were plenty of places for a man with Gunner's skills to conceal himself, and the old oak would be a fine one, Jake noted.

"The sheriff's boys will be here as soon as we call him," Virgil said with some truth. He hadn't exactly told them what he was up to.

Jake pulled the sleeve back on his Drake Mossy Oak pullover to check the time, and Virgil noticed. "How much time we got?"

"Forty-five minutes," Jake said nervously.

"Let's get out and look like we belong here."

They both walked to the back of the truck.

"Can you tell I'm carrying?" Jake asked.

"You look like a preppy redneck that could be carrying," Virgil said. "And I probably look like I belong to that plumber's truck." Virgil started walking down the side of his boat as if he were thinking of selling it. "My ex-wife used to ask me if her dresses made her ass look big."

"Now that's a dangerous question," Jake said, realizing that Virgil was trying to relax the tension.

Virgil started laughing. "I'd say, 'No, but your ass is making that dress look huge!'"

Jake laughed. "Do you ever wonder how come you aren't married anymore?"

"Sometimes," Virgil grunted.

CHAPTER 26

Fabian watched the city of Columbus roll by from the backseat of the rental car. He had thoroughly enjoyed his tour of some of the town's grand old houses that had been miraculously spared during the Civil War. Fabian loved history, and each home had a story to tell. There were dozens of stately restored mansions to see, but he'd only had time for Shadowlawn, Rosedale, and Ole Magnolia.

Up front he could hear the GPS giving Rook turn-by-turn directions to the meeting place. From his window he saw Dick's Sporting Goods, and then Rook immediately turned left.

"We'll be there in just a few more miles, boss. It's near the end of this road," Rook said in the same tone he used every day. He was trying hard to act normal, but his mind was frantic with worry.

Fabian sat in his usual silence. Every vehicle he saw looked suspicious, but he had no reason for concern. This was not a dangerous deal, beyond the considerable danger of being caught with millions of dollars of counterfeit money. At his age he would never see freedom again if he were caught. Fabian had lived all his years and committed countless crimes without ever seeing the inside of a jail cell. He felt invincible, but he also knew that Northeast Mississippi wasn't his home turf.

The backwater of the Columbus Lake reminded Fabian of parts of Louisiana where he frequently duck-hunted. He loved those places. Every year after Christmas he and his brother, along with several close friends, would stay at a remote camp and duck-hunt all week. Fabian went mostly for the wine and companionship. He loved the stories the men would tell, each trying to one-up the last, each trying to impress the others with a more expensive shotgun, a high-tech jacket or, sometimes, a new mistress. This year they would all be captivated by Fabian's priceless original artifact. He couldn't wait.

Rook saw the boat landing, and it looked as it had from the Google Street View he had seen when preparing. He scanned the area hard for anything that resembled the Secret Service, and nothing stood out except for an old van that appeared like it could've been dumped by the restrooms a month ago. The agents wouldn't tell him details of the raid but assured him they would be there watching and would react at the appropriate time. Rook wasn't concerned for his safety during the raid, but he did worry that he would be compromised and there would be retaliation from the Antoinettes. His only comfort came from the agents, who promised him witness protection if they were able to take the Antoinette crime family down. Rook didn't completely trust the agents, but he prayed that they were true to their word.

Watching everything carefully, he turned the rental car into the parking lot and parked in the center. The parking places were much longer than normal so they could accommodate vehicles with boat trailers.

Fabian noticed the two men studying an old boat near the ramp. They appeared to be a buyer and a seller. At the other end of the parking lot was a rattletrap van, which he studied with suspicion before deciding no thieves sophisticated enough to have caught wind of this exchange would be caught dead in such a thing. The Bolivars and Perry Burns were nowhere in sight. Fabian reached for his cell phone, while Rook wished he could throw his out the window.

* * *

Chance drove up and waved at his sister to follow him. He had a slender cigar in his mouth and a cocky, wild-eyed look on his face. His attitude aggravated her, but she pulled in behind him into the parking lot of the boat ramp. They both pulled next to the rental car, and Chase made eye contact with the man she determined had to be Fabian Antoinette. His driver didn't smile, and his sunglasses blocked any eye contact; his only response was to nod his head slightly when she looked at him.

Wanting to set the pace of the conversation, Chase quickly exited her car. Fabian was immediately impressed by her looks. Rook stepped out of the car and glanced around, looking for the agents. Everyone else thought he was just being cautious.

Larger than life, Fabian stepped from the car in his designer clothes. "Rook, apparently it's going to rain today."

Everyone looked up. The sky was clear and no rain in sight.

Fabian pointed at Chance's cigar and said, "I always heard that when you saw a pig with a stick in his ass, that meant it was gonna rain." Fabian broke into a giant smile and slapped Chance on the back. He watched Chance's face for a reaction and didn't see one or really care.

Chase feared her brother would lose his temper, but Chance just wanted the money. The crazy old coonass could call him whatever he wanted as long as he bought the helmet.

"Where is my old friend Perry?" Fabian asked after more-formal introductions.

"Apparently, he had a family emergency that needed his attention back home," Chance explained.

"That is unfortunate."

"It's not necessary for him to be here for this," Chase said. "We have what you want."

"Ah, my dear, you are correct. I do have what you want."

Chase was ready to tell her story that she had rehearsed many times. "Mr. Antoinette—"

The New Orleans native immediately interrupted her. "Please, call me Fabian."

Chase blushed, pointed west, and continued: "About a half mile from here down this road is a park, and across the river is the lock and dam that regulates the water level. At one time this whole area was a huge Indian community. They say there was a major site right on the banks of the Tombigbee where Tibbee Creek flowed into the river. Right over there—most of it's underwater now from where they built the lock and dam and created the lake here.

"That village is what caused Hernando de Soto to be here during the 1500s as he explored this country. That's how all this came to be federal property. Back in the day when they were building all this, my father was digging on some high ground to set a septic tank, and that's when he found the helmet that you are about to purchase. Dad knew it was a very significant find and immediately hid the helmet. It stirred a shitstorm, and all sorts of investigators were looking for it. They wanted to put it in a museum. But my dad had a streak of bad luck and ended up in prison for something else. My brother and I have finally decided that it's been long enough that we could sell to a discreet person like you."

Fabian smiled as he soaked in the story, believing the beautiful female's every word. "Your father was a very smart man. He recognized an opportunity."

"Fabian, it's finally time my brother and I profit from our father's fast thinking."

"Honey, you have no idea how excited I am to see this thing."

Thinking only of the money that would soon be hers, Chase opened her trunk and stepped back. Chance pulled the wooden box closer to the edge and flipped open the brass latches. Slowly he folded back the top and revealed a bright-red velour cloth.

Fabian stared at the cloth with anticipation. Rook surveyed the surroundings and tried to control his breathing. Chase and Chance were totally focused on watching Fabian's reaction.

No one except Chance noticed that behind the box lay two expensive scoped rifles, hunting gear, and a game camera. Chase had forgotten they were in her car. Chance scratched his head with curiosity but focused his attention on their buyer.

CHAPTER 27

Jake and Virgil were trying to view the discussion from their vantage point about a hundred yards away while acting like they were interested in the old boat. Virgil and Gunner spoke softly through a wireless device that Gunner rigged up for them. Knowing the scene would be scrambled by Fabian's bodyguard, they didn't bother to try to record anything. Jake's adrenaline was starting to kick in, and more than once he felt the semiautomatic pistol on his hip just to make sure it was still there. He noticed Virgil was calm and relaxed. *A seasoned pro,* he thought with admiration.

They watched the trunk pop open and knew the deal was in progress.

"Get ready, boys," Virgil whispered. "Jake, crank the truck and be ready to roll." Virgil's plan was to block the vehicles in when they made their move. The boat would help them block more area.

"What if they back up?" Jake asked.

"Let's hope they don't."

Jake casually walked to the truck and readied himself. They had a lot of asphalt to cover fast without drawing attention when Virgil gave the signal.

In the stinking stakeout van across the parking lot, a pair of Secret Service agents were listening through parabolic microphones pointed at the criminals while simultaneously filming everything that occurred. The agents chattered excitedly over their radios with the other two agents up the road, all of them waiting for the optimum moment to converge on the scene and seize their holy grail: undeniable evidence with which to build an airtight case.

One-half mile away the judge sat in his Land Rover awaiting Jake's call. Even though the outside temperature hovered at just under forty, sweat beaded on his forehead, and he clicked on the air conditioner. After seeing Chase and Chance pass by, he'd driven down as close as he dared. On the passenger seat next to the day's newspaper was a Browning Hi-Power 9mm pistol. The judge glanced at it and then at a picture of his wife taped to his dash. He knew very well that desperation made men act in unexplainable ways—he'd seen countless examples during his time as a judge—but only now, as he wiped sweat from his brow, did he clearly understand the power of desperation.

* * *

When Chance unfolded the red cloth, Fabian could be seen taking a deep breath in anticipation. The helmet looked authentic. Smeared with dried mud, it looked as if it were five hundred years old. Chance stepped back and smiled. *Easy money.*

Stepping closer, Fabian Antoinette methodically unfolded his bifocals. Gently he reached to touch the helmet and then thought better of the idea. Soaking in every visible detail of the artifact, he stared and then slowly stood up straight.

Watching him intensely, Chance and Chase stole glances at each other. The two con artists were holding their breath, waiting on Fabian's response.

Smiling slowly at Chase, Fabian quickly folded his glasses and returned them to his coat pocket. He then nodded an approval to Rook, who opened the trunk of the rental car to retrieve the two bags of money.

Chance and Chase were trying not to smirk as they made eye contact. Chase noticed the two men in the truck were about to leave but paid them little attention.

Two similarly sized but different cases were now sitting in front of the twins, consuming their complete and undivided attention.

Fabian had learned years ago when he and his brother had started the counterfeit business that if he provided the money to someone in a distracting case, it helped to divert them from scrutinizing the money too soon. They were happy enough to be getting money; the fancy case picked out just for them further endeared him and bought time.

"For you, my dear, your father's reward, one point three million, is in this lovely Louis Vuitton case, as I promised," Fabian said softly as he handed her the case.

The gesture was not lost on Chase, who appreciated expensive brand names, but she was intensely curious as to what was in the other bag. *Doesn't matter. The one point three million is in my case!*

Fabian then turned to Chance and handed him the black backpack. "I thought you would appreciate a good backpack. I'm sorry it isn't as luxurious as your sister's, but you'll find that it too is packed with one million three hundred thousand dollars."

Chance and Chase looked at each other with shocked expressions.

Fabian turned to each of them with his hands outstretched. "What's wrong? I thought that's what we agreed on, no?"

Not wanting to say anything, Chance unzipped the top of the backpack, revealing stacks of hundred-dollar bills. As soon as he saw them, he quickly zipped the pack shut. *Holy shit!*

Smiling while shaking her head, Chase quickly composed herself. "No, Mr. Antoinette, that's exactly what we agreed on," she said as she handled the money in her case. "We're just extremely happy to see the money." *The damn fool paid us double! He must have thought each of us wanted one point three!*

* * *

Jake anxiously waited on Virgil, who was standing outside the truck, to give the signal. The truck was cranked and in gear with the nervous wildlife officer's foot pressed tightly on the brake. He could overhear him speaking to Gunner on their wireless devices. Jake held a small radio in his hand, and while Virgil was talking to Gunner he clicked the "Talk" button.

"It's about to go down, Judge, over," Jake said in a whisper, and waited for a response.

He was still waiting when Virgil jumped in the truck and whispered excitedly, "Go, Jake."

They had decided that Jake would drive normally, as if he were going past the parked vehicles, and then at the last second slam on the brakes. They hoped this would put them as close to the criminals as possible when they jumped from the truck. But it was really hard to drive normally under the circumstances. It was all he could do not to floor it as they pulled over, and when Jake slammed on the brakes he was so keyed up that he jumped out of the truck before putting the truck into park. It started rolling forward just as he heard Virgil hollering for everyone to put their hands up, and Jake had to dive back inside and slam the transmission into park.

"Game wardens, hands up!" Virgil yelled again at the criminals as he held his badge up. "Jake!"

"I'm right here!" Jake was just about to draw his weapon when he realized that Virgil had not. He glanced at the criminals, and they were all standing in shock. None had their hands up.

The Bolivars had each grabbed their cases and were holding them tight. Fabian stood still, wondering why game wardens were harassing them. Rook may have been the most surprised in the bunch. This was the first he had heard about game wardens taking them down.

Inside the plumber's van, the Secret Service agents were just about to freak completely out. Nobody knew what was going on, so they bailed out of the van to get answers. Dropping into a run, with their badges held before them, they started hollering, "Hands up! Secret Service!" from about three hundred feet away. The criminals and the wardens alike looked at them in total bewilderment.

At that moment Chance decided he had seen enough. He slung his pack onto his back and took off running. This caught the wardens by surprise.

Virgil knew he couldn't keep up and hollered, "Jake, I have these guys. Go get him!"

Jake looked at the Secret Service, now only 150 feet away, then back to Chance making tracks the opposite way, and took off after him on foot.

"Nobody move!" Virgil hollered, holding his badge up with one hand and his pistol now in the other.

The Secret Service guys, who had been running and talking into small radios, began screaming "Put that gun down!" at him, not knowing who or what he was.

"Watch him, Gunner!" Virgil said to his cover man in the nearby woods. "Don't let Jake get in trouble!"

Gunner was watching Jake chase Chance, who had a pretty big lead already, down the road toward the lock and dam, which was a dead end. Gunner tracked the pair and readied his rifle to protect Jake if needed.

The agents arrived in a flurry of heaving breathing and barked orders. They were in button-down shirts with ties. Neither even considered running after Jake or Chance, as their dress shoes were hardly ideal for running on asphalt, or any other surface for that matter.

The agents had their firearms drawn. "Everybody show your hands! Put your weapon down!" they screamed at Virgil, who finally did as he was told.

"Everybody calm down," Virgil said in his best authoritative voice.

"You shut up, and don't move!" the lead agent said to him in an agitated voice.

The agents secured Fabian first, then moved to Rook and were purposely a little rough with him to help sell the notion that he had no knowledge of the bust. Rook pitched in, trying to act as if he were resisting.

Then the lead agent turned to Virgil and asked, "So who are you?" To which Virgil explained to everyone's satisfaction.

"So who are the runners?"

"The guy in the rear is my partner, Jake Crosby. The guy he is chasing is her brother and accomplice," Virgil said, pointing at Chase.

"Secure her," the lead agent said after doing a double take at Chase. She didn't seem threatening, but he knew better than to take chances. He turned back to Virgil. "Accomplice in what?"

"They are selling a stolen antiquity of the state of Mississippi."

The lead agent considered this, then holstered his weapon and put his hands on his knees to catch his breath. "No shit. Well, we're after these assholes." He nodded at the two men from New Orleans. "They are the best counterfeiters in this part of the South."

While he was talking, an unmarked sedan had screeched to a stop behind them, and now two more identically dressed agents emerged from it.

Pointing at Virgil, the new lead agent asked, "Who is this guy?"

"He's a game warden."

"That's interesting," the new lead agent said as he surveyed the scene. He looked at Chase and then focused on his prize. "Well, well, well. Fabian Antoinette and his hired muscle," he said, staring straight at Fabian. "As slick as you are, you let a game warden take you down?"

"This is a misunderstanding. I want my attorney" was the only thing that Fabian muttered, and he glared at Rook as if to say, *Don't say a word.*

Looking at Chase Bolivar, the first lead agent asked if she minded if he looked in her bag, a request that earned him an immediate *Go to hell* look.

"I haven't done anything wrong."

"We'll be the judge of that."

"I have a partner in pursuit of another suspect," Virgil explained. "Could you let me go check on him, or at least one of your men go?"

The new agents looked at the other two. "He does, sir," the younger of the first pair said. "They went that way."

The second lead agent pointed at his junior agent. "You take the van and go check on him." Then, looking at Virgil, he said, "You need to stay right here for now."

Virgil exhaled deeply. He didn't like being told what to do.

"We need to Mirandize them," the other young agent said, reminding everyone of protocols.

"Let's do it," the second lead agent said, "and in the spirit of cooperation, let our new friend here arrest her, and we'll take these two. That work for you, Warden?"

"That works fine as long as I get the brother too."

"Yes, indeed," the lead agent replied. His interest was strictly in the counterfeiters.

The group stood silent for a moment. Fabian was fuming, and Chase was defiant. Rook was more anxious with each passing second, though he'd been cheered by Fabian's earlier look instructing him to remain silent, which suggested the man still considered himself his employer.

The sound of a siren could be heard traveling toward them, but it was still a ways off.

"Somebody you called?" the second lead agent asked, referring to the siren.

"Not me," Virgil replied as he cuffed Chase and then began explaining her Miranda rights. A quick search revealed she had no weapons, but Virgil noticed three EpiPens on her dash.

"You allergic to something?" he asked, being cautious.

"Just you," she spat back.

"I have that effect on some women," Virgil said with distinct sarcasm. When she was secured, he glanced up to find Jake and Chance long gone from sight. Suddenly he was overcome with worry for his partner. He knew that Chance Bolivar was capable of anything.

Seeing him looking that way, Chase informed Virgil that Jake would never catch him. "Chance chases his dogs through the woods all night. He can run for hours."

"Just shut up," Virgil replied.

"And even if he does, you'll find out we haven't done anything wrong. You're going to be the joke of the department."

"You have no idea what's going on, do you?"

"I know you're making a huge mistake."

Virgil laughed. "No, I think you and Chance have made all the mistakes, enough mistakes to get the feds involved. I'll let the sheriff explain it all to you."

Chase was stunned as she comprehended that there were federal officers present. "You're crazy."

Virgil stepped away from Chase and spoke into his wireless. "Gunner, can you see Jake?"

"They're gone, Virgil," Gunner responded immediately. "They went straight into those woods and disappeared. I had no chance to keep up."

"Dammit!" Virgil weighed his options. "Hey, come watch this prisoner, and let me go after him," he told Gunner.

"I'm on my way!"

"Hurry up," he said, watching Chase glare murderously at him. "I'm worried about Jake."

The second lead agent spun around and saw Virgil leaving. "Hey, where are you going?"

"I got someone coming to watch her," Virgil replied as he pointed at Gunner emerging from the woods. "He's on my team," he added, jumping into the truck and slamming the door. He knew the other officers were looking for Jake and Chance, but he had to go help. He knew the area much better than they did. Already in motion, he called out through the open window, "I'm going after my partner!"

"I'll help you!" a young agent offered, and ran toward Virgil, who braked just long enough for him to jump in.

* * *

The ambulance flew to a stop beside Judge Rothbone's Land Rover, and the EMTs jumped out and into action. A passing woman had stopped her vehicle when she'd heard the judge's horn blaring and saw him slumped over the steering wheel. The lady was still standing in front of her car with a concerned look on her face while she talked to someone on her cell phone.

The EMTs quickly evaluated their patient and worked to stabilize him, as he was pale, unconscious, and his blood pressure was sky high.

It wasn't until they were waiting to read the heart monitor that both noticed the pistol on the seat beside him. Their first thought was suicide, but they didn't have time to discuss this, since their patient proved to be in full cardiac arrest. The hospital was only a few minutes away, and the medics were urged to bring him in as quickly as possible, while the doctors would prepare for their arrival.

While they were loading the judge into the ambulance, a Columbus police officer arrived to direct traffic, and they alerted him to the pistol. They didn't know who he was yet or why he had a pistol on the seat next to him, they said, but the officer said he would secure the firearm.

As the ambulance rolled away with the judge, the officer looked inside the Land Rover. The pistol was loaded, and he also found a few legal papers in a folder that looked important. He secured the items in his cruiser and called for a tow truck.

Shutting the Land Rover driver's door and walking away, he never heard the handheld radio on the vehicle's floorboard crackle to life, or Jake Crosby's plea for help.

As he sat in his patrol car facing the Land Rover, the officer typed the vehicle's tag into his onboard computer. He had a gut feeling this guy was someone who could be a problem to him if he mishandled anything. The ambulance's siren had faded completely when he got his answer: Judge Ransom Rothbone of Monroe County, Mississippi.

"Holy shit!" the officer said with a large exhale. He quickly grabbed his cell phone and dialed his supervisor.

CHAPTER 28

Jake had been chasing Chance for over half a mile in a sprint, and the exertion was wearing on his forty-plus-year-old frame. He hadn't gained any ground, but he hadn't lost that much either. Reality was setting in that he couldn't keep up the pace, though. It was brutal. He also knew Chance was running into a dead end in the thick woods that bordered the lake on the north side. If he made it through the swampy woods, on the other side was a marina, complete with boat storage, and then the park that overlooked the river. After that all that was left was the Columbus Lock and Dam. Chance would be trapped, and his run for freedom would be in vain.

Jake's mind raced and his lungs burned as he struggled to match Chance's grueling pace. It occurred to him that if Chance got too far ahead of him, he could get to the marina and steal a boat. There would be no one to chase him on the river. Or he could hide in a boat, like the Boston bomber had. Jake knew the stakes: he had to keep up and not let Chance out of his sight.

After another two hundred yards, the aching in Jake's legs threatened to just shut him down, especially in the leg he'd broken in the drainpipe. He was beginning to lose ground and he needed help. Since he was in plainclothes, he didn't have his shoulder radio to use to call for assistance. More important, the same radio could send a GPS location to the operators in Jackson that would immediately summon assistance. He cussed himself for not being better prepared.

Then he remembered the radio in his pocket to talk to the judge. Still running, he found it in his pocket and mashed the "Talk" button.

"Judge! I need help . . . I'm in pursuit of Chance Bolivar on foot . . . and he is approaching the Columbus Marina . . . Send help. I'm thinking he may try and steal a boat!" Jake said as best he could while running and not taking his eye off Chance. He was obviously losing more ground.

"Judge! Judge, can you hear me?" Jake was almost out of breath, and talking while he ran was difficult.

The radio remained silent.

"Dammit!" Jake exclaimed. Gritting his teeth, he kept running.

* * *

Chase leaned against her car in handcuffs. The two remaining Secret Service agents placed Fabian and Rook in the backseat of their unmarked sedan and stood outside the car discussing the afternoon's events while watching Gunner cross the lot to them. They were jacked up on adrenaline and energized by busting the South's best counterfeiter. Everybody was also concerned about Jake and the agent sent after him, and they'd used their cell phones to call 911 for police backup. After that they called back to their New Orleans office and gave the go-ahead to pick up Fabian's brother and execute the search warrant they'd asked for in advance.

Inside the sedan, the attitude was intense. Fabian was furious and was trying to understand how he had gotten himself into the situation. The handcuffs were extra tight and added to his anger. Rook remained quiet, hoping that Fabian wouldn't sense he was part of his problems. The man at times seemed clairvoyant, and Rook knew he would keep analyzing this event until he thought he understood what had happened.

When Gunner jogged up in full camo, including face paint and state-issued body armor, the agents looked him over with a critical eye but accepted him as part of Virgil's team.

"Is there anybody else in the bushes watching us?" the first lead agent asked with a laugh.

"No, it's just us," Gunner responded. "I guess you guys were the ones following Fabian at the Jackson Hilton last week."

"You noticed us?" the other lead agent asked with surprise.

"Yep," Gunner said as he studied the prisoners.

The two agents looked at each other with disbelief. They had considered themselves careful.

Seeing their reaction, Gunner said, "I guess I got lucky."

Still handcuffed and leaning against her car, Chase was listening to everything that was being said while glaring at Fabian, who was spewing fury in the car. She was fuming mad at him but also at herself for never having considered that the money would be counterfeit or foreseeing any of many ways this deal could go wrong. In fact, that was what she had liked about it: it was safe, and she was unaware of any laws that she had broken.

The warden had shocked her with the news that the movie prop was stolen. She had not seen that one coming, but she knew buying and selling stolen property was the least of her worries. The rifles she had forgotten in the trunk of her car were her immediate nightmare. She had no concern for Chance at all, only herself and explaining the firearms and accessories that were lying there for all the law enforcement officers to see.

* * *

Virgil regretted sending Jake after Chance, but he really didn't have a choice. There was no way he could have kept up with him. Jake was their best opportunity. Now Virgil and a Secret Service agent were in Jake's truck riding down Wilkins Wise Road, looking for the two of them. There were not many places Chance could go. The marina was probably the best bet.

"You guys been on this case for very long?" the agent asked, trying to end the tense silence.

Virgil kept scouring the edge of the woods for his partner but answered, "Uh . . . about a week or so."

"Is it a big deal? The artifact?"

"Yeah, it was a bigger deal when we thought it was real, though. We just recently learned that it's actually a movie prop stolen from a memorabilia collector in California."

"I don't see your partner anywhere," the agent said as he helped survey the area.

"Yeah, this ain't good. I can't believe I have lost him," Virgil said with a sigh.

Then Virgil had an idea. He pulled his cell phone from his pocket and dialed Jake. Right after the phone could be heard ringing in his ear, he heard Jake's phone ringing in the cup holder.

"Dammit!" Virgil grunted. They had broken so many rules in this case. He hoped they didn't come back to haunt him. The frustrated warden looked at the agent and shook his head. "Keep your eyes peeled. We gotta find him. That guy he's chasing is one mean sombitch."

* * *

Chance wasn't sure where he was running. He was just trying to get away. He knew the area up ahead didn't offer many options. The backpack was heavy, but he was in decent shape. He was accustomed to running through the woods chasing his dogs at night, and he had endurance. The excitement of having over a million dollars cash on his back provided the incentive to find a way to elude the man chasing him.

Occasionally glancing behind him, Chance could see Jake Crosby in pursuit, but he clearly wasn't keeping up. Chance figured they would expect him to run to the marina and steal a boat. However he managed it, he had to get to the other side of the river and buy himself some time to hide the money. If he could hide the money first, then it wouldn't matter if they eventually caught him.

He set a hard pace and continued running toward the dam. If he were lucky, there would be sightseers there, allowing him to steal a car and drive out of here. His devious mind envisioned someone leaving the keys in their car while they peered over a viewpoint. If that didn't work, he would cross the river on top of the dam. He hoped the water wasn't roaring over the top. Dread filled his mind, because he knew the danger—one slip was all it would take, and if the fall didn't kill him, the raging cold water would.

Chance was not going to be overtaken or give up. He was hard-wired to endure and fight to the end. He'd make it as hard on them as possible. If this guy was going to catch him, he would have to earn it.

Cussing his lack of options, he knew he needed to gain some distance to give him some time.

He wondered how they had been set up. He knew Virgil and Jake were game wardens and had been shocked to see them. What interest could they have in them selling the artifact? *It doesn't make sense.*

* * *

A team of doctors swarmed around the unconscious judge in the Baptist Hospital trauma room. Their training confirmed what the medic's monitors had indicated—he had suffered a myocardial infarction. They worked frantically to stabilize his blood pressure and his oxygen levels. As with any patient there was much concern for his well-being, and when word spread through the ranks that their newest patient was Judge Ransom Rothbone, eyes widened. Nearly everyone had heard of his reputation and respected the man.

The Columbus police chief had to sit down when he heard the news of his friend of over forty years. Once he composed himself, he personally called Mary Margaret Rothbone and gently explained the grave situation. She too was shaken, and couldn't talk for a moment. He had already arranged for a county deputy to pick her up and drive her to the hospital. He begged her to wait on the officer and not drive herself. She resisted at first, but finally she saw the wisdom in a driver. She also realized she needed the time to locate Rosemary and tell her.

* * *

As Jake was approaching the edge of the woods, he was forced to stop and try to catch his wind. The cold air burned his lungs with each gasping breath. With his hands on his knees, he looked for Chance and couldn't see him. Frustrated, he grabbed the radio once again.

"Judge Rothbone!" he shouted. "If you can hear me, please respond!"

Nothing.

"Judge!"

Silence.

"Shit!"

Jake felt for his cell phone, which was almost always in his chest pocket, then remembered it was in the console of his truck and cursed again.

His injured leg ached. This was by far the most strain he had placed on it since rehab. But there was nothing to do but start running again toward the marina.

He'd taken only a few steps when he saw Virgil turning into the marina.

"Yes!" Jake screamed. "Virgil!"

Virgil had the driver's window open and swiveled his head toward Jake, then yanked the wheel and charged off across a rough field with his boat trailer bouncing wildly in his wake. When Virgil braked beside him, Jake sagged against the truck door and immediately started to explain the situation.

"I lost him. I just couldn't keep up," Jake said in an exhausted voice. "My bad leg's killing me."

"That's okay, Jake. The cavalry's on its way, and we'll find him. He can't go far. We got his sister plus the other two men, and he's gotta be around here somewhere."

All three men were studying the marina. It was the obvious place he would run, since there were plenty of places to hide in and around the boats.

"Get in! Let's go!" Virgil said in a commanding tone. "We can't let him get on the river."

Jake was thankful to sit down and catch his breath.

CHAPTER 29

Chase Bolivar now sat in the back of a police car and watched the officers search her trunk. They huddled around the artifact for a few minutes and listened to a man in camo she had never seen before.

When they pulled the rifles and backpacks out of the trunk, her attitude changed from anger to dread. There were still a lot of dots to connect, but they would run the serial numbers on the guns and find out they belonged to the recent robbery victims. She needed to quickly create a cover story and alibi. She needed to determine a way to deflect attention to Chance.

As she watched an officer check out the Browning rifle, she began to tremble. When they held up the voice changer, panic overwhelmed her. The handcuffs locked behind her accentuated the fact that she was trapped and in no kind of control of the situation. There would be lots of questions to answer, and she had been so brazen for so long that she hadn't developed any predetermined answers.

The backseat smelled like body odor and vomit and was separated from the front seat by a mesh of steel wire. It reminded her that armed robbery in Mississippi carried with it a sentence of three years to life for each count. She wouldn't be eligible for parole for at least twenty years, and maybe never, since she had committed the crimes with a firearm.

She shook harder and her heart palpitated as she realized she might never get out of prison. Just like her father—the man she had spent so many years hating—she might spend the majority of her adult years incarcerated. *I might die in prison . . . just like Dad.*

Never once had this thought crossed Chase's mind. Never once had she contemplated the potential consequences of her actions. The irony of it wasn't wasted on her. Tears filled her eyes as she wondered how this had happened. How had she become just like her father? Massive waves of panic flooded her, and Chase Bolivar suddenly found herself having a full-blown anxiety attack in the backseat of a black-and-white police car.

* * *

Jake, Virgil, and the young agent spread out to search the marina, which was indeed ripe with places to hide. After a quick glance around the ranks of dry-docked boats, Virgil immediately wanted to call for a police dog and more officers to assist. Jake chose to trust his hunter instincts, leaning low as he walked to study the damp ground for footprints. The Secret Service agent was concentrating on areas with gravel in order to keep his wing-tipped dress shoes clean.

When Jake saw a set of fresh, muddy boot tracks, he had a gut feeling they had been left by Chance. He followed them with his eyes to where they headed over a rise toward the park.

He glanced back at Virgil, who was searching a yacht called *Victor's Secret*, and considered his options. He didn't know for certain that they were Chance's tracks. Nonetheless, waving at the agent, he pointed at the tracks and then took off running again, following them up the rise.

At the top Jake saw the plumber's van on the nearby frontage road, along with an agent beside it pointing eagerly toward the lock and dam. Jake wiped sweat out of his eyes and could see Chance running at a steady jog away from him. Looking back, Jake saw the other agent talking to Virgil and pointing at Jake. Knowing they'd seen him, Jake focused on Chance and continued the pursuit.

Where is he going? There's nowhere to go!

Jake ran straight at Chance as fast as he was able. Keeping up had been difficult before and could only be more so now, but he wasn't quitting. He grimaced each time his right leg hit the ground but concentrated on Chance and pushed through the pain.

When Chance hadn't found a convenient vehicle to steal, he'd turned his attention to his last option: the dam. The Columbus Lock and Dam, with the strength of steel and concrete, quietly impounded the Tombigbee River and created the 8,900-acre Columbus Lake. There were five consecutive gates that could be opened to relieve floodwaters and assist with the river's natural flow. On the other side was a lock that allowed the passage of barges, raising or lowering the water level to twenty-seven feet so they could move cargo efficiently to its destination. There were tall fences everywhere and highly visible warning signs that said to stay back or stay away—this is a dangerous structure, and drowning in the current is a real threat. On the river, boats weren't allowed within eight hundred feet of the immense, silent structure.

Chance looked at the dam ahead and knew he had to get across. To do so, he had to climb fences and the concrete structure, none of which intimidated him. If he could get on top, he could balance his way across the dam. After that, getting across the lock would be relatively easy. The other side of the river represented freedom. It would only be brief, because they would surely find him. He couldn't run forever. He just needed to hide the money where he could retrieve it later. Hiding the money was paramount in his mind.

Chance looked back at the warden approaching at a fast jog. He was still several minutes away. Whoever he was, the guy was persistent. Something about him was familiar, but Chance couldn't place it, nor did he try. He was focused on self-preservation and getting that money hidden.

Standing at the edge of the giant concrete structure, with the smell of muddy water being held back by the dam permeating the air, Chance realized he had become his old man. Just like his father, he was planning to hide a fortune in cash that he could reclaim when the heat was off of him. How had this happened? What were the chances? Maybe his son and daughter would spend their lives looking for their daddy's hidden fortune. *Maybe that's our family's curse.*

While he tried to catch his breath, he spat on the ground and blamed his dead father for all of his problems.

* * *

The stainless screws in Jake's femur were being tested. He worked out and had participated in physical activity during his warden training, but running for so long on the muddy, uneven ground was the most strain by far that he had placed on the repaired leg.

Jake was about four hundred yards from Chance, who'd come to a halt at the dam, and was closing steadily on him. He could smell the muddy river and could tell Chance was eyeing the structure, looking for a way across the river. The idea of trying to cross the dam was absolutely crazy to Jake. On one side were tumultuous river currents swirling around an obstacle that could pull him under in seconds, and on the other was a thirty- or forty-foot drop straight onto the exposed concrete apron of the dam.

When Jake saw Chance start to climb the fence, he stopped running to analyze what he was up to. He needed to anticipate what Chance was going to do but liked nothing about what he was seeing. Breathing hard, he watched Chase drop over the first fence and attempt to climb the concrete structure. Glancing back, Jake could see the agent in the plumber's van running toward him. Another look farther east revealed Virgil and his help were nowhere in sight.

"That son of a bitch is going to do it!" Jake exclaimed to himself. Then, turning toward the running agent, he yelled, "Call for backup! Have 'em send units to the other side!"

The agent waved an acknowledgment, then wheeled and sprinted back toward the van.

Jake took a deep breath and took off running again.

* * *

The two older Secret Service agents watched Fabian and Rook in the back of their car. Ideally, they would want to separate them, but they didn't have that luxury. They would worry about that later. Right now they were waiting on the other two agents so they could return to their home offices. They had considered taking the two men to the federal detention facility in Aberdeen, which was the closest one, to process them, but after a brief discussion they decided to take them straight back to New Orleans.

They listened to Gunner explain to the police the Mississippi game wardens' interest in the Bolivars and were fascinated that Fabian, the great con man, had gotten caught in the web of a con.

Gunner enjoyed the excitement of the bust and being around the law enforcement officers. It made him miss being on active duty, experiencing the thrill of a team working together. As he stood savoring the success, he suddenly wondered about Perry Burns. *Where's Perry Burns?* He scratched his head and made a mental note to ask Virgil.

* * *

Chance climbed the fence to the dam and stood at the concrete wall looking frantically for a step up. The engineers had obviously designed the structure so it would be impossible for someone to scale the wall without tools or climbing gear.

Once he decided there was no easy way to scale the wall, he checked on his pursuers. The dogged warden was getting close. Chance looked back at the wall and then at the muddy water. He could swim across, or at least he thought he could. The water would be cold and the currents strong. Surely they wouldn't follow him.

He was about to jump in when he had an even crazier idea that would quickly give him some distance from his pursuers. He could swim to the first gate, climb over, and slide the thirty feet down the apron like a water slide and then swim to the other side of the river. He figured no one would follow him. Chance made up his mind and immediately jumped into the water. The cold, muddy water nearly took his breath, but he shook off the initial shock before inhaling air and swimming to the gate. Driftwood packed against the dam, and Chance had to force his way through it. When he reached up to grab the top of the gate with his hands, he found the cold concrete smooth and hard to grab. His feet struggled to find a purchase on the slick side. Finally, he found a seam with his boots that gave enough grip for him to push himself out of the water. Straining against the extra weight of the soaked backpack, he eventually swung a leg over the top and straddled the huge gate like a horse's back. Catching his breath, he looked down the opposite side. The drop was heart stopping. It was almost straight down, with the base swelling out like a giant concrete sliding board.

Looking back, he saw the warden at the fence. Chance was tired, but his pursuer looked exhausted. Chance was confident his next move would give him the distance he needed. From his vantage point he could see a barge in the lock. If he hurried, he might be able to climb aboard as it started its push south. With that thought, he swung his leg over, made eye contact with the warden, and smiled, and then, with spooky self-assurance, plunged out of sight.

* * *

The eight-foot fence stopped Jake's forward progress. Leaning into it with his hands in the chain links, he watched Chance pull himself out of the water and up on the top of the first massive gate. Jake looked up and saw three strands of barbed wire at the top of the fence. His chest heaved as he caught his breath, and he knew he had to climb the fence.

Across the river, on the far side of the lock, a tower similar to what you see at a small airport was ideally located to assist river traffic as they passed through the lock. Jake could see a man he assumed to be the lockmaster watching the events through binoculars on a balcony. The lockmaster, always vigilant against threats, had already called 911 and reported the incident. He was about to lock his tower down if either of the two men got any closer. Homeland Security had given him exact protocols to follow if anyone breached the fences of the lock and dam.

When Chance dropped out of sight, Jake was horrified but knew what he had to do. The toes of his boots fit into the chain link well enough to allow him to climb up to the top of the fence. Once at the top he pulled the barbed wire lower until he was able to swing a leg over. His pants caught in the wire twice, and his jacket snagged, but he yanked it free and managed to climb down the other side, feeling lucky he hadn't ripped himself up on the barbs.

Jake didn't like the idea of chasing Chance down the spillway, but it was his job. He couldn't just stand there and watch Chance get away. It would be easy to say that he wasn't a dangerous criminal and wasn't worth the risk, but Jake saw it as a chance to prove his worth as a law enforcement officer and demonstrate that he could overcome obstacles. It was what he was supposed to do. Without any more thought, he threw off his jacket and jumped into the cold river.

* * *

Virgil and the young agent arrived at the parking lot at high speed and screeched to a stop. They were halfway across the grass to the dam when they saw Jake jump into the river. Virgil was taken aback, and the young agent started pointing at Chance, who had survived his plunge down the apron and was now bobbing in the water between it and the closest side of the lock. Along the sides of the lock was a long pile of large gray rocks stacked to prevent erosion. As they watched, Chance made it to the rocks.

"Holy shit!" Virgil screamed. "We need some backup! We need a boat!"

"I radioed the Columbus Police, and they have units on the way. What about your boat here?" the agent asked, looking back at Jake's truck and the boat on its trailer.

"There's nowhere to launch it below the dam! The bank's way too steep!" Virgil rushed back to dig a throwable flotation cushion from his boat, and pointed at Jake. "We gotta get him out of the river. Between the current and the cold, he'll drown! Keep your eye on Chance over there. We gotta watch where he goes."

Running as fast as he could, Virgil made it to the fence and knew at a glance that he couldn't get over it. He watched helplessly as Jake struggled to pull himself atop the first gate.

"Jake, stop!" Virgil screamed. "Don't do it! He's not worth it!"

Jake made it up astride the gate, but teetered there breathing heavily, barely able to balance himself.

Virgil was only about ninety feet from him and knew Jake could hear him clearly. "Seriously, Jake! Let him go. We know where he lives, and we got Chase, the artifact, and the money. Let him go. It's not worth it."

* * *

After making it to the rocks, Chance had an idea. He had spent so many years looking for his father's hidden money that he knew a good hiding spot when he saw one. Along the side of the lock were a hundred yards of giant gray rock with steel support bars for construction barges to tie up to. Muddy water swarmed all around. Chance was at least 150 yards from his pursuers, and he didn't think they could see him clearly, especially if he went underwater.

Holding himself against a steel tie bar that was just under the surface, he pulled off the backpack and squeezed a ten-pound rock into his pack to ensure that it sank, then took a deep breath, unlatched the buckles, and dove. When he'd gone as deep as his lungs would bear, he attached the backpack to the tie and released it. It glided quickly down the tie bar to the bottom, where it would wait on him to retrieve it.

When he surfaced, his pursuers were paying more attention to the warden, who'd followed him to the top of the gate. Chance recognized the guy as the one who was limping badly. He knew he would have a hard time keeping up with Chance in the cold water.

Chance made a mental note of exactly where he was before starting to swim away. Shivering from the cold water, he knew it was beginning to affect him and that he needed to get out soon. However, he was very pleased with his spur-of-the-moment hiding spot. He was confident the police had not seen what he was doing and nobody would ever accidentally stumble upon it. Chance could retrieve it later at any time during the night, and no one would ever notice him. The cold, dark water would be a giant liquid safe, preserving the stash of cash for his return. For a split second as he paused to catch his breath, he considered the ludicrous turn of events whereby Fabian thought they both wanted $1.3 million. *Thankfully that crazy coonass brought my money in a heavy-duty backpack.*

Feeling cold yet satisfied, Chance just needed to swim to the other side of the river. He didn't care what happened now.

CHAPTER 3Ø

Straddling the gate, Jake was shivering from the cold water, and the exertion of the pursuit was taking a toll on him. He heard what Virgil was yelling at him and he exhaled in relief. Once atop the gate, he'd very quickly realized he did not want to slide down. Virgil was right. They had what they wanted, and they would eventually catch Chance. Jogging down the stairs to a concrete walkway at the water's edge, a Secret Service agent was getting in a better position to observe Chance, who'd now struck out swimming for the river's far shore.

"Jake, come back over here!" Virgil exclaimed. "Don't go after him. Just swim back!"

Virgil could see that Jake's shivering was getting more violent.

"Can you swim back? I can toss you this cushion."

"I can make it," Jake said as he tried shifting his body to take the pressure off his aching leg.

Virgil spun the cushion like a Frisbee anyway, and it landed in the water five yards from Jake.

Relaxing from the intensity of the chase, Jake realized he had done all he could. It was over. No need to push further. The bust had been a success. There was one loose end, but with the help of the local police they would catch Chance. Even the judge would be happy that the Bolivars wouldn't be bothering him for a while.

"I'm coming," Jake called out to Virgil.

"Well, come on then. I'm getting cold just looking at you!" Virgil wanted his partner back on solid ground. He was in a very dangerous situation. The boiling currents below could trap a man underwater longer than anyone could hold his breath.

Jake almost laughed, but the view below him down the apron sobered him right up. Leaning forward, he began to swing his good leg in order to pull his body up for the drop back into the water on the upstream side of the gate. It was going to be awkward, but it was the only way to get back into the water. The top of the gate was only a foot wide, and the steel was cutting into his bum leg. Getting off the gate and swimming back was the best idea Jake had heard in a long time.

"Come on, I'll buy you a cup of coffee!" Virgil hollered in an encouraging voice.

Jake placed both hands on the gate and leaned forward flat atop it to swing himself back over. Suddenly losing his grip on the slick steel, Jake slipped and in panic reached to catch himself with his other hand, but it was too late. The weight of his body dropping was too much for his wet hands to control. Jake dropped straight down the back side of the dam, just as Chance had, only Jake was turned sideways.

When Chance had dropped, he'd deliberately hugged the wall and slid down it feetfirst. His momentum had shot him into the water like a water park slide. Jake fell straight down sideways and bounced when he hit the apron, knocking the breath out of him.

Virgil blinked his eyes in disbelief. One second Jake was there catching his breath. The next he was gone. Virgil began screaming and ran toward the steps that led down to the back side of the dam.

Jake had already been spit out into the river on the other side when Virgil finally arrived where he could see. With his hands on his knees, trying to catch his breath, Virgil watched Jake as he battled the current.

The Secret Service agent on the walkway had looked away from Chance just in time to see Jake splash into the muddy water and submerge. When he didn't see Jake pop up after a few seconds, he immediately started stripping off his coat and shoes to jump in the river.

The local police officers had already called for a water rescue team, but it was going to take a few minutes for them to navigate upriver from where they launched.

When Jake surfaced, confused and with his side burning, the current had carried him forty yards from the dam. He coughed up muddy water, then spit and breathed deeply to fill his lungs with air while he could. Wiping his face, he struggled to orient himself. He was closer to the lock and the pile of rocks than the other side. He couldn't see Chance but was determined to get to those rocks and hold on for help.

His bad leg made swimming difficult, and he had to thrash with his arms just to stay afloat. His head dipped under a few times as he tried to fight the current with his weakened limbs.

Chance hadn't seen the warden fall, but he did hear all the commotion behind him, and when he turned he saw the man pop up in the current, looking disoriented. He was clearly in trouble.

It wasn't in Chance's nature to help anyone in law enforcement, but even as exhausted and bone cold as he was, his tactical mind was still whirring madly away. He knew he wasn't getting away clean today. They knew who he was and where he lived. He didn't want to look over his shoulder waiting on them to come get him for a dinky charge of misrepresenting the artifact. That's all they had on him. That and resisting arrest, which he could probably now nullify if he helped the officer. Hiding the money was all he wanted to do, and that had been accomplished.

Chance spun around and started swimming out to intercept Jake, who was approaching him rapidly with the current.

The agent was just about to jump in when he saw Chance change his course. Not knowing if he intended to help or harm Jake, the agent feared the worst and dove in. He hadn't realized that from his angle the current would never allow him to swim straight to them. Though he could see the pair, he was swiftly carried below them.

Virgil arrived at the concrete walkway out of breath. Watching keenly, he absorbed every detail.

When Chance finally caught Jake, there were a few seconds of tense anxiety. Nobody, including Jake, knew Chance's intentions. Thanks to the fall, Jake was not in any condition to overpower the man he had been chasing.

Virgil was the first person on the bank to determine that Chance was indeed helping Jake and screamed for someone to bring a rope as Chance struggled in the current to return to the Columbus bank side.

A young police officer who had calculated the current and jumped in forty yards upriver was making good time to get to the pair. He had a yellow rope tied to himself, and Virgil watched it spool out to the men. By the time he got to them, it was obvious to the trained officer that both men were in bad shape. Chance looked hypothermic, and Jake was struggling to keep his head above water. The officer barked at Chance to hang on to Jake, then secured Chance with an elbow around the neck and commenced the struggle back to the riverbank. For once in his life glad to see a police officer, Chance did what he was told and latched a death grip onto the back of Jake's collar.

As the men on the bank pulled them in by the yellow rope, Virgil noticed the rescue boat approaching and waved it toward the agent who'd miscalculated his dive into the river, who was closer to the boat than the bank, still caught in the current.

As the three men approached the riverbank, Virgil waded out in the water to help. Securing Jake safely on the bank first, he then turned to help with Chance. In another moment everyone, including the police officer, was lying on the bank, gasping for air. Other officers brought blankets, and a few bystanders had gathered to watch the scene. None of the police knew the good guys from the bad guys, but the officers all knew Virgil, and he quickly sorted everyone out for them.

At last Jake sat up and wiped the cold water from his face.

A moment later Chance rolled onto his stomach and heaved up a good quantity of brown water. Having paid attention to Virgil's explanation of what was what, an officer was about to cuff Chance when Virgil stopped him.

"Chance, that was a mighty good thing you did out there, and it will be noted in my report. But we still gotta arrest you."

Spitting on the ground, Chance nodded that he understood and then considered the rock pile on the side of the lock. A sly smile formed on his lips.

Virgil handed a pair of handcuffs to Jake. "You deserve to do the honors."

"Where's the backpack?" Jake asked Chance between coughs.

Chance groaned as he sat up and realized he had seen Jake at the Hilton. "I had to take it off when I started swimming for your sorry ass. I couldn't swim with it on."

No one questioned the validity of the story. They knew they were fortunate to get everybody out of the water alive.

Jake slowly stood up and took the cuffs. He made eye contact with Chance just like they had out on the river. Each man understood the other's intentions. Chance held out his hands and Jake applied the handcuffs and, pausing to catch his breath a few times, quoted the Miranda rights word for word. His first arrest was now official.

Jake was soaking wet and shivering. Exhausted, he placed his hands on his knees and looked at Virgil.

"I promise they ain't all this hard," Virgil told him with a smile while looking down at his own wet pants. "Let's go. I'm getting kinda chilly."

* * *

When Jake and Virgil walked up the hill to the parking lot, they found it full of law enforcement personnel. The Lowndes County sheriff and the Columbus police chief were talking to Gunner. The Secret Service agents had regrouped and stood talking to the one who'd been fished out by the rescue boat, who was now draped in a blanket.

Fabian Antoinette and Rook still sat stoically in the backseat of the unmarked sedan with government plates. In the back of a nearby police cruiser, Chase was over her anxiety attack and was furiously scheming.

An ambulance had arrived and the medics were giving out warm blankets to the wet men and checking their vital signs.

The sheriff had a huge smile on his face, which surprised Virgil. Usually the top brass was mad about something he had done, as he was never known to follow procedures. Virgil and Jake were halfway to the cars when the sheriff came out to meet them. The local officers had taken the prisoner on ahead.

"Well, you got the robber, boys! We checked the guns and gear in the back of the Bolivars' car, and it matches exactly to the recent robberies of the hunters. There was even a voice changer back there. How did you know it was him?"

Virgil looked at Jake with widened eyes but quickly recovered and turned back to the sheriff. "We've been working day and night on that case and following every lead."

"That's some damn fine police work, boys."

"Thank you, sir," Virgil said with a furrowed brow, trying to understand the situation.

It was Jake who got there first. He remembered the ponytail from the photo and seeing Chase jogging with her hair held in the same fashion. "Sheriff, you said 'him.' We think it may have been her," Jake said with confidence. "Or at the least it was a team effort."

The sheriff stared at them for a few seconds, then at Chase sitting in the backseat of the patrol car.

Virgil nodded. "Check out her cigarette butts. I think you will find they match what was found at the crime scenes."

"I'll be damned. I just assumed . . . We'll get to the bottom of it pretty quick. You boys go get warm and dry. We'll have 'em all at the police station. Those two ain't going anywhere."

"Keep the Bolivars separated," Virgil added.

The sheriff nodded and smiled at the wardens as he walked away toward his suspects.

* * *

Morgan had realized that Jake had left for work and was not in his warden uniform or his official work vehicle again. She couldn't make sense of it, and it had worried her all day. Jake didn't talk to her about much anymore. He was self-absorbed, and she sensed he was keeping things from her. Secrets were something she didn't appreciate.

When Jake walked through the front door, he could hear Covey crying and loud music reverberating from Katy's bedroom. The exhaust fan buzzed above the stove while Morgan cooked supper with Covey riding her hip. Excited Jake was home, Kramer's tail beat against the wall with a steady rhythm, and his toenails clicked on the hardwood floor. Everything seemed as it should to Jake, except the temperature of the house was noticeably cooler than usual.

"Supper smells delicious," he declared as he entered the kitchen in his bare feet.

"I've been keeping it warm. I've tried to call you, but it just goes straight to voice mail," Morgan said with more than a little agitation in her voice. It had been a rough day.

"My phone got wet," Jake explained as he noticed a portable heater in the corner of the kitchen. "So why is the house so cold?"

Morgan hadn't looked up from the pan of spaghetti sauce yet. "Your dog chewed through the electrical wiring outside for the heat pump, and now we don't have any heat!" she exclaimed, then popped the wooden spoon on the pan and turned to see her husband's reaction.

She was instantly surprised to see him so disheveled. His clothes were soggy, his hair was a mess, and he smelled like muddy river water. "What in the world happened to you?"

"It's nothing. I fell in the river this afternoon," Jake explained, as if the afternoon's events were no big deal. Looking down at Kramer, whose tail steadily swished back and forth as he smelled Jake's legs, Jake finally caught up to what she'd said about the dog and the heat pump. "Did he get shocked?"

Morgan sighed. "I have no idea, but I doubt it. We couldn't get that lucky. The heating guy came and checked the damage. They had to order a new wiring harness."

After rubbing his face with his hands, Jake again looked down at Kramer. His tail slowly stopped wagging as he sat at Jake's feet.

"But it should be here tomorrow afternoon," Morgan explained with a trace of sarcasm.

Kramer now dropped his head and cut his eyes away from Jake.

She thought about handing Covey to Jake, but his shirt still looked wet, so she slid the baby into her high chair. "I'm tired, Jake," she said when she turned back to him. "This job keeps you gone all the time, and I don't know where you are or what you're doing, and I am worried about us."

Jake exhaled deeply and looked at his wife, who had both Ragú sauce and a suspicious stain that was probably baby throw-up on her blouse. Her hair was frizzy from her standing over the cooking pasta. Jake smiled at the sight of her. The baby was about to start crying again, and Jake could hear music that he didn't understand permeating with a rhythmic thump from the other side of the house. Morgan needed a break. She looked like she had endured a rougher day than he had.

"You do *know* that I love you so much."

The remark had more feeling to it than usual. The emotion of the words caught Morgan by surprise, and she looked at him as if something were wrong.

"What's happened?" she asked.

"Nothing. I just realized standing here, looking at you, how much I love you."

Morgan shot Jake a suspicious look. "What happened today?"

"Nothing," Jake answered plainly.

"Nothing happened? You're all wet, Jake. You're not in uniform, and your truck hasn't moved all day."

"It was just another day at the office."

Morgan placed the spoon down, wiped her hands, and walked over to her husband.

"I love you too, Jake. But if we are going to make this marriage work, you have to be honest with me. Honest about everything."

Jake sat down on a barstool and grabbed a bottle of wine and refilled Morgan's glass. He quickly considered what Virgil would do in this situation, and then with that thought secure he smiled and decided to do the exact opposite.

He turned the wine bottle up and took a pull. His mind flashed to something he had recently read about how timing influences who you happen to meet in life, but it's your heart that chooses who you are with each day.

Jake handed Morgan her glass of wine. "You're right," he told her. "Sit down, and I'll tell you everything."

EPILOGUE

Six months later

Rumors of a million dollars in cash floating down the Tombigbee have every fisherman from Columbus to Mobile, Alabama, searching for the backpack, and has given birth to another urban legend at the expense of the Bolivar family.

Chase was convicted of three counts of armed robbery and one count of false pretense and faces forty years, with a possibility of parole in twenty. In prison her only peace comes from teaching a Pilates class each morning to inmates and a few guards. The rest of the day she contemplates her actions and grows increasingly bitter. Two weeks in, she met Blanche Whorton, a.k.a. Eva Marie Mitchell, her father's long-lost Gypsy paramour, who is in prison for exploiting the retirement funds of vulnerable older men in nursing homes. Chase and Blanche have lots to talk about.

Judge Rothbone spent ten days in the hospital recovering from his heart attack and open-heart surgery. Soon after the incident he was immensely relieved to learn that Rosemary and her new friend, the resourceful young attorney Samantha Owens, had the finances of Mary Margaret's surgery under control. Though the judge was unable to travel to France for the surgery, the two young women happily tended to Mrs. Rothbone's every need. The judge never returned to the bench, retiring instead to take care of his wife and his grandson, Luke, and to train bird dogs. People who have seen him say he has never looked better. When the judge sits alone, he laughingly ponders the irony of how, though his lifelong horrible eating habits had certainly caused his heart attack, they'd just as surely kept him from making the biggest mistake of his life.

Virgil continues to serve as a game warden and remains frustrated that he hasn't been promoted to lieutenant. It could have something to do with Virgil's recent review with his supervisors, in which he insisted that Stevie Wonder wasn't actually blind. "Go to YouTube, type in 'Is Stevie Wonder really blind?' It's all there on video. You'll see. Paul McCartney knocks over a microphone and Stevie catches it." Miraculously, his questionable surveillance techniques on the Bolivar case were never exposed. Both Virgil and Jake received commendations from the governor for apprehending the robber so quickly. For fun, one night a week Virgil is a guest chef at the Old Waverly Clubhouse, where his jalapeño-stuffed pork tenderloin is a crowd-pleaser, and his banana pudding routinely sells out. Virgil is considering a new career that allows him to showcase his culinary skills. He also has a crush on the club's bookkeeper.

Fabian Antoinette and his brother remain free on bail while they await their trial for counterfeiting. The brothers have a team of attorneys preparing a stout defense full of continuances. Their story has become popular news in the Louisiana newspapers, causing much grief and daily seclusion for Fabian as he considers that greed was his ultimate downfall. He still can't believe the irony, that something counterfeit actually led to his demise.

Rosemary Rothbone has spent the last six months taking care of her mother and father. The surgery in France went off without a hitch, and her mother's recovery was speedy enough that Rosemary was able to show her mom many of the sights in Paris that she saw as a college student on one of her study abroad programs. Upon returning to Mississippi, Rosemary accepted a job as Samantha's legal assistant, and she now loves going to work every day.

Jake continues to enjoy being a game warden and protecting wildlife and was thrilled to receive a commendation from the governor for his role in the arrest of the mysterious robber. While Katy and her dates are a great source of unrest for Jake, he and Morgan have settled into a routine that has fostered a healthier marriage: he shares with her his daily activities, some thoughts, and a few dreams, and although she worries, she feels better knowing. Many times he has remarked that he wishes he had learned this simple lesson years earlier.

Kramer finally "finished" his training. The trainer graduated the dog in a manner similar to the way teachers graduate difficult students they don't want to deal with anymore. He still drinks from the toilet and suffers from separation anxiety. Most recently he bit the preacher and a fifteen-year-old boy Jake didn't trust around his daughter and forced two Mormon missionaries to call 911 from a magnolia tree in the front yard. Morgan and Jake have never felt safer.

Chance Bolivar sits in the Lowndes County jail awaiting trial, just like his daddy's hidden fortune sits waiting on the next person to find it. He thought the crime of false pretense was his only concern until a duck hunter realized the tire tracks leading into the gravel pit were suspicious. Now Chance faces murder charges, with a court-appointed lawyer, since he doesn't have access to his cash. Desperate, he is considering calling his late father's attorney and making a deal.

Chance has been pissed off ever since he learned the money in the backpack wedged at the bottom of the river is all counterfeit. He wishes he could use it to pay that worthless lawyer Billy Joe Green to get him out on bail so he could flee the country. Living in a Brazilian Confederado hideout after paying his big-shot attorney with fake hundreds to spring him would be the best use of the counterfeit money he could possibly think of.

The old money that has consumed everyone's dreams for years—and still does—rests at the bottom of an old well inside a big black waterproof gun case, awaiting Chance to retrieve it. He worries about it almost every hour of every day. If he told anyone about it, he knows that they would only steal it. He trusts nobody. He sometimes smiles when he thinks about his old man's stolen fortune. Maybe he'll tell his kids someday. Maybe he won't.

ACKNOWLEDGMENTS

Many a late night and weekend were burned while this story crept out of my mind onto the pages. A thank-you is owed to my wife, daughter, and family for putting up with me. I also want to thank my Mossy Oak family and AFC families for their support. Thanks to Kyle Jennings, Terry Goodman, the Thomas & Mercer team, and JoVon Sotak for believing in me, plus David Downing for his editing skills. My readers amaze me with their support. Thank you for letting my stories participate in a bit of your personal time. I hope y'all enjoy this one.

ABOUT THE AUTHOR

Bobby Cole is a native of Montgomery, Alabama, and president of Mossy Oak BioLogic. He is an avid wildlife manager, hunter, and supporter of the Catch-A-Dream Foundation. Cole is the author of four novels: *The Dummy Line*, *Moon Underfoot*, *The Rented Mule*, and *Old Money*. He lives with his wife and daughter in West Point, Mississippi.